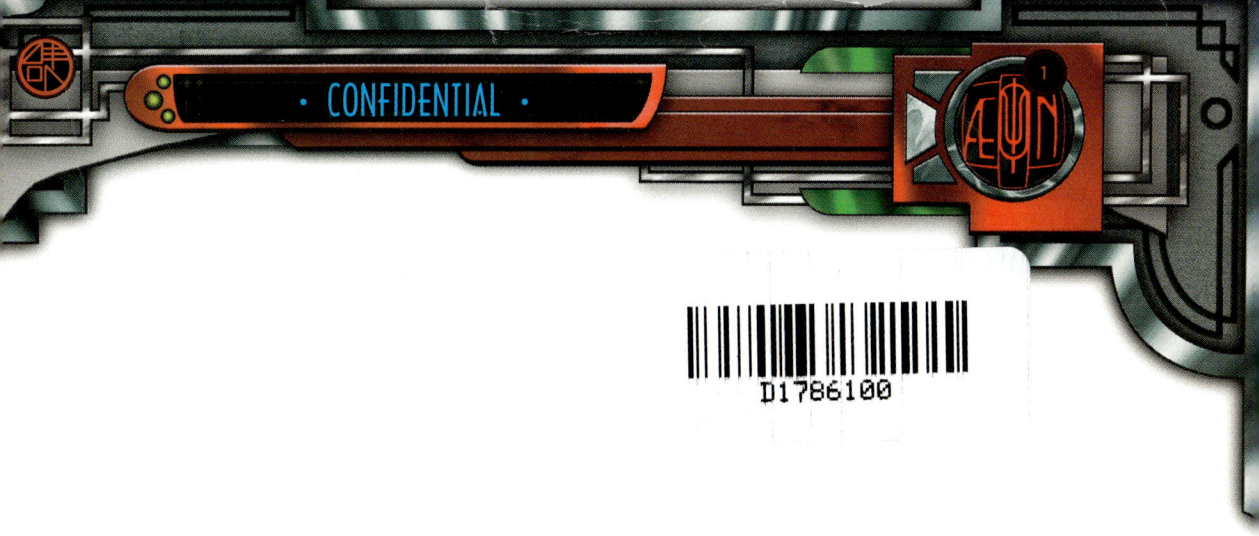

>>> FILE DUMP <<<

FILE DIRECTORY

1.0   REPORT TO FIELD OPERATIVES — 4.30.2120   2

2.0   REPORT TO FIELD OPERATIVES — 5.6.2120   57

This information is property of the Æon Trinity. Place your palm on the viewplate for authorization scan before continuing. Unauthorized access of these files is a criminal offense.

>>> FILE DUMP <<<

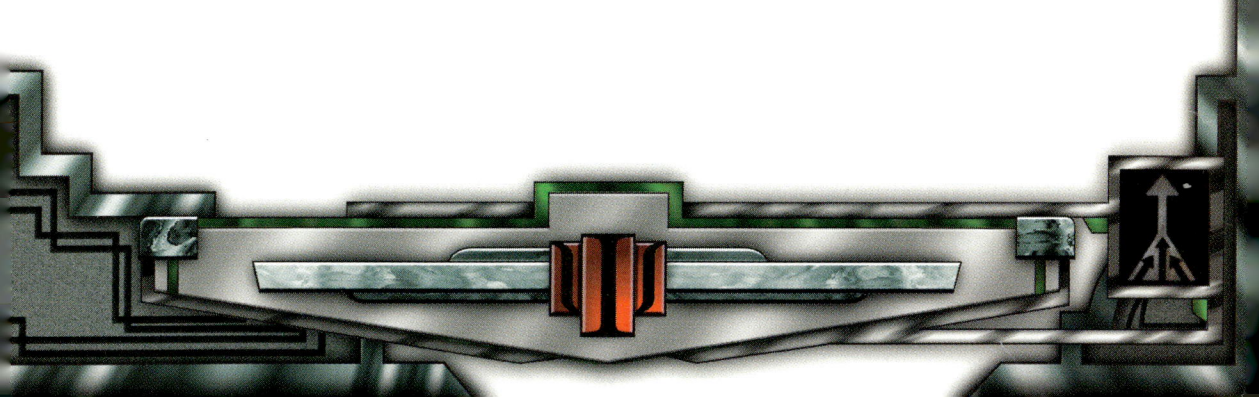

REPORT TO FIELD OPERATIVES

ÆON TRINITY TRANSMISSION [NEPTUNE DIVISION]

European Terrestrial Office, Deputy Office Director Emma Bailes

Gentlemen and Ladies —

The shit has well and truly hit the fan. The situation we are dealing with has the potential to make the Chitra Bhanu crisis of 2109 look like two kids fighting over a sim game. For years we've relied on the psi orders to defend us from the Aberrant menace, and on the public to trust the orders to do that job. The public's trust was shaken by the betrayal of the Chitra Bhanu; it was shaken further when the Upeo vanished and the orders failed to stave off the *Esperanza* crash. But even after all that, Joe Hologram, the man on the street, could trust those heroic psions to make things better.

Not any more, my dear associates. With news of members of both the Æsculapian and Orgotek orders involved in the illicit Huang-Marr Biorg Project leaking from a dozen sources, we may well see the public lose any and all faith they ever had in the psi orders. Once word gets out that docs and teks were toying with taint, playing with Aberrants on Luna, and using live human subjects, for God's sake — we could lose everything. *Everything*! Humanity would turn on the orders, believing them to be just as bad as Aberrants. We'd see another war, and the survivors would be easy pickings for the freaks, the Chromatics or whatever else is out there.

That *cannot* be allowed to happen. We stand at a crossroads, people, and what happens in the next few weeks may well determine all of our fates. You, my dear field operatives, are an integral part of our salvation.

Our first order of business is to determine how deeply the Æsculapians and Orgotek are involved in this taint-related research. Æon associate Robert Wei, a member of China's Ministry of Psionic Affairs, has allowed Proteus operatives to take part in the interrogation of captured Huang-Marr conspirators upon their return to Earth. Triton Division is researching information uncovered in the investigation that resulted in the capture of those same conspirators. Special Agent Hector Ramirez is in charge of directing operatives to follow our strongest leads: information that implicates high-ranking Æsculapians in this taint research.

We must know the full scope of the cancer that is the Huang-Marr Project and we need to know it fast. Then we must burn the tumor out. We must find every last psion involved in this monstrosity and deal with him, ASAP. If we demonstrate pub-

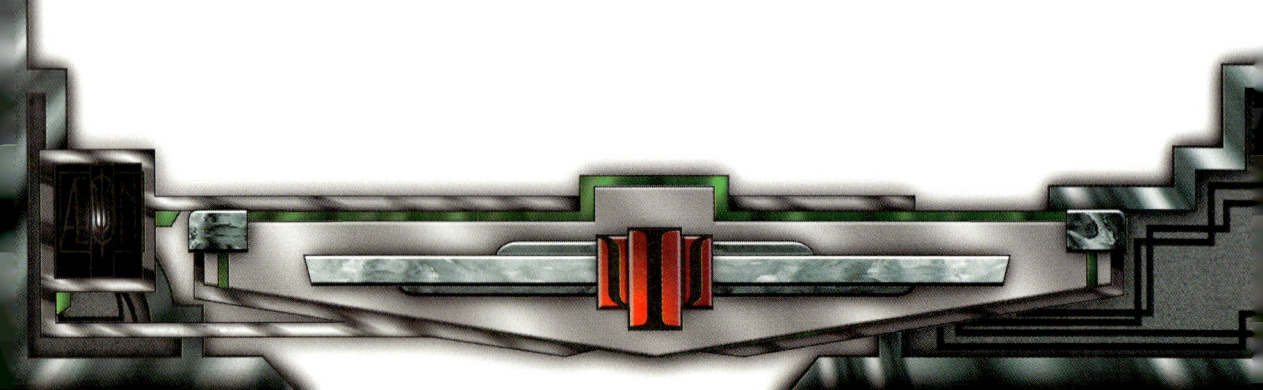

licly and effectively that there were just a few bad apples in the orders — ones that we've pruned — then maybe we can prove to Joe Hologram that the rest of the orchard is healthy. If we do that, and quickly, we just might get out of this scrape in one piece.

I cannot overemphasize the seriousness of this situation. We have rogue psions running around, possibly with high-level support within two psi orders. We have experimentation on human subjects — experiments utilizing taint! — running unchecked, and word of new taint-influenced bioware that blows standard-issue equipment out of the water. We have a high-ranking Æsculapian dead and in disgrace, a renegade and probably insane test subject of his hiding somewhere — not to mention missing suspects, missing corpses, misdirected funds and God only knows what else.

In fact, we understand that one of the project's suspected originators, Dr. Abel Marr, was just killed in an accident in Basel only days ago. Marr's untimely demise is very suspect, and may just be one of many. It's possible that the individual coordinating the Huang-Marr Project — so far known only as a computer agent called "Minerva" — is tying up loose ends in gruesome fashion.

That's where you come in. As Special Agent Ramirez has likely explained, you must follow the strongest leads we have on the biorg project, all the while keeping a lid on things. You've proven yourself competent and reasonably discreet in the past. This assignment calls for you to exercise both qualities. Based on further investigation of the late Dr. Grabowski's minicomp, as well as continued interrogation of the few surviving conspirators, the Trinity feels certain that this "Minerva" is also based in Basel.

You must go into the lion's den — the Montressor Clinic, headquarters of the Æsculapian Order — and discover the identity of Minerva as well as that of any accomplices. Apprehending the Huang-Marr conspirators is your top priority, but you must act with utmost discretion. Special Agent Hector Ramirez, although pursuing other aspects of this crisis, serves as your Æon contact. Don't expect handholding on this operation — the dam has a lot of leaks and you're only plugging one of them.

The future of humanity rests, in large part, on your shoulders. I know you're up to that responsibility. If you're not, well, let's see if you can fake it until this is all over. In the meantime, best of luck.

B'hatzlichah
Bailes
European Terrestrial Office 23:09:70 4.30.2120

Hope Sacrifice Unity

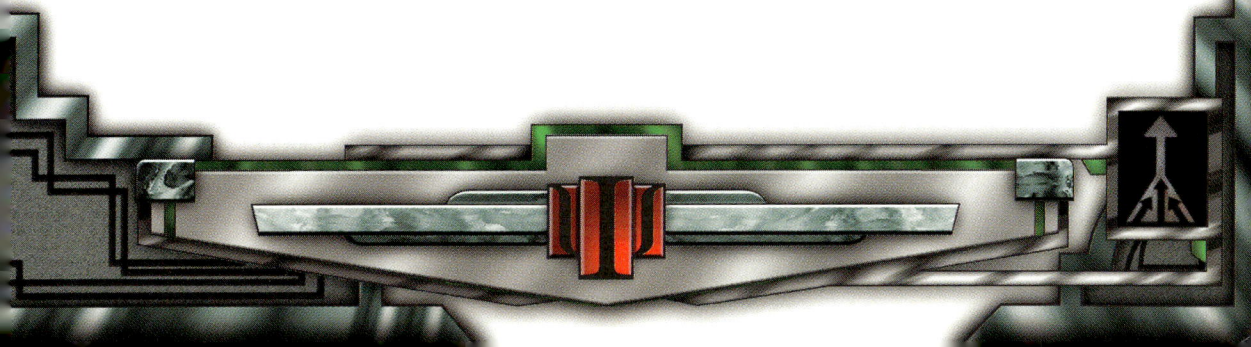

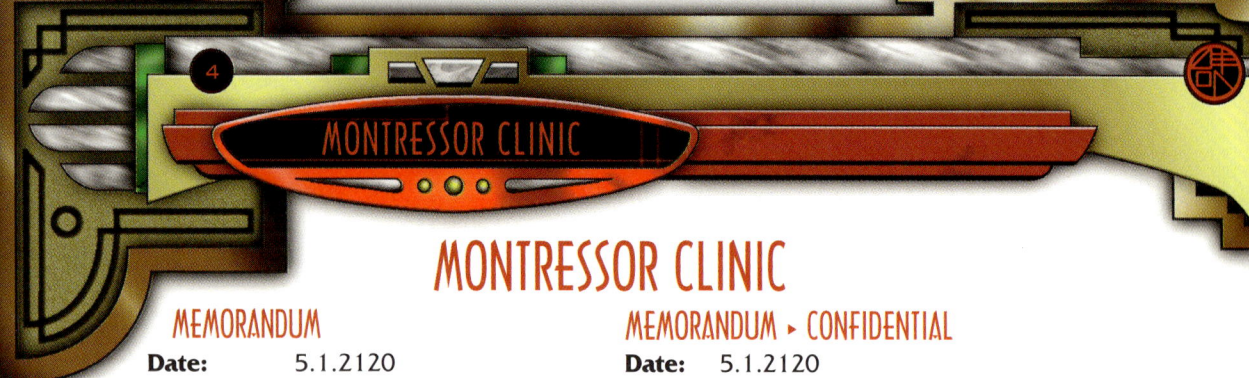

MONTRESSOR CLINIC

MEMORANDUM

Date: 5.1.2120
To: Staff
From: Dr. Matthieu Zweidler, Senior Director
Subject: Visitors

As some of you know, we will be visited shortly by very special guests. From the 4th through the 11th, we are playing host to psions associated with the Æon Trinity, some of whom had peripheral roles in the unpleasantness on Luna, at Beaulac Clinic and Boltzmann Station, and in the tragic destruction of Mars' Summit Center. These psions will stay with us, touring the facilities and acting as *ad hoc* ambassadors from the other orders. We must take this opportunity to confirm that there are no secret cabals of "mad scientists" here.

I am sure some of you have heard less-than-flattering rumors about the events leading up to the unfortunate death of Dr. Jerzy Grabowski, the clinic director at Beaulac, and about the role of Æon investigators in that matter. I also understand that some of you take the rumored — I repeat, *rumored* — improprieties at Beaulac as fact. Whatever the true circumstances that took place on Luna, there is no cause to mistreat the former Lunar personnel who now work here; allegations against them have yet to be proven.

Rest assured I am looking into the entire matter extensively. In the meantime, I urge you all to cease such speculation as fruitless and inaccurate, and allow your peers to work as they are accustomed to; that is, with professional respect and courtesy.

Otherwise, I look forward to the arrival of our visitors. All staff will of course offer every courtesy to our guests, and will cooperate fully with any *reasonable* requests they make.

Zweidler
SFZ/lt

MEMORANDUM ▸ CONFIDENTIAL

Date: 5.1.2120
To: Security Staff
From: Jakob Neihaus, Security Director
Subject: Visitors

As you know, we'll be baby-sitting a horde of "heroes" who royally cocked things up at Beaulac. We'll spend a week chaperoning a band of Trinity lackeys who'll poke their noses into every aspect of our operation in hopes of catching us with our pants down. They found something dirty up on Luna and now they're coming Earthside, determined to find something dirty here.

This is not a "fact-finding" mission or a "goodwill reception" no matter what kind of spin Doc Matt put on it in his memo. These people have an agenda. They'd love us to be the next Chitra Bhanu, and they won't be happy until they find something — anything — that they can use against us.

So we have to be perfect. We already run a tight ship; it has to be tighter. I don't want these Trinity assholes finding a single thing that they can complain about. That means perform your duties like your job depends on it — because it does. Tighten door checks, admitting and discharge security. Clean up the free clinic and make it look pretty for the photo ops. Shut down anything you find that's unauthorized and report to me that you've done so. (And yes, Devereaux, that means your "medicinal" pot farm is out of here.) Starting today, nobody sneezes in this place without you being there to hand them a tissue.

Two of you will escort our guests at all times; assignments will be on the duty roster by the end of today. One member of Black Company will be there, too. I want no sniping or grumbling with the Company, gang. We're all on the same page for the next couple of weeks. You can get back to busting those psych goons' chops when *Strike Team Psion* has left the building.

Weapons drill is at yellow, I repeat, *yellow* for the duration of our visitors' stay. If there's trouble, we want to be able to handle it before those Trinity jackboots have to so much as muss their hair.

Neihaus
JN/de

Olympus Screamer

"Lift a rock on the Rock and we're there"
TODAY'S HOT TOPICS!

...The late Dr. Jerzy Grabowski, former head of Olympus' Beaulac Clinic, was interred today on the Lunar surface. Most of the guests stayed in hoppers rather than pay their respects in vacuum, but the mourners got a surprise. A procession of pirate-burrow denizens stomped over in vac suits and jumped around on the Good Doctor Grabowski's grave. It seems he'd championed shutting the pirate burrows down, and these irate citizens interrupted the funeral for several minutes to let Grabowski know they'd outlasted him. Contrary to his usual form, the late Dr. Grabowski had no comment....

...Due to persistent rumors of cheating perpetrated by the Novy Petrograd Bandits, the Lunar Baseball League Commissioner's office prepped an investigation into the Wroclaw Sector team's latest contractual blunder. Wroclaw manager Leonid Semyonovich supposedly produced immigration records proving that the Bandits imported players from higher-g's. Sure enough, new Novy P-grad first baseman "Alain DuChamp" looks remarkably like washed up former Yankees first sacker Bobby Vatcher. "DuChamp" went into his patented fist-pumping routine right after poking a homer at Wroclaw Sector's Schilltronix Dome, and Semyonovich went nuts. No official statement yet from Bandits owner Pyotr Ilgauskas, but General Manager Elias Richter indicated that the Bandits "are ready to cooperate fully with the league office in hopes of clearing up these allegations as soon as possible." "DuChamp," on the other hand, was his usual incoherent self during post-game interviews....

...Over a month after the "Freak Alley Aberrant" murdered Dr. Jerzy Grabowski, hysterical sightings of the creature are finally diminishing. United Luna Police Force sweeps never found a thing, but that didn't stop people from screaming about another freak in the Underworld. The cops officially concluded that the damn thing is dead or at least gone, and folks are finally calming down. Those reporting a "Freak Alley Aberrant" are regarded as loons, drunks or morons — just like those who file the dozen Aberrant sightings each day. Olympus police confided that they have eyewitness reports of the "Aberrant" tearing apart an Orgotek factory complex, shooting itself into orbit, stealing Grabowski's remains, and even cruising Luna Park to see the sights....

TRITON ARCHIVE

ABERRANTS REMAIN AMONG US
— Anti-Aberrant Defense League leaflet

There is conclusive proof that Abberants still wak among us!!! They are here and they have infiltrated every government. They pull the strings of the vast comspiracies that have conspired to rob us of our FREEDOMS and make us SHEEPLIKE in the face of the ABBERANT MENACE!

In 2109 a COMNSPIRACY of Abberants, acting on orders from Dives mal and the SECRET MASTERS falsely FRAMED the noble Chitra Bhanu! Working thruout the universe in their unmarked black hoverships, these ABBERANTS and CONSPRATORS planted evidence that the Chitra Bhanu were in league with both ABBERANTS and ALIENS, enacting their plan to MURDER these peace-loving psions!

In 2114 this CNSPIRACY decided to destroyu more of our defenders! They had ther ALIEN allies destroy the *Esperantza*, and MURDERED the Teleporters WHILE WE WERE NOT LOOKING!

WE were not vigiliant enough then, but we know NOW that Abberants ahve targeted NEW ORDERS for destruction! They have planted SPIES deep within the other orders and are ACTIVATING them. SOOON they feel we will turn on the orders and destroy them, leaveing us defenseless! YOU must learn what you can do to help fend off the Abberant menace!

GRABOWSKI FUNERAL >>> PROTEUS ARCHIVE

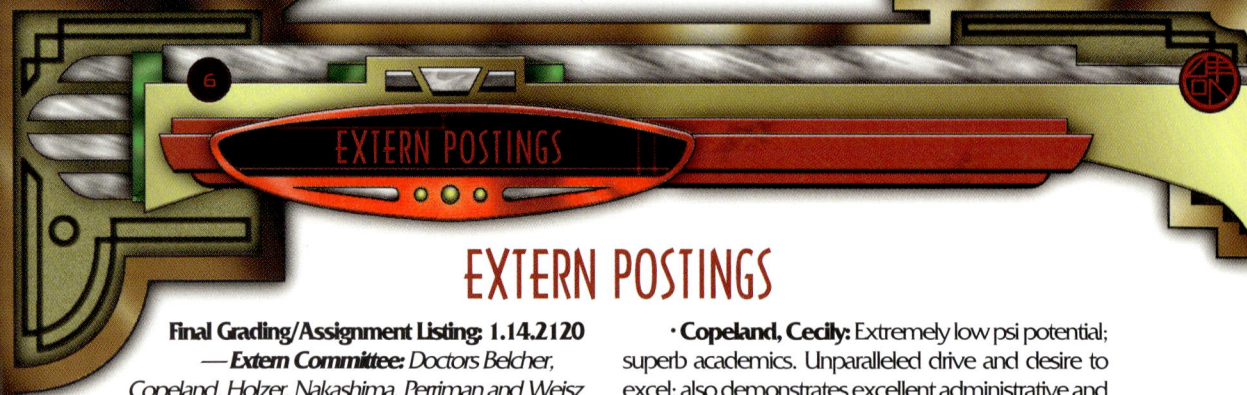

EXTERN POSTINGS

Final Grading/Assignment Listing: 1.14.2120
— **Extern Committee:** Doctors Belcher, Copeland, Holzer, Nakashima, Perriman and Weisz in attendance, Doctors Kotsay and Sheff absent

• **Alvarez, Selene:** Alvarez's test results consistently place her in the top 5% of her class. She demonstrates superb bedside manner and strong Iatrosis aptitude. Spent additional time above and beyond required hours in the free clinic. Alvarez's advisor indicated that she wanted to return to Venezuela to work there at some point. Two cousins are currently Norça psions. **Posting:** Port-au-Prince

• **Braipanasul, Rajesh:** Braipanasul is the youngest member of his class. He possesses tremendous psionic potential, mostly untapped. Instructors feel that he may be suitable for Algesis work; Black Company has expressed an interest after further training. **Posting:** Basel

• **Copeland, Cecily:** Extremely low psi potential; superb academics. Unparalleled drive and desire to excel; also demonstrates excellent administrative and organizational skills. Will make clinic director someday; expresses interest in working off-planet. From Federated States, has limited perspective as a result. **Posting:** Addis Ababa

• **Finn, Daniel:** Possibly the most average student of the past decade. Median test scores on everything — academics, psi potential, you name it. Totally affable; wouldn't complain if we posted him on the Lunar surface without a vac suit. Will make a fine GP someday, far from the front lines. **Posting:** Rochester

• **LaSalle, François:** Excellent Iatrosis potential. Was visiting relatives in Quebec when *Esperanza* struck; still experiences occasional survivor's guilt. Not recommended for frontline situations until that issue is dealt with. **Posting:** Basel

• **Muller, Heinrich:** Has a surprising interest in things spiritual. Would expect him to stay closer to grounding in hard sciences. Psi potential unquestionable; focus and dedication to studies lacking. **Posting:** Port-au-Prince

• **Sang, Lee Dae:** Ranks in upper 20% of class in academics, but lags slightly in psi potential. Shows a real knack for Algesis, but not the inclination to use it; should be discouraged from learning too much about that mode. Some sentiment for sending him to Port-au-Prince, but his scientific curiosity should be engaged by extended time here. Will probably end up in research. **Posting:** Basel

• **Thompson, Alison:** Completely botched the medical portion of her studies; lowest test scores we've seen in years. From the United Kingdom and is apparently into the "Old Ways," whatever they are. Strong psi, but Zweidler would blow his stack if he saw her technique. [*I have. I did. Get her out of here. —Matthieu*] **Posting:** Port-au-Prince

Matthieu, I'll announce these postings Thursday, unless you have objections. —Alfonse

Looks fine to me, except Alvarez. Get her further from Norça's home territory. I don't want her cousins recruiting her as their personal medic. —Matthieu

---

ARE YOU AN ORGAN DONOR?
— public service announcement

Hello, my name is Doctor Roland Stoltzfus. I work at the Montressor Clinic in Switzerland, and I'm asking for your help.

The world today is a more dangerous place than it has perhaps ever been. With the return of the Aberrants, humanity's ongoing extraterrestrial expansion and new technologies arriving here every day, there has never been a greater need for blood or organ donors. Thousands of people who could otherwise be saved are dying because we don't have the blood supplies or the organs to save them.

But there's something you can do to help. Go to your local clinic or hospital and give blood. It only takes a few minutes, it's painless and it saves lives all over the Solar System. And, while you're there, fill out an organ-donor card. Agreeing to donate your organs after your death means that part of you will live on through someone else.

Every day, we fall farther behind the demand that harsh reality places upon our facilities. Every day, the crisis grows. Please, become an organ donor. The life you save may belong to someone you love.

— *This message was presented by OBC, the Montressor Clinic and by your local branch of the Intersolar Red Cross.*

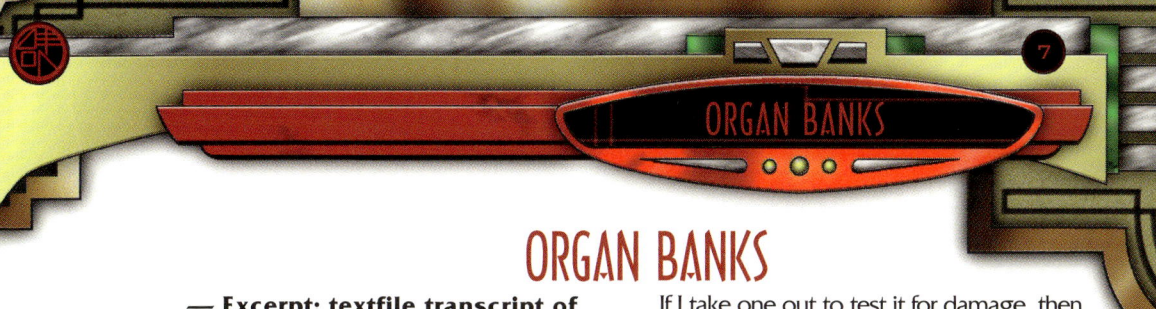

ORGAN BANKS

— **Excerpt: textfile transcript of Montressor Clinic security footage**

\>>> Two men in clinic uniforms enter restroom. Employment files designate the individuals as Serge Rivera and Edwin Ledee. Audio picks up conversation in progress. <<<

LEDEE: …won the bet with Wockenfus in Shipping.

RIVERA: Impossible. No way he would have done that.

LEDEE: I'm telling you, he waited until the new guy left the room, then unzipped and took a whiz right into the kidneys.

RIVERA: Oh, man, what happened?

LEDEE: The pH alarm went off, so we dumped some KOH in to balance it out. Then Melian fiddled with the vids so the incident got wiped. Wockenfus paid up and we scrammed before the new guy came back.

RIVERA: The kidneys look okay?

LEDEE: They looked like kidneys usually look. If I take one out to test it for damage, then there's all sorts of paperwork, and the whole thing comes out — with Melian getting fired as a result. Besides, kidneys are built to handle that sort of thing, so a little extra won't hurt.

RIVERA: I hope so. If Stoltzfus catches wind of this….

LEDEE: Never mind Stoltzy; he hasn't been awake for years. The new guy is the one we have to watch out for — he'll pitch a fit.

RIVERA: Tuten?

LEDEE: Yep. He's got a carbon-monofilament extrusion up his ass.

RIVERA: Did you notice that he was walking funny the first couple of days he was here?

LEDEE: Yeah. Looked like he'd been off-planet. Faded fast, though. Probably native Earther.

RIVERA: Whatever. He's an asshole, wherever he's from.

LEDEE: Goes with the job, man, goes with the job.

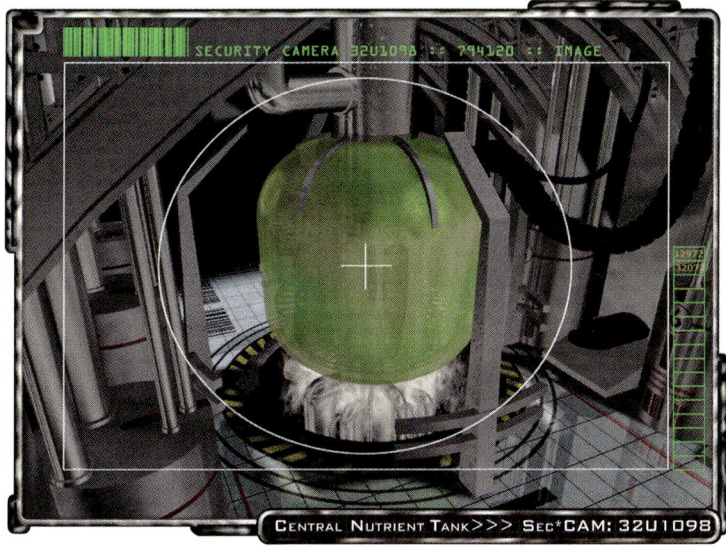

This came in on one of the Organ Bank security cameras. Some wise guy moved the camera from the liver nutrient chamber to the men's room. It took two weeks for anyone to notice, but in the meantime we got this recording. I think you'll agree that there are some serious concerns here.
— Neihaus
P.S. — I've forwarded a copy to Roland, for whenever he wakes up.

Montressor!

— Miranda Soto, The One to Watch © 2120 OBC

Once again, *Montressor!* sets the standard for ongoing drama in holovids. While other serials (*Marianas, Langrange Delta-Niner* and *Sanhedrin Station*, to name three) have garnered more attention this season, the writing and acting on *Montressor!* consistently draw the discerning viewer back to this fictionalized Basel, and the lives and loves of those who dwell there. *Montressor!'s* relationship with its viewers can best be described as a marriage; there may be dalliances with others, but in the end we always come home.

Undoubtedly part of *Montressor!'s* initial appeal was the connection to the famed clinic. "How much of the show was real?" we wondered. "How much would we be allowed to see?" Well, despite Proxy Zweidler's steadfast refusal to appear on the show (he's a constant offscreen presence, however, and the comlinks have been buzzing with rumors that he will finally step onstage shortly), the vid's producers have been granted unparalleled access to behind-the-scenes life at the real Montressor. While head scriptwriter Alain Berends won't say how many of his scripts are drawn from life ("Certain of the people on the show were, how you say, inspired by rexs and patients whom I and others associated with the show met — but that's all I can say"), rexs outside the clinic give *Montressor!* high marks for its authenticity. "Just like I remembered," was the comment from one Æsculapian of my acquaintance. "I caught myself reacting when the code-blue alarms rang on the show."

"If they were going to do a show about my clinic — and they said they would, with or without my approval," Dr. Zweidler said, "I thought that my cooperation would at least make it the best show possible. It would allow humanity to see the sacrifices that doctors and nurses here make for them every day. All that I asked in return was that the show be done well — I intensely dislike things that are done poorly or partially."

This was the proxy's one and only comment on the show, though sources close to Zweidler suggest that he is quite pleased with *Montressor!*, its string of Raymi awards and the licensing fees the show pays to the clinic's general fund.

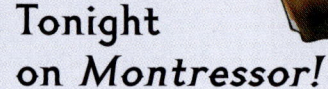

Tonight on *Montressor!*

— OBC program guide

Ross E. Schreck, Angela Kahane (R): Doctors Maline (Schreck) and Guderiene (Kahane) rekindle their romance; while in surgery, Dr. Takashi discovers that his patient has taint; Nurse Gould helps a dying patient at the free clinic fulfill his last wish; Dr. Bailey confronts Alodar Mirac (guest-star Janosz Steyer) over rumors of illicit research at the clinic; Administrator Yaus prepares the clinic for an upcoming visit from Qin observers; Doctors Abdelnaby and Erwin face their impending separation as her reassignment to Port-au-Prince approaches.

Ground Broken at Three Æsculapian Satellite Clinics

— Sheila Desbrough, Follow the ¥ © 2120 GN

BASEL — Work began on three more Æsculapian-sponsored clinics this morning; one on Ceres and two on Earth. The *Rossi* Station clinic was on the drawing board for over three years, with construction delayed by Aberrant attacks, financing difficulties and petitions from other off-Earth sites. The two Earthside sites, however, were rushed through the approval process despite a staggering number of competing bids from municipalities eager to play host to an Æsculapian clinic.

São Paulo and Brisbane won the new clinics. "It's both an honor and a relief to know that the brave doctors and psions of the Æsculapian Order will be on hand in our city should the worst happen," São Paulo mayor Irene Maldonado said during the groundbreaking ceremony for the de los Santos Clinic. "We welcome them to São Paulo with open arms and grateful hearts." Brisbane's ranking citizen was more succinct: "We're glad you're here, and I hope to God this is the last time I see you."

Economic studies have estimated the impact of a top-flight clinic on a local economy to be in excess of ¥42.5M. Between the clinic's actual business and corresponding secondary injections of cash into the local economy (hotel stays, restaurant visits for patients' families, increased property values, job creation), an Æsculapian clinic is a major shot in the arm for any locale. Add the prestige factor of having a clinic staffed by actual psions, and landing one of these coveted practices becomes something any self-respecting city aspires to. The Æsculapian Order does not solicit considerations when establishing new sites. Still, when cities desperate for a clinic make suggestions, who can blame Dr. Zweidler and his associates for listening?

So for today, Ceres, São Paulo and Brisbane are happy. Other regions (reputedly York, Maracaibo and at least three Lunar sites) must work through their disappointment and plan their proposals for the next round of clinic assignments.

Medicine, after all, is one business that will persist as long as the species does.

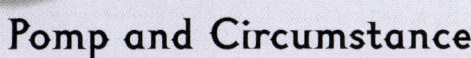

Pomp and Circumstance

—Cori Heisler, The Painful Truth © 2120 MMI

The venerable Montressor Clinic, headquarters of the docs, is decked out in its best, waiting for the arrival of the heroes of the "Beaulac Clinic Crisis." (*What exactly did these heroes do?* I ask myself. The Æsculapians, Orgotek and even the Æon Trinity's normally effusive PR people have been suspiciously closemouthed about the actual events that took place on Luna only two months ago.)

The reclusive Dr. Zweidler himself will attend the welcoming ceremony to thank the psions for their services on Luna. Despite the unseasonably cold (even for Basel) spring day, the clinic will hold the welcoming ceremony on the outside landing platform. Yours truly will be there for the greetings, but we've been informed that the media won't be allowed to follow inside!

"There won't be anything to see, really," said clinic spokesflak Pierce Monahan. "They're just getting the basic tour." That may be so, but we here on the outside wonder what special sights psions will see that "blanks" won't!

And let's hope that Dr. Zweidler and his staff know what they're doing, inviting these psions in. If the rumors trickling down from Olympus are true, we should all pray history doesn't repeat itself. The last time these psions visited an Æsculapian clinic, it sounds like the whole place nearly fell down around their ears!

ÆON TRINITY FACTBOOK: EARTH

Select Region by Touching

North America   South America   Australia
    Asia   Africa   Antarctica
Pacifica   **Europe**

>>> Data Transferring... Check Out Today's *Retrospective* with Warren Shaw... Loans for offworld transfer available from Bank of Christchurch... Data Transferring... Rex Pharmacies, the lowest prices for prescriptions this side of the Clinic!... Transfer complete <<<

Select Region by Touching

Iberia   British Isles   France   Germany
Benelux/Holland   Italia   **Switzerland**

>>> Transmission Halted... New Data Transferring... Bad Credit? No Credit? You can still afford luxury on Luna!... XXX ADULTS-ONLY HOLOS AVAILABLE. TOUCH ME TO FIND OUT HOW... Transfer complete <<<

• TRITON ARCHIVE •

SCHILLTRONIX ANNOUNCES SUCCESSFUL BLIGHT PROJECT ALLIANCE WITH ORGOTEK

— Schilltronix press release, 6.19.2119

Schilltronix Corporation is proud to announce a joint venture with Orgotek in constructing a series of research bases around the North American Blight Zone. The stations will be constructed in sequence over the next year-and-a-half, each with a different research focus. All, however, are directed to the ideal of eventually reclaiming the Blight for agricultural purposes.

Schilltronix will account for approximately 30% of the estimated ¥4.5B cost of construction and maintenance of the six-station ring, as well as 25% of operations costs in exchange for rights to any strains of Blight-resistant plants produced by the project, in addition to other considerations. Orgotek will pay the remainder of the costs and have rights to soil treatments, new fertilizer compounds and other hard technologies developed to counter the Blight.

Orgotek CEO Alex Cassel and Schilltronix CEO Stefan Coutrai signed the historic agreement today at Schilltronix corporate headquarters in Geneva, Switzerland.

ÆON TRINITY FACTBOOK: EARTH: EUROPE: SWITZERLAND

OVERVIEW

Location: Central Europe, East of *Esperanza* crash zone
Area: 41290 km^2
Land Area: 39770 km^2
Coastline: 0 km. Landlocked
Climate: Temperate, but varies with altitude. Winters are rainy/snowy and often cloudy. Summers are humid and sometimes rainy.
Terrain: Three distinct geological zones. Alps comprise S corner of region, the Jura the NW. Intermediate region is a central plateau marked by large lakes, plains and small hills.
Natural Resources: Minimal. Salt and timber, hydropower and limited hydroponics
Land Use: Arable Land: 8% Permanent Crops: 3%
Meadows and Pastures: 36% Forest and Woodland 18%
Other: 35%
Irrigated Land: 370 km^2
Environmental Issues: Overcrowding along W and NW borders, esp. in urban regions due to *Esperanza*-zone refugees. Some ancillary damage from the orbital-station crash. Air and water pollution, esp. from manufacturing base along Rhine and increased use of fertilizers. Deforestation becoming prevalent. Open-air burning producing some air pollution. Biodiversity in marked decline.
Natural Hazards: Avalanche, landslide, flash flooding
Population: 8090125 11:16:2119 census
Age Demographic:

0-15 yrs:	16%	1294420	52% female
16-64 yrs:	64%	5177680	51% male
65 yrs+:	20%	1618025	63% female

Increase in elderly population can be attributed to presence of Montressor and affiliated clinics in providing care.
Population Growth: 0.73%
Net Migration Rate: 11.16 migrants/1K population
Ethnic Divisions: German 61%
    French 26%
    Italian 9%
    Romansch 1%
    Other 3%
Languages: German, French, Italian, Romansch
Literacy: Age 15 and over: 98% (source: 2112 survey)
Labor Force: 4.06 million (864,000 foreign workers, predominantly Italian and French)
By Occupation: Services 52%, Industry and Crafts 30%, Agriculture and Forestry 8%, Government 6%, Other 4%
>>> Transmission interrupted! Try Again/End/Print/Quit <<<
>>> END <<<

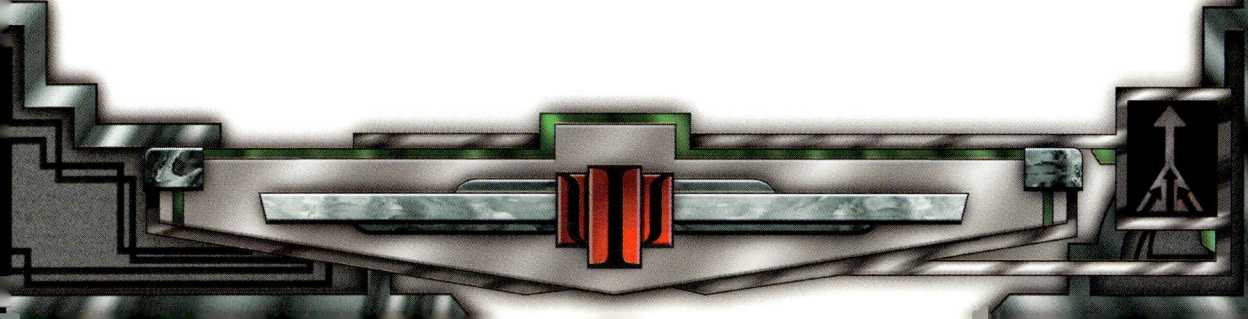

BLACK COMPANY

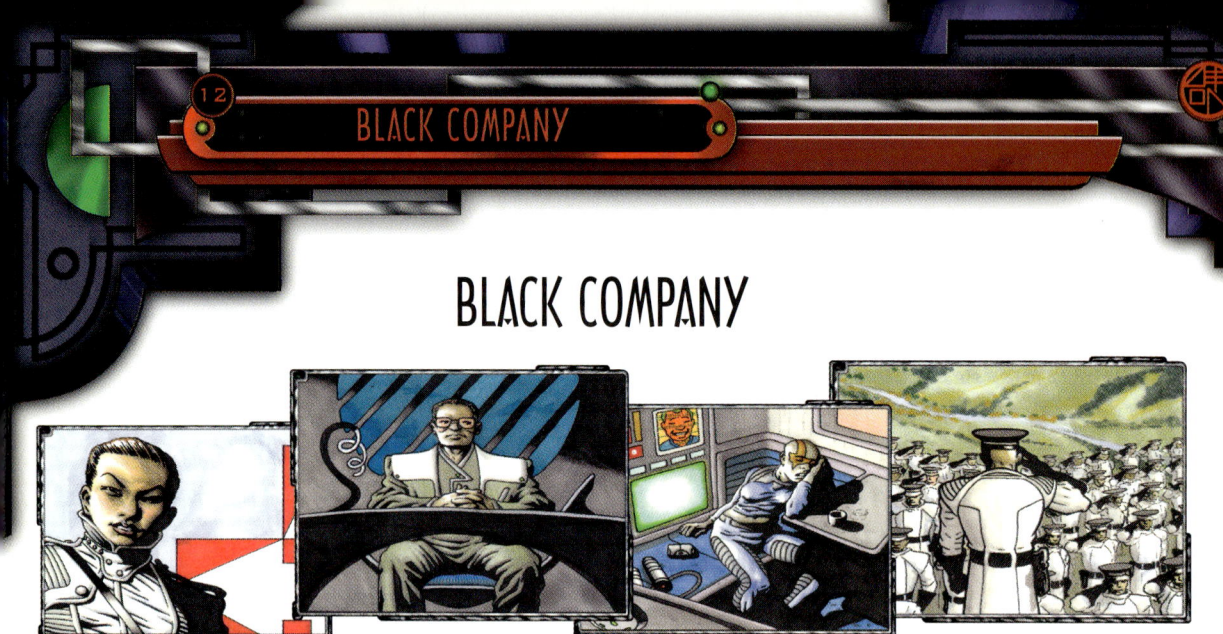

Greetings, citizen. My name is Aprille Glück. I'm contacting you on behalf of my employer, Dr. Matthieu Zweidler.

It's come to Doctor Zweidler's attention that you're unhappy with your current order. That you're feeling stifled. That you're looking for something *more*, something you can't get where you are now.

Maybe it's a chance for promotion.

Maybe it's a new brand of excitement.

Maybe it's security.

Maybe it's more money.

If this is what you're looking for, you'll find it all in the Black Company.

What is the Black Company? Named to honor the Swiss *freikorps* that were Europe's military elite for centuries, the Black Company is a group of top-flight psions recruited from all over the world who work together to protect the Æsculapian Order's interests.

BLACK COMPANY RECRUITMENT HOLOSIM > ÆSCULAPIAN ORDER

Headquartered in Basel, at the famous Montressor Clinic, the Black Company works directly for Dr. Zweidler and *no one else*.

Think about it. You're that close to the top. Do you get that in your current order?

Black Company duties cover a wide range: providing honor guards for visiting dignitaries, protecting Æsculapian clinics in combat zones, fighting Aberrants who take potshots at a hospital. And when you're not on direct assignment, your time's your own.

The pay is excellent. The living quarters — provided by the Æsculapian Order, of course — have all of the latest amenities. The best medical care available to humanity is right there for you. And there are many fabulous perks.

You don't have to decide now. But think about what you've got, and think about what we can offer.

We'll be in touch.

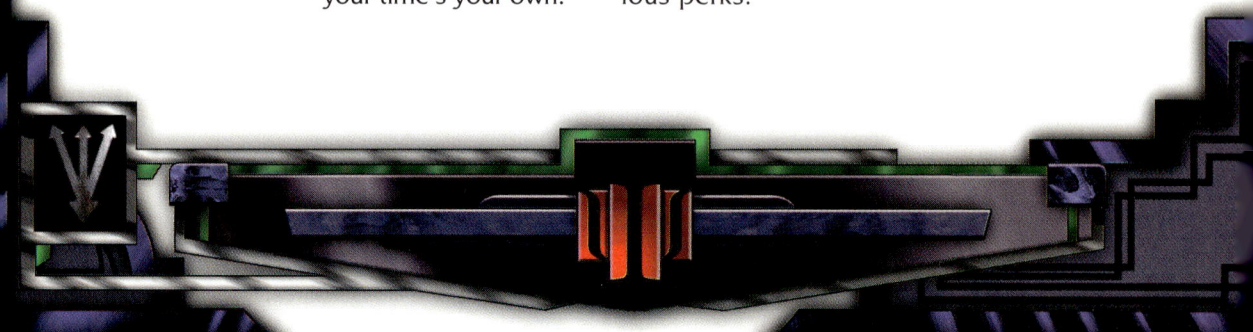

HUANG-MARR PROJECT BRIEFING

— recovered from Æsculapian databank [Basel]

Mission Statement: The goal of the Huang-Marr Biorg Project (henceforth "the project") is to develop bioware applications that can be surgically implanted and subsumed into a psion's natural armature.

Goals: Ideally, the bioapps developed for the project will be undetectable. Furthermore, increases in psi yields of up to 400% are anticipated.

Timetable: The project is to produce a working prototype by 2.15.2119, with laboratory and field testing to commence by 8.1.2119. Testing is to continue until 7.1.2120, with commercial production to commence by 12.1.2120.

Rationale: It is a simple fact that our psions, even the very best, are orders of magnitude lower in power than all but the weakest Aberrants. It is ludicrous to expect our best to go into combat at a decided disadvantage every time. Sooner or later, we won't have numbers on our side. Defeat is inevitable under such circumstances.

The logical solution to this problem is to make sure that our psions are better armed. Standard bioware is the first step in the right direction, but even that leaves the best-armed psions bearing ordnance that's markedly inferior to their opponents' capabilities. The logical step, then, is to make better bioware, bioware more thoroughly integrated with a psion's natural abilities, thereby providing a more efficient amplification of power. And, if necessary, bioware that has auxiliary or augmented power sources.

It is our intent to create bioapps that give our psions equal standing with their enemies. Ideally, we can build on preliminary research already finished by Drs. Huang and Marr to implement a full-scale manufacturing process within the year.

Mandate: Parties within both the Æsculapian Order and Orgotek have provided monies, facilities and test subjects for the project. High-ranking officials of both groups are fully committed to making certain that this project succeeds, *regardless of the cost.*

Security: The project must operate in strict confidentiality. This confidentiality is enforced by whatever means necessary. What we are doing is in violation of the statutes of every governing body in human space. We are risking, and in some cases, ending subjects' lives. We are working with the deadliest genetic sequence known to mankind, and we are using it to craft weapons of awesome destructive capability. If we are discovered before we have a chance to demonstrate the benefits of our work, we will be disgraced, imprisoned and in all probability executed.

Needless to say, this is hardly a desirable outcome. If we are discovered, the sacrifices we are making — our time, our work, our consciences — go for naught. Therefore, it is imperative that the project operate under utmost secrecy. By reading this document, you have agreed to work with us in this most vital endeavor. You cannot go back. There is nowhere to go but forward.

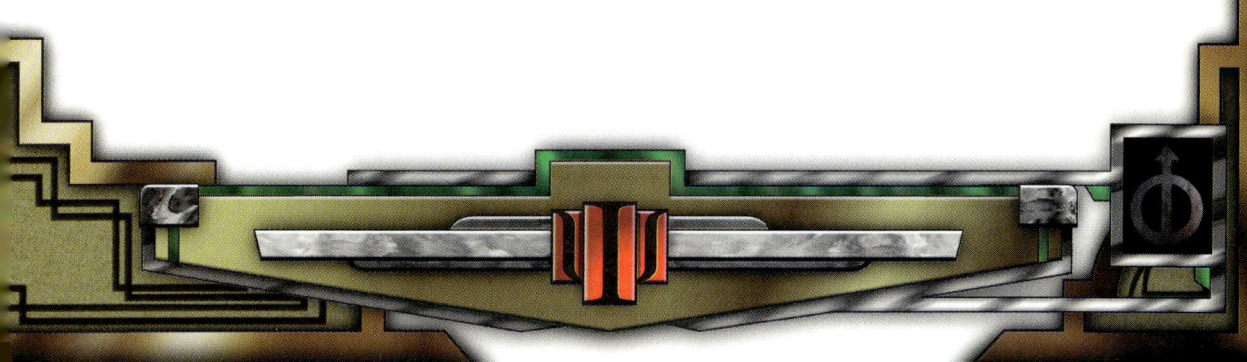

PROJECT BRIEFING

History: The project was founded on the research conducted by two independent Æsculapian psions, Dr. Ella Huang and Dr. Abel Marr. Veterans of the Nerve Studies Clinic, each became interested in researching ways to improve the interface between psions and their bioware. Their work led them to research done by Celia Wu, an Orgotek corporate researcher, and eventually to each other. Meanwhile, the grant proposals that Marr filed came to the attention of Dr. Gustaf Beitz of the Æsculapian Order after the latter returned from treating psions injured in the Aberrant attack on *Tethys* Station. Beitz immediately saw the potential applications of Marr's work, and he brought Huang and Marr to Basel to arrange funding. They drew up a research plan and brought Wu in on the project; she arranged for Orgotek support as well.

Unfortunately, by late 2117, it became clear that the project had stalled. While Wu, Huang and Marr managed to extract increased efficiency from the standard bioapps they worked with, it simply wasn't enough. It was at this point that Beitz suggested taint be included in the biotech operating matrix. Wu balked and left the project, but Huang and Marr considered the stakes and agreed to continue work. The two recruited staff and threw themselves wholeheartedly into their work. Wu died later in a tragic skimmer accident near Rochester, Minnesota; she was replaced on the project by her assistant, Horace Meeks. Satellite labs were set up on Luna, Mars and elsewhere on Earth. Orgotek participation increased in exchange for rights to the manufacture and sale of any bioapps the project produced.

Which brings us to the present. Technically, we are criminals. In truth, we are pioneers, the Galileos of this new age, defying accepted conventions in order to serve the greater good.

Welcome to the project.

Recovered from: //æsculapian.org/montressor/main.users/mangels/save_fil

File matches [6] others found on system. Located in:

//æsculapian.org/montressor/bcomp.users/mandel/save_fil

//æsculapian.org/montressor/main.users/huang/save_fil

//æsculapian.org/montressor/main.users/marr/save_fil

//æsculapian.org/montressor/sercure.users/lacombe/save_fil

//æsculapian.org/montressor/organbanks.users/Tuten/save_fil

//æsculapian.org/montressor/nerve.users/polonsky/save_fil

• TRITON ARCHIVE •

MEMORANDUM

— recovered from deleted files in minicomp of Dr. Jerzy Grabowski (post-mortem)
• Eyes Only • Confidential •
• Eyes Only • Confidential •
Date: 2.6.2120
To: Project Heads
From: Minerva
Subject: The Future

We are compromised. To that effect, consolidate operations immediately. Move >>> data lost <<< delay. Lunar personnel are to be transferred to Mars or Earth through Basel and dispersed from there. Equipment and experim[ental data is to] be shipped likewise while extraneous subjects are transported or destroyed. The details of the cleanup, I [leave in yo]ur capable hands.

We cannot afford to stop our work now that we are so close to success. The results from the testing centers have been ext[remely encouraging, and] demonstrations have been enough to ensure continued cooperation from our frie[nds in] >>> data lost; degraded too much to allow successful reconstruction <<<

— contents recovered from deleted files within the
Æsculapian Organ Banks databank [Basel]

3.14.2120

Minerva's kept his/her promises thus far. I'm in at the Organ Banks under the name of Reinhardt Tuten — "Rootin' Tuten," they call me, and it's annoying beyond belief — with a complete dossier, background and history. Of course, it had to be the Organ Banks, and I can't believe that Grabowski let it slip that I was headed here. Still, hopefully the investigation will blow over shortly and I can get back to doing what I'm supposed to, instead of checking on warmed-over livers in month-old nutrient baths. Still, everyone here has something to hide, so no one asks any annoying questions. It's perfect, as long as it's short-term.

3.16.2120

Astonishing. The staff here seems equally divided between sociopaths and incompetents. The former are here, working primarily on extractions, because the corpses they take donations from can't complain. The latter are here because it's harder than one would think to screw up this job, and because no one except Catalanotto knows how many organs come in and out of this place. Actually, I'm not sure even he does, and that may be a good thing.

Catalanotto himself is an interesting study. He runs this place with an iron fist, which he primarily uses to scratch his ass. Today a short-timer named Diaz dropped and cracked a transfer container. Catalanotto went ballistic; security had to restrain him from assaulting her. Diaz is here on a three-month rotation because she lost a high-profile patient at Addis Ababa; I don't know what she was expecting, but surely it wasn't this.

3.18.2120

Catalanotto doesn't know. The records are hopelessly out of date. The interesting thing is that, simply from a visual scan, the numbers in the computer are low. One would expect it to be the other way around, with organs missing like in some sort of holovid "organ-smuggling" ring. That's not the case. There are actually *too many* parts here.

Someone's being sloppy with personal effects, too. Randle wore a Nippon Ham Fighters hat on shift. That's against regs and I called him on it, which got me precisely nowhere. The interesting thing, however, is that the hat was originally the property of a John Doe that the cleanup teams brought in off the road around New Year. Effects of John Does are supposed to be sterilized and sent to the free clinic.

It's a small thing, but it rankles.

3.20.2120

Finally adjusting to Earth gravity again. The others are whispering about my stride and my limp — any of them with half a brain must know I've been on Luna. That means I have to worry.

3.24.2120

The situation is worse than I thought. Admissions is hopelessly out of date. We don't know how many organs we have here, or of what kind. That means bad matches are going out the door. That means patients are dying on the other end of those shipments.

How the hell did this happen? Every other Organ Bank I've visited has been at top efficiency. This is right under Zweidler's nose, for God's sake. How can he not know? And Stoltzfus? Where the hell is he when all this is going on? Relaxing in Beijing while contractors finish the new banks there. Nice work if you can get it, Roland.

A body came in yesterday afternoon, brought in by a man on the shipping staff named Wockenfuss. The cadaver's ID card didn't list him as a donor, but Rivera started cutting.

Cause of death was "blunt trauma to the head." The body looked like it had been bludgeoned for half an hour with a baseball bat.

What the hell is going on here?

4.3.2120

Vaughn spilled KOH into one of the vats today, then tried to cover it up. I raised hell; Vaughn's out the door and a half-dozen hearts had to be destroyed because of contamination. I'm pushing for a full audit, but Catalanotto doesn't want to go through with it. I think he's afraid his dirty laundry will come out.

4.8.2120

An unpleasant surprise on the comlink today. Minerva downloaded my bolt-hole information — it's through Schilltronix's latest contracted site — and leveled some very thinly veiled threats. My request for the audit had somehow climbed past Catalanotto on the chain of command and landed on Minerva's desk, where he — yeah, *he* — promptly squashed it. The audit would draw attention to the Organ Banks, and to the man who asked for it — me. And I'm supposed to be laying low.

Of course, this gives me one more clue as to Minerva's identity. I'm sure that Minerva's a he. It's either Stoltzfus, Delemont or Beitz. They're all squatting over Catalanotto in the chain of command.

4.13.2120

I don't like this. Minerva is putting more pressure on me. He knows about the transcripts of the data logs that I've set to release to Heisler and Shaw if I die, so I don't think I'm in any immediate danger. Still, the direct attention of a man like Minerva is disturbing. More warnings to back off on my efforts to clean up the banks.

That bothers me on a level that the Huang-Marr Project never did. Some of the biorg work was… regrettable. Disturbing, even. But we were doing it with a goal in sight, an ultimate end that would make all of the suffering worthwhile. I believed that then, and I still believe it now. Making humanity safe from Aberrants is worth a lot of lives, a lot of pain and a lot of sleepless nights on the part of a few lowly researchers.

But this, this is just waste. This is lives being thrown away out of sheer laziness and carelessness. There's no end in sight, no goal that this is working toward. What I'm witnessing here — and what people like Catalanotto and Minerva seem willing to sanction — is far more a betrayal of my ideals as a doctor than the biorg project ever was.

4.19.2120

Diaz feels the way I do. I wish I could confide in her a bit more, but there's no sense getting her in trouble. I'm safe; she's not. In the meantime, however, she's working on getting Admissions tightened up. I'm doing some work on safeguarding the actual banks — there's been an ungodly amount of contamination.

One interesting tidbit: Minerva thinks Malachi Ross has somehow gotten off Luna. It's an interesting theory, but I don't see how it concerns me. God should roast Jerzy's soul for that screwup.

4.30.2120

More pressure from Minerva. Diaz is being transferred out tomorrow, a month early. She's ecstatic; sees it as a reward. I know what it is — an attempt to deny me allies.

5.1.2120

Diaz left. It doesn't matter.

I know who you are now, Minerva.

>>> file ends <<<

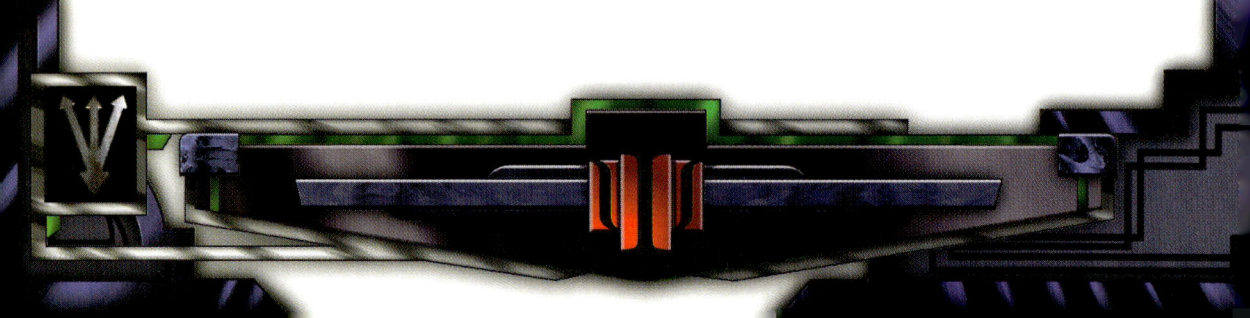

FOR STORYTELLER EYES ONLY!

This section is for Storytellers only; it provides the information, plot hooks and statistics needed to run the second installment in the **Darkness Revealed** series for **Trinity**. Players should stop reading *now* and restrict themselves to perusing the full-color setting section.

What Is This?

Friends in High Places is the first episode of **Passage Through Shadow**, the second book in the **Darkness Revealed** adventure trilogy. This episode can serve as either a continuation of the series begun in **Descent into Darkness** or as a stand-alone story that can be your players' entry into the Trinity Universe.

The **Darkness Revealed** trilogy, comprised of **Descent into Darkness, Passage Through Shadow** and **Ascent into Light**, throws characters into the middle of the most momentous events of the 22nd century. The characters' interactions literally have the power to affect all of humanity. Their actions are of the greatest import, not only to the psi orders and the Æon Trinity, but to the human race — even to the entire cosmos. Great and terrible things are afoot, and the characters may well be the fulcrum on which the weight of history rests.

Darkness Revealed is an epic series, but one that operates from moment to moment. Viewed from a distance, the characters' actions might be grand stuff, but here those events are broken down into small-scale, immediate, personal incidents. In some instances, particular events may seem mundane on the surface only to have subtle yet profound repercussions elsewhere. The flow of the plot derives from the choices that the characters make, not from any "master plot" that *must* be followed.

Each episode in this book is split into two sections: full-color setting and black-and-white rules information. The former is "color text" in more ways than one — it consists of interesting background information pertinent to the story. Players should read the setting material before — or at appropriate points during — the episode. The setting sets the stage for the scenario and provides useful information for characters to use in the course of the story.

The black-and-white rules portion of the episode — such as the material you are reading now — consists of Storyteller-specific material. From here on in (or at least until the beginning of the next episode), you get a plot synopsis, specific episode and source material, suggested ways to advance the plot, hints for nudging things along, and even Storyteller-character writeups. This is the meat of the adventure, the part that really tells you what's going on.

Either way, good luck. The Trinity Universe is about to change forever.

The Plot

The following is a synopsis of *Friends in High Places*. Later sections cover the details more fully.

What Has Gone Before

The characters are pursuing leads uncovered during the events of **Descent into Darkness**. In that volume, a series of disappearances on Luna caught the attention of the Æon Trinity, which sent a group to investigate. What the characters found was bigger than anyone expected. Individuals within the Æsculapian and Orgotek Orders had collaborated on something called the Huang-Marr Bio-organic Interface Project (generally shortened to the "Huang-Marr Project" or simply "biorg project"). This illicit program used taint to create bioware implants that boosted psions' abilities to terrifying levels; these implants were even tested on abducted human subjects.

The Olympus branch of the project was already shut down by the time the characters began their investigation. Materials and personnel (including one of the project's chief scientists, Dr. Heinrich Mangels) were shipped off Luna and information was destroyed. However, there was still enough evidence to track down and detain the project's apparent author, Æsculapian clinic head Dr. Jerzy Grabowski. An escaped experimental test subject (former rex Dr.

Malachi Ross) broke into Grabowski's cell and murdered him before he could be questioned.

With Grabowski dead and Ross vanished back into Olympus' underbelly, the investigators had few leads. The most promising was Boltzmann Station, a nearby Lunar colony with possible ties to the Huang-Marr Project. After digging through a quagmire of intrigue and coverups, the Æon Trinity confirmed that Boltzmann was home to another branch of the biorg project, with conspirators at the Linma Telcom communications complex and the Æsculapian Covenants Clinic. Research there involved working directly with Aberrants! A mysterious espionage unit known only as "Option-8," seemingly related to Orgotek, hindered the team's investigation. Still, with the assistance of Boltzmann Station security personnel, the investigators shut down the site and captured all but four of the conspirators. Patrice and Andromeda Willom, husband-and-wife Orgotek scientists, escaped in a capsule to Mars. The other pair, the Æsculapian Serevitek Kriso and the Aberrant Anders Nash, left in a similar capsule.

With the Huang-Marr conspirators on the run, the investigators gave immediate chase. The characters' transport came upon the ice-hauler *Freya* and discovered the ship had picked up Kriso and Nash's capsule. Nash had already killed the crew and taken control of the ship. Kriso, at this point more terrified of his Aberrant companion than of what the Æon Trinity might do to him, promised to divulge all he knew of the biorg project if the team would save him. After a hard battle with Anders Nash, the investigators made it safely to Mars.

The team set out to find the Willoms, the chase leading them to Summit Center on the dead Olympus Mons volcano. The investigation became a race against assassins gunning for the team and for the Willoms. The ensuing battle literally sent Summit Center tumbling down the mountainside. But even in the chaos of that sudden descent, the investigators fought off the Option-8 assassins and apprehended the Willoms.

Overview

At the start of *Friends in High Places*, the Æon Trinity feels certain that biorg research has been shut down. It has evidence linking dozens of individual Æsculapians to the illicit research, and operatives are being sent to apprehend those docs. Evidence points to Orgotek as well, but that order's ties are more nebulous. Æon operatives (under Hector Ramirez) are checking into those leads.

Amid this time-consuming research, the characters are sent to Basel to pursue the masterminds behind the Huang-Marr Project. By far, the biggest lead is the mysterious "Minerva," who appeared to the Huang-Marr conspirators as a computer agent modeled after the Roman goddess of wisdom. The characters are to ferret out "Minerva," Mangels and any other hidden conspirators, while disrupting unconnected Æsculapians as little as possible. The investigators' mere presence at Montressor is bound to generate numerous rumors no matter what the outcome. It's just as important for the characters to be subtle as it is for them to find the remaining accomplices.

Even from the beginning, it's evident that this isn't a simple reconnaissance mission. The public death of Dr. Grabowski, followed by the notorious battle with an Aberrant and the destruction of Summit Center on Mars, has the media very interested about what's happening within the Æsculapian Order. The Montressor staff is reluctant to admit the characters, fearing public scandal could tear the order apart. The team must be subtle and persistent to avoid the media and clinic security long enough to bring the facts to light.

The characters discover the tension between Basel-traditionalist and Port-au-Prince-bound Æsculapians. They learn of the friction between regular clinic security and the elite Black Company. They unearth the barely suppressed fear that the entire order may be purged pending the outcome of the characters' investigation.

After learning of these general facts, the team finally acquires vital information: There's a link between the vitakinesis order and the Schilltronix corporation. Schilltronix proves to be the conduit between the Æsculapian and Orgotek conspirators, channeling resources between Basel and the North American Blight Zone.

Dr. Heinrich Mangels also pops up, blowing his own cover as an Organ Bank technician named "Reinhardt Tuten." The very thing that made Mangels perfect for the Huang-Marr Project makes him terrible at hiding in the Organ Banks. Mangels takes great pride in his medical talents and scientific skill. However, he can't stand incompetence, which is exactly what he sees every day in the Organ Banks. Eventually, Mangels' attempts to excise the corruption within the Organ Banks brings him to the characters' attention.

Before the characters can move on Mangels, Dr. Malachi Ross reappears. Controlled by

Grabowski into becoming a biorg test subject, Ross escaped his confinement on Luna, killed Grabowski, and roamed the lower levels of Olympus for weeks trying to hold onto his sanity. Ross' mind finally eroded until the only thing that remained was the burning thought, "Make them pay." He returned to Earth to track down his Huang-Marr colleagues and exact his final vengeance upon them.

Ross crashes Montressor's security and comes after Mangels, killing his former co-worker after a tense chase. The characters find themselves face to face with a completely out-of-control, powerful psion, and are forced to take Ross down. In the aftermath, the characters have virtually every piece of the puzzle. They uncover Beitz's identity as "Minerva," the location of what seems to be the last hideout of the Huang-Marr conspirators in North America, the fact that only a few docs are involved in this corrupt enterprise, and irrefutable proof in the form of Dr. Malachi Ross that the Huang-Marr Project exists.

Still, despite all this telling information, the characters aren't out of the woods yet. They must deal with the aftereffects of their investigation, as well as with the death of Ross and Mangels, and with the capture of Beitz and the few remaining conspirators. This leads into the dramatic events of the next episode, *Signals and Flares*.

Theme

Friends in High Places is about loyalty and who commands it. Which takes precedence: one's species, one's order, one's friends or the mythical Truth? Recognizing your ties to one demands that you betray the others — so which path do you chose? The characters must understand that they are interlopers. It's foolish to expect someone to turn his back on the people he has worked with for years, just because some snot-nosed investigator says he should. The characters need to learn who or what the Montressor staff is loyal to, and how to best reconcile those loyalties with the mission set by the Æon Trinity. The characters should also consider how Æon's interests may conflict with their own individual morals.

There are also questions of humanity's loyalty to the orders. One, the Chitra Bhanu, was already destroyed as a nest of traitors. Another, the Upeo wa Macho, vanished under mysterious circumstances. Now, the Æsculapians — the most humanitarian and trusted of the orders — stand accused of working with the ultimate enemy and of betraying sworn oaths. The motives of the corporate-minded Orgotek may be understood more easily, if not forgiven. But if the Æsculapians can't be trusted, who can be? If the characters don't handle this matter well, the answer may well be "nobody," and the consequences will be dire.

Loyalty should impact on the characters' own Allegiances. They're more than just traits on character sheets; Allegiances represent shared philosophies. In the course of the investigation, each character should find cause to question or reaffirm his Allegiance.

Mood

There's a lot of bitterness and frustration at Montressor. The clinic is regarded as a shining beacon to the healing arts, but in practice is an impersonal administrative machine. The discrepancy between the dream of the Æsculapians as benevolent healers and their reality as bureaucratic automatons can be maddening. Proxy Zweidler is often more concerned with his status as a leading figure in human affairs than with ensuring that docs care for the sick and infirm. His directors follow

Culture Clash

The differences between life inside the clinic and in the bustling city beyond cannot be overstated. Montressor is *in* Basel but not *of* it; the only rules that apply inside the clinic are those made by the clinic's denizens.

When the characters set foot on clinic soil, they enter a self-contained world with rigidly proscribed social rules and classes — rules they do not know and classes they are not a part of. When characters break those rules, they are shunned or mocked — often with no idea why. When they cross social boundaries they didn't know existed (voluntarily hanging out with Organ Banks staffers, for example), they suffer the consequences in the refusal of others to cooperate with them.

Allies and even friendly contacts are hard to come by; the characters should feel that they are alone in alien territory. In a very real sense, they are.

their own agendas, often at odds with one another. And a basic philosophical schism between the Basel rationalists and the Port-au-Prince spiritualists threatens to split the order.

Some in Montressor still hang onto the dream and try to bring reality back in line with it. Others want to tear the whole system down and start again, preferably with themselves in charge. And there are a few, mostly in positions of power, who have no idea that anything is wrong.

The characters should realize that the denizens of Montressor are, for the most part, neither as angelic as they are made out to be nor as damned as one might suspect. They're just people trapped in an impossible situation, doing the best they can. In fact, it's a situation little different from the characters' own.

The Setting

The action in *Friends in High Places* takes place in and around the Montressor Clinic in Basel, Switzerland. Basel is a cosmopolitan city, the second largest in Switzerland, and is still struggling to deal with the flood of French refugees that washed into town after the *Esperanza* disaster. Still, the city maintains its legendary charm, and much of the surplus population has been literally farmed out to the rural half-canton of Basel (distinguished from the entire district of Basel-Stadt, which contains the city and a few surrounding towns).

Basel's civic government is very proud of the city's reputation, and jealously protects both Basel's good image and the city itself. The city's police force (boosted with a selection of psions thoughtfully provided by the clinic) is extremely — and sometimes excessively — zealous in keeping the city peaceful. While there is a black market in Basel, it's been driven deep underground and thus is difficult for outsiders to access.

Indeed, the whole city is difficult to access, in a manner of speaking. While tourists and visitors are welcome (tourism and hospitality — especially relating to families of those being treated at Montressor — are the city's largest industries), they are welcome in only certain parts of the city. Outsiders who stray from the specifically tourist-friendly galleries, shops and cafés are likely to find closed blinds, close-mouthed locals and a more chilly "*Wilkommen*" than brochures promise. *Come visit us*, Basel entreats, *but see only what we want you to see*.

Smaller communities in Basel-Stadt echo that sentiment. The locals aren't hostile, but they are very protective of their privacy.

Montressor Clinic

Montressor Clinic is renowned throughout human space. Literally the most famous hospital in existence, Montressor is a symbol of all that is good and true about the medical field, and about its foremost practitioners — the Æsculapians.

The clinic is not in Basel proper, but is located on Wartenberg Hill in the outskirts of Muttenz, one of the towns subsumed into the larger Basel metropolis. In truth, the clinic might as well *be* Muttenz; that section of the city has become financially dependent on Montressor. Clinic-employee housing, shops and restaurants frequented by clinic staff, and hospitality services for the families of those undergoing treatment are the extent of the economy in Muttenz, but that suits the locals just fine. Montressor's largesse is sufficient to make Muttenz more than comfortably prosperous.

The clinic is built into a monastery that was originally constructed in the 10th century. The place had a bad reputation with the locals — until

Black Markets

The team should want for nothing in terms of equipment that the Æon Trinity or the orders can't provide. At the same time, the characters shouldn't need any gear (say, buckets full of grenades) that Ramirez or the orders would refuse to provide — or so the authorities say.

However, the black market serves a more important function than outfitting the characters with major ordnance. The characters can get information on arrivals and departures in the area, access codes for the clinic or corporations, even insight into local politics — who's been seen drinking heavily lately, which clinic personnel do others bitch incessantly about, sudden changes of management or new areas of commercial development. If the characters fail to find leads at Montressor, the black market serves as another means to get vital information.

The other interesting feature of the black market is its link to the Æsculapians' fabled Organ Banks. A little digging (a standard **Investigation** roll) turns up the open secret that "accidents" and "object lessons" find their way into the banks. The dissection and donation of crime victims' bodies may benefit the needy, but it hinders the Basel police's forensic efforts.

they figured out that they could make money from tourists by exploiting it. The monastery spawned legends of everything from hauntings and vampires to more historically likely accounts of misbehavior conducted by the monks. The monastery proper was closed in 1784, and changed a variety of hands and purposes after that. It was a high-end, discreet cosmetic-surgery clinic before Dr. Matthieu Zweidler and several of his associates bought the place in 2084. They refurbished the existing clinic space, added operating theaters and a research wing, and opened the Montressor Clinic (named after Zweidler's mentor in medical school) in 2086.

Today, the clinic has expanded far beyond the original building. The newly renovated monastery is the centerpiece, with five additional structures as part of Montressor's holdings. Additionally, there is a large amount of open land, an internationally acclaimed golf course, and assorted ancillary sites associated with the clinic. The facility also retains bits of pieces of real estate all over the Basel-Stadt region, particularly in the city. Many hotels catering to tourists and patients' families are actually owned indirectly by Montressor.

The monastery houses the administrative center — not just of the clinic network, but of the entire Æsculapian Order. It also contains outpatient facilities, operating theaters, the famous free clinic, an emergency room and patient facilities. Down in the basement, as numerous holovids can attest, rests the order's Prometheus apparatus, tucked safely behind numerous safeguards and security devices (although the chamber people see on vids is just a prop meant to placate the masses). The clinic's research wing has been moved to its own building, as has the Organ Bank (along with its attendant administration). Classrooms and psion-training facilities (and the morgue) are in a fourth building on-site, with dormitories for students, employees and security personnel occupying the last major structure on the compound.

Covered and open walkways extend between the various buildings of the Montressor campus, and there is underground access through the steam tunnels as well. Smaller buildings on the grounds include caretaker sheds, garages and a clubhouse with an attached restaurant for the golf course. For all intents and purposes, Montressor is self-contained.

A Clinic Divided

To outsiders, the Montressor Clinic staff presents a unified front of dignified, altruistic professionalism. In truth, staffers fall into one of two camps: the Basel "rationalists" or the Port-au-Prince "spiritualists." Even within these factions, employees are Balkanized to a disturbing degree, with a hierarchy of stars, pariahs and wannabes.

Basel-trained docs, particularly old ones, bear an antipathy for rexs with a more "spiritual" or intuitive approach to medicine. The latter are usually sent to the Port-au-Prince clinic. Those who return to work in Montressor are systematically excluded from positions of real power in the administration. This is not a matter of color; instead, the Basel docs feel very strongly that progress is accomplished through only strict adherence to the scientific method.

Docs of Indian, Asian, African and American descent — who are just as analytical and formal as Zweidler himself — are exiled to Port-au-Prince for using "home remedies." Resentment among Port-au-Prince alumni grows due to Basel's dismissive and patronizing attitude, though flare-ups have been only verbal thus far.

Despite such internal friction, the clinic considers itself a closed world, and any attempted intrusion is met with a unified response. Still, characters could try to exploit the divisiveness to their advantage.

Ground access to the clinic is by road only. There was some discussion of a rail line, but that idea has long since been abandoned. Montressor also has a trio of landing pads for hoppers and helicopters, allowing quick access from Basel's airport. The pads allow direct — and illicit — business to bypass the official spaceport.

Knossos

"Knossos" is the nickname that Montressor employees have assigned the maze of steam tunnels and service crawlspaces that runs throughout Wartenberg Hill between the clinic's various buildings. The tunnels are about three meters high, and few are any wider than that. Carved into the rock of the hill, most tunnels are faced with plasticrete and lined with pipes carrying steam, water, heat, filtered air, sewage and other necessities throughout the clinic complex. The tunnels are humid and hot, with the hiss of escaping steam and the plink of falling water echoing throughout. Standing water is everywhere, making any pursuit somewhat easy (characters gain an additional die to **Awareness** or **Survival** rolls to hear someone splashing).

There aren't many security sensors among the accessways. The only entrance to the tunnels is from a secured clinic building, so things are a bit lax down below. Ceiling lights are placed every 10 meters. Large pipes are suspended from the ceiling as well, providing excellent hiding places — as long as one doesn't hoist himself onto a poorly insulated steam pipe.

Montressor personnel use Knossos for trysts, smoke breaks, low-grade drug sales and whatever minor crimes or misdemeanors come to mind. There are a few rooms down in the tunnels as well, some of which are recreation areas with pool tables and the like. The vast majority are just storage closets for the physical plant.

The Organ Banks

Montressor's Organ Banks are the largest single repository of human replacement organs in all of human space. The actual storage facilities are below ground, in huge vats of oxygen-rich nutrients. The original Organ Banks relied on cryogenically frozen organs, 30% of which could be damaged before being used. Montressor researchers pioneered a method of keeping organs alive and healthy in biotech nutrient baths (the vats are made of durable hardtech plasteel) while waiting for needy patients. The Organ Bank sublevels are quite warm and are permeated by the stench of the nutrient bath — which a visitor once described as "the smell of Cajun blackened jello."

The Organ Banks are equipped with a loading dock offering access to both the road to Basel and to a nearby landing pad. This accessway allows for fast dropoff and pickup of organs. Outgoing materials are shipped in storage canisters weighing between 10 and 30 kilos. (Off-planet shipments are provided with redundant layers of protection, which add to canister mass but which protect against the rigors of takeoff acceleration and radiation.) Such packages contain a single organ, monitoring equipment and a bath of nutrient gel supersaturated with oxygen.

There's also a morgue-cum-dissection lab right off the loading docks, with freight-elevator access to the organ vats themselves. The lab is designed for chop-work and organ preservation. There are, of course, stringent measures in place to confirm that donors are in fact dead before the banks staff goes to work on them; to date, no accidents have been *recorded*.

DARKNESS REVEALED:

Low Interest and the Banks

At first glance, it seems odd that losers, dropouts and screwups are delegated the important work of storing, shipping and keeping human organs healthy for emergency transplants. After all, if the Organ Banks do such important work — and are constantly used by the order as a shining example of the fine efforts that docs perform — doesn't it make sense to have the best and brightest on staff there?

Not really. The banks have such simplistic procedures compared to the other areas in which the order is involved that they're considered the safest place to put marginally competent employees. It doesn't take superior talent to remove organs from cadavers, file them and dump them into auto-regulating nutrient baths. It also doesn't take much brain power to prep the organs for shipping or to make sure that readouts on stored organs are within acceptable parameters. Most of the time, the job doesn't even require doctors, much less fully trained Æsculapians. "Stab 'em, slab 'em and dab 'em" is the phrase that most banks workers use to describe their job, and it's not far from the truth.

The order's directors don't want washouts and loose cannons running around giving Æsculapians a bad name — either as official docs or as former employees. It's safer to keep the "problem psions" in positions of little responsibility and low visibility, but still under the order's thumb.

Thankfully, the Montressor Organ Banks' often dysfunctional staff is not indicative of Æsculapian banks in general.

The vats themselves are separated by blood type of donor and then further by individual organ type. Each organ is examined for disease, structural damage and genetic defects. The findings go into a comprehensive database, which has genetic-typing information designed to find the best possible matches for each and every part. The banks also keep extensive records of bone marrow types from anyone who's ever undergone serious treatment at an Æsculapian clinic — marrow tests are part of the cost of a stay.

Administration at the banks consists of checking in donations and arranging for shipments out — not to mention supervising the same functions at satellite banks around the globe and throughout the Solar System. After all, it makes a lot more sense for an Organ Bank on Luna to ship to Earth's L5 point than it does for Basel to do so.

Montressor assigns its least-capable personnel to the Organ Banks. The collection of misfits, washouts and ambitionless drudges is kept far from the high-pressure work inside the clinic proper. So long as there are no egregious errors at the banks (like someone turning the heat too high on a vat and deep-frying all the AB+ organs), Montressor administration is content to look the other way and ignore the banks as much as possible.

Unless they're in administration (which is above ground, well-ventilated, and relatively stench-free), clinic personnel exiled to the banks are among the most unpopular at Montressor. This is due not only to their incompetence, but also to their nutrient-gel stench that never seems to fade.

Security

Regular Montressor Clinic security is composed of normal humans under the direction of Jakob Neihaus, formerly of the European Commonwealth's Special Forces group. While there is no policy in place mandating that only normals serve on Security, it's an open secret that the commander prefers to work with "regular humans" as a result of his military experiences. Neihaus' department consists mainly of locals (he raids the Basel police department heavily for new recruits, much to the city's chagrin), but they are highly trained, heavily armed, and possess an *esprit de corps* that dwarfs that of the psion-staffed Black Company. Furthermore, the entire security staff has something of a persecution complex stemming from the preferential treatment that psions get, resulting in a "we try harder" attitude that gets solid results.

Clinic security is impeccably professional, extremely thorough and not at all willing to take guff from outsiders. Security guards delight in busting anyone they catch poking around without permission, and Neihaus has already whipped them into a frenzy of resentment over the team's intrusion. In essence, Montressor security hopes to catch the characters screwing up so the interlopers can be shown the door at the first possible opportunity.

Black Company

Black Company is named after the Swiss mercenary *freikorps* that were the terror of European battlefields for centuries. Soldiers who fought like demons, the Black Companies (so named for their lack of identifying standard) showed no mercy to any opponent and no loyalty to any save their own and their clients.

The modern Black Company is a worthy successor to this notion of corporate loyalty and combat amorality. Recruited by Zweidler's Head of Security Aprille Glück from the disaffected and undisciplined of the Æsculapians and other orders, the members of the Black Company are all top-flight psions. A surprising number have auxiliary Modes; all have extensive combat and security training. While there are a few Black Company Æsculapians (divided evenly between combat medics and Algesis specialists), the majority are recruited from the Legion, the Norça and Orgotek.

Black Company's orders are simple: Do whatever Zweidler and, by extension, Glück tells it to do. If that means clinic security, fantastic. If that means fighting Aberrants, fine. If that means bodyguarding a high-ranking Æsculapian official, or even Zweidler himself, no problem. With the Black Company, it's all a matter of following orders.

Regular Montressor security harbors a great deal of resentment for Black Company for several reasons. Black Company is an elite group, knows it and acts like it. That attitude wears thin with the folks who handle day-to-day operations. Black Company ops are paid much more than what regular security is, and they make no bones about showing off their wealth. There's also a prevalent suspicion that Black Company is engaged in some sort of sub-

Uniforms

Both regular security and Black Company operatives wear white uniforms, with Black Company regulars distinguishable by their rank insignia pins (made of polished obsidian) and their black gloves and boots. Dress uniform requires a cap; white for regular security and black for Black Company.

While Black Company ops have their pick of weapons (if they chose to take any), regular clinic security carries Orgotek Electric Eel tasers or Aris Whistlers. Door guards and those stationed in emergency rooms bear Voss 63Ks, in addition to a taser or Alchemy webgun.

Both security and Black Company guards wear armor vests, while officers might wear bioweave armor. Supervising officers have HUDsets, which they use frequently.

versive or illegal activity — there are just too many members around for their relatively light duties in Basel.

It's ironic that most resentment against psyqs at Montressor occurs among the very humans paid to keep them safe.

Schilltronix AG

Schilltronix (named after the *schiltron*, the traditional Swiss military formation of massed pikemen in squares) is a publicly held corporation, the Æsculapian Order retaining a majority position through dummy corporations. While Schilltronix owns some manufacturing (licensed bioapp technologies, mostly in orbital plants or within the boundaries of Switzerland using cheap European labor), it focuses on ecotech and construction investments. The North American Blight Project's monitoring and agricultural research stations, in particular, do a great deal of business with Schilltronix. The company also operates a few subsidiary corporations that are devoted to orbital-crystal growth and habitat construction, but the Blight is Schilltronix's cash cow.

Most of Schilltronix's business is perfectly mundane. However, the Huang-Marr faction secretly used Schilltronix's resources in the biorg project's development. Schilltronix is only marginally aware of this wrongdoing, but it's not inclined to investigate further as long as the bottom line looks good.

Huang-Marr's contact inside Schilltronix is Ilse Wanamaker, Vice President of New Projects. Ilse used her authority at Schilltronix to facilitate Huang-Marr's goals. In return, Schilltronix had an option on certain advances the project made, with a licensing fee assigned to Orgotek, and guarantees of Orgotek investment in the corporation (Orgotek's involvement was thanks to Horace Meeks, the primary electrokinetic researcher linked to the biorg project).

Where to Go?

If the characters want to investigate someplace other than Schilltronix or the clinic proper, Basel and Muttenz are the likeliest subjects. The team might head off to the Waldhaus to interrogate a clinic rex on vacation, or might go down to the IBB (the local engineering school) to get a handle on recent graduates being tapped for involvement in Huang-Marr. The castles are wonderful places to meet informants — or to set up ambushes. St. Arbogast's and its neighboring charnel house provide good backdrops for clandestine meetings.

Basel-Stadt

The city of Basel proper is built on a small hill called the Münsterhügel, with urban areas radiating from there to encompass many of the small towns that once surrounded the hill. Riehen, Allschwil, Binningten, Obwerwil, Muechenstein, Reinach, Aesch and of course Muttenz are among the once-independent communities that have been swallowed, either *de facto* or *du jure*, by the city's expansion. The whole metropolis goes by the name of Basel for convenience, though longtime residents of the small towns cling adamantly to their communities' original names. Even today, old-time Muttenz residents correct anyone with the temerity to claim that the Montressor Clinic is in *Basel*.

The other main geographic feature of the city is the "Rheinknie," the bend in the Rhine where the river turns from west to north. The Münsterhügel is located at the bend in the river, and the combination of the two serves in many ways as the city's heart. No fewer than four bridges (most notably the Johanniterbrücke) cross the river at this bend, with others spanning the Rhine up- and downstream. The area around the Rheinknie is considered "Downtown"; it's where tourist attractions, parks, hotels and restaurants are located.

The city has transformed somewhat since the 20th century. Industry has moved out of town, while service and tourism have come in to pick up the slack. International consulting firms and high-tech headquarters take up space next to an expanding university and medical-school base, and galleries, museums and historic districts cover more ground than ever.

Muttenz, on the other hand, is a slightly different story. The center of the region, clustered around the Church of St. Arbogast (the only fortified church remaining in Switzerland), consists of refurbished historical houses — many serving as bed-and-breakfasts. Outer neighborhoods remain industrial, and the port at Auhafen still thrives. Auhafen is the last upriver port on the Rhine, and as such handles all cargo coming into Switzerland along that route. Salt mining at Schweizerhalle perpetuates industrial work there, and a few chemical plants are tucked discreetly amongst the refurbished houses in the region.

The Montressor Clinic shares Wartenberg Hill with the ruins of Wartenberg Castle, which is something of a tourist attraction. The south wall and much of the tower of the castle, which date back to the 13th century, still stand, providing an impressive counterpoint to the converted monastery that houses the clinic. Two other castles — Middle Wartenberg and Vonder Wartenberg — are also close by. The Waldhaus, tucked away in the remnants of a nearby forest, is the only getaway in the area not owned by or otherwise linked to Montressor. As such, it is frequented by clinic personnel.

Psi Use in Polite Company

The characters may be tempted to use psi — most notably Clairsentience or Telepathy — during their investigation (whether to peer into a secured area or to sense what a suspect is thinking). That's one reason why they're shadowed by Black Company during their stay at Montressor; the psion guards' natural Attunement picks up the characters' psi use. Even though Black Company probably can't sense what effects the characters use, the guards report any surreptitious activity, resulting in an official complaint to Æon. If there are repeated incidences, they're all that is needed to show the characters the door.

What's the big deal? Although not officially illegal, using psi in such an intrusive manner without asking permission is considered inappropriate; much like walking into someone's house unannounced or swiping someone's wallet and digging through it.

But as long as no one knows, what's the harm, right? True enough, but characters do well to remember that psions can sense subquantum ripples when psi energy is channeled nearby (see Attunement in **Trinity**, page 191). If the characters plan to apply their psi abilities, they had better ask first or make sure no one is around who can sense the attempt.

Ramirez stresses these points very strongly to the characters before sending them into the field. The stakes are too high to allow for amateur mistakes.

Running *Friends in High Places*

Getting the Characters Involved

If you are using **Passage Through Shadow** as a direct sequel to **Descent into Darkness**, there's no problem with integrating the team into events. Impressed by their work, Special Agent Ramirez probably wants to keep his successful operatives on the trail of Huang-Marr. The flip side to the equation, of course, is that the characters are still low-ranking psions who can be disavowed or otherwise written off if they take a misstep. Ramirez and his superiors are well aware of the potential for disaster involved in poking around Montressor, and want to avoid another Chitra Bhanu situation (a fact that would make the docs breathe easier, if they only knew).

The characters return to Luna to discuss recent events with Ramirez, which naturally leads to their opportunity for a higher-profile assignment. Proteus handles further questioning of the conspirators apprehended in **Descent**, Triton pursues the informational leads, and Neptune takes care of the rumors of psi-order corruption that circulate in the media of late. Yet someone needs to find who was behind all of this. Ramirez phrases things optimistically, making the characters' impending journey into the lion's den seem like a fantastic opportunity. If the psions pay attention, they are aware of how they're really being used.

Ramirez asks the characters to visit the Montressor Clinic under the guise of a "goodwill visit" to repair some of the PR damage from the discovery of the Huang-Marr conspirators. While they are there, the characters are under orders to poke discreetly into everything they can to find "Minerva" — the one seemingly behind the biorg project — as well as look for any other conspirators still on the loose. At this point, it seems likely that Huang-Marr has been shut down or at least put on hiatus due to the team's efforts on Luna and Mars. If the characters find any active work going on, it is a bigger surprise to Ramirez than to anyone else. His interest lies primarily in finding the guilty parties and bringing them to justice, and in controlling the situation before a witch-hunt develops. He suggests starting with checking out personnel recently transferred from Luna — Dr. Heinrich Mangels being the strongest lead — as well as equipment returned from Beaulac. Catching up with these elements should make backtracking to "Minerva" that much easier.

Throughout the briefing, Ramirez repeatedly warns the characters to be polite and delicate in their dealings at Montressor. Zweidler and his staff are extremely powerful, both as psions and as political creatures, and they can pull strings to get a team of nosy psions shipped off to guard a methane glacier on Titan. Furthermore, wild accusations of Æsculapian guilt won't serve anyone's interests. If they are disbelieved, the characters will be discredited permanently — despite suggested improprieties, the docs are still much-loved by humanity. On the other hand, if the accusations somehow stick, the consequences could be disastrous — panic, riots, people refusing medical care from perfectly innocent psions, and even the persecution of every doc in settled space.

If the characters uncover more conspirators or further evidence of corruption, they must report back to Ramirez before taking offensive ac-

Screwups

Continuity is still possible if the team botched things on Luna or Mars. Ramirez plays up the "one-last-chance" angle. The Trinity agent emphasizes how high-profile the mission to Montressor is, and how all past errors will be forgiven if the team pulls this one off. (Not forgotten, mind you — Ramirez is too canny for that, and wants to keep something in reserve to hold over the characters' heads.) If the psions seem recalcitrant, Ramirez has no compunctions about pulling out the old "Everyone else wanted to bury you, but I fought for you guys and, dammit, here's your chance to prove I was right about you. Besides, you guys owe me" shtick. He guilts, cajoles and does everything short of hitting the characters over the head with a brick to get them to go.

The one thing that Ramirez does not do with errant psions is state: "The fate of humanity rests with you!" — although he hints at it. If the characters screwed up at Olympus Mons, the last thing they need is more pressure now.

tion. There are good reasons for this — Montressor is a hospital, for God's sake, and an uncontrolled melee could cause hundreds of casualties. This isn't some holovid, after all; the characters' actions have repercussions. Furthermore, if corruption extends as high in the Æsculapian hierarchy — or as far into Orgotek — as Ramirez suspects, the entire team is heavily outgunned by some of the psions involved. Any attempt to bring the fight to, say, Zweidler, or of gallivanting off to take on Cassel is likely to end with the psions exploring heretofore unknown meanings of "screwed."

Still, Æon is very interested in using hard evidence discovered by the characters to determine if the biorg project was sanctioned by the orders or if the conspirators operated on their own. The worst-case scenario is that two entire psi orders are corrupt; the best case is that Zweidler and Cassel simply can't control their people. Either way, it's bad, and the Trinity needs accurate data so it can plan a response. Montressor is the best place to start.

The characters must go in, wave for the cameras, and most of all be subtle. Of course, subtlety is not always a hallmark of character teams. Should the psions disregard this part of their orders (intentionally or otherwise), feel free to make sure they pay the consequences in reputation, rank, liberty and in other regards.

Missing the Point

Friends in High Places is composed of a series of encounters and locations that can be run in a fluid fashion, designed for the characters to uncover and act on certain bits of information. If the characters are any good at sleuthing, they learn how high the Huang-Marr conspiracy reaches in the Æsculapian Order, and where the taint-ridden project's trail leads.

Unfortunately, your players may ignore the very real threats facing humanity and may concentrate on things that make sense to only them. Whatever phantom leads they pursue, you'll eventually want to get things back on track. You have a couple of choices — simply let them go wherever their hearts lead or nudge them back.

Getting things online involves subtly tying the team's efforts back into the main narrative. When working to expose the entire Æsculapian Order as corrupt, the psions may find an internal investigation already underway that refocuses them. The characters are welcome to help — within the parameters that the order dictates. The team might decide to leave the area on a wild-goose chase, only to have the vehicle break down — could it be sabotage? It's worth checking out back at Montressor.

Remember that events described in this book unfold even without the characters' help. The upcoming reception or sightings of Ross at Montressor could bring the team back online. Additionally, whatever the characters do has consequences — for instance, trying to discredit the docs incurs the wrath of powerful and wealthy people, from the Æsculapians to the Æon Trinity. The characters shouldn't believe that they have unlimited power.

However, keep in mind that ramrodding a team into the main plot is a bad idea. People and characters resent being pushed around, and rebel at the earliest opportunity. If you can provide suitable in-game inducements — bribes, threats or tantalizing hints — to get the team to look where you want it to, everyone's happy. The trick is be subtle, allowing the players to think that an idea was theirs.

Newcomers

Elements of this episode are designed as a continuation of **Descent into Darkness**. However, *Friends in High Places* can be adapted to new characters quite easily, with just a few changes.

If you introduce characters to the **Darkness Revealed** series with this episode, Special Agent Ramirez of the Æon Trinity remains the hook. (His statistics are in **Descent into Darkness**, but you shouldn't need them). He gets recommendations from the characters' instructors or other contacts in the various orders — Backgrounds are perfect for this — assembles the team for a briefing and introduces himself before laying out the situation. His speech to the new recruits should cover the following bases:

• Who he is (a representative of the Æon Trinity), and what he can offer the team in terms of support and employment (involvement in matters of great importance to the universe, possible fame and attractive salary);

• That Æon needs someone to go looking into matters at Montressor. The previous team is following other leads and the characters' teachers/peers/bosses/friends/whomever recommended them as the best (this can, of course, be ironic or simply a bald-faced lie at Storyteller discretion);

• The extreme delicacy of the project, and how he trusts the team's discretion;

- How this really is a fantastic opportunity for them to get their own "personal in" with the Æon Trinity;
- And why, if they refuse, they'll probably find themselves assigned to the lonely *Mimas Orbiter 2*.

At this point, Ramirez goes into what he really wants the psions to do (refer to Getting Your Characters Involved, above), all the while soft-pedaling the real seriousness of the situation. After all, he's never worked with these psions before and doesn't know how they're likely to react under pressure. He turns the characters loose, sees how they play matters and then applies the screws or encouragement as needed.

The players shouldn't feel forced into going along with the plot, but working with Ramirez should appear to be the characters' best available option. Æon wants the team, and whatever Æon wants, Æon gets.

Behind the Scenes

Although the characters' previous efforts exposed the Huang-Marr conspiracy, some of the main schemers remain hidden. Æon has Proteus interrogating captives, Triton following up information trails, and the characters themselves pursuing the strongest leads at Montressor.

Even so, the remaining conspirators don't wait to be caught. Gustaf Beitz ("Minerva," the man behind everything), has already shut down the half-dozen other project sites and is working systematically through each remaining conspirator. Those whom he determines can be trusted are relocated to *Eyrie*, an orbital station, while others suffer "unfortunate accidents." If the characters take too long in their investigations, Beitz and his lackeys could erase all traces of the conspiracy!

Æsculapians

Docs pursue a number of private projects unknown to the world at large, or even to the other orders. Huang-Marr is by far the most extreme secret endeavor ever indulged within Montressor's halls. Those few rexs who heard of the biorg research treated it like the order's other "mystery projects." The truth of the events from **Descent into Darkness** is just trickling down to Montressor. Despite the shock and anger generated in many of these individuals, they keep their mouths shut. This type of scandal could turn the Æsculapians into the next Chitra Bhanu. The few rexs in the know consider the project an Æsculapian problem. *Docs*, not some outside party, should investigate and resolve the matter quickly and quietly, forestalling public panic and possible retribution upon the order as a whole.

Thus, Æsculapians, regardless of their respective loyalties, give up little information. The team is stepping on rex toes by coming to Montressor, and if the docs can handle things better and faster than these Æon intruders can, Zweidler and company should be left to do so. Indeed, a number of docs resent the notion of outsiders poking around their precious clinic, following red herrings and searching for scapegoats. Some rexs even have personal grudges against the characters for their recent efforts on Luna and Mars, which damaged the careers of friends and loved ones and tarnished the Æsculapians' reputation as a whole. The very few who know why the psions are really there are caught between siding with their order and being true to their consciences.

The Æon Trinity

Æon has broad goals: It wants Huang-Marr and everyone involved with it. The Trinity would prefer to keep things completely quiet and out of the public eye. Events have made things too public to allow for that, however, so Æon now strives for speed over subtlety (although it continually stresses to characters the need to keep a low profile). Ramirez has virtual *carte blanche* to assist his team, though the characters don't know that and he doesn't tell them for fear of them becoming lazy. Æon and Ramirez are desperate for results — they have people pursuing every other lead other than the ones that bring the characters to Montressor. If the characters don't get results, another team will take over.

The Media

The media doesn't know the truth of the biorg project, but it knows that *something* is up. In the aftermath of **Descent into Darkness**, all manner of rumors spread — corruption within the orders, bizarre new psions with incredible powers, conspiracies of psions taking control of the UN, psions planning on subjugating humanity, and even that psions have joined forces with Aberrants. The media isn't foolish enough to give credence to all of these, but it's pursuing each possibility aggressively. Since most fingers point at the Æsculapians and Orgotek, it's only natural to focus attention on them. The characters are obviously in Basel to check into these matters. Every major media rep is on hand to get the scoop of the decade. Even Cori Heisler sniffs around.

The Huang-Marr Conspirators

The axis around which everything in this episode operates is the Huang-Marr conspiracy. The confederates still believe in the project and its potential, but have stopped research for now. They've devoted their attention to riding out the storm of scrutiny now upon them. Led by Dr. Gustaf Beitz (also known as the mysterious "Minerva") of the Montressor Clinic, the conspiracy has a small staff for such a far-reaching group — due in part to the death or capture of a number of the conspirators in **Descent into Darkness**. The only ones who matter at this point are Mangels, Beitz, Huang (Marr is dead by the time the action opens) and Meeks. As events in *Friends in High Places* show, the characters have the best chance of flushing out Mangels and Beitz and following them to their compatriots.

Mangels was moved from Luna to Earth when the Beaulac Clinic biorg site was dismantled. His relocation was originally planned as a routine transfer through Montressor's Organ Banks and then to a new field site (perceptive players may note Grabowski's "farewell email" for Mangels on page 8 of **Descent into Darkness**, which indicates Mangels' new assignment). Beitz decided further caution was called for even before Mangels' shuttle touched down in Basel, though. Mangels' name was scrubbed from the manifest and a "new" individual was assigned to the Organ Banks — "Reinhardt Tuten," simply Mangels under a pseudonym.

This transfer was supposed to be only temporary, since Beitz decided that Mangels' trail was too obvious and planned a tragic accident for "Tuten." However, before the plan was set into motion, Mangels revealed his blackmail scheme. He'd made duplicates of all of his work on Huang-Marr; if he died, the copies would go to Warren Shaw (of OBC's *Retrospective*), Cori Heisler (of MMI's *The Painful Truth*) and General Solveig Larssen (the Legions Proxy). With the characters exposing the biorg project as well, Beitz had his hands full shutting down even more damning aspects of the conspiracy. Mangels was left in Montressor's basement until Beitz could think of a way around the blackmail.

Beitz would much prefer to do unto Mangels as occurred accidentally to Marr, but Mangels' blackmail ensured his survival for the moment. Huang, in the meantime, was transferred to *Eyrie* Station — the bolt-hole that Beitz also used when he decided that things had become too hot to bluff through.

Meeks is supposed to wrap things up at the Orgotek biorg site in the North American Blight Zone and then slip up to *Eyrie* as well.

Arrival at Montressor

The characters, however they are induced into going to Montressor, go in style. They are flown in comfort directly to the clinic's landing field, where they are greeted by what can politely be described as a media circus.

Multiple holovid reporters are there with their crews, tripping over each other as they seek the

What the Public Knows

The Huang-Marr Project is not general knowledge — yet. The public *is* aware of the following:

- Dr. Jerzy Grabowski was suspected of being the corrupt ringleader at Beaulac Clinic (before his murder).
- Apparent Aberrant worshippers killed a number of people at Boltzmann Station before being stopped by Æon Trinity operatives.
- A disgruntled Nordamerican citizen sabotaged Summit Center on Mars in protest of China's political dominance.

The root causes of these events are still a mystery to anyone not directly involved in **Descent into Darkness**. Still, it has leaked that there were some sort of secret experiments at Beaulac involving Æsculapian and possibly Orgotek personnel. There is also word that high-ranking psions were involved in the Mars sabotage, and that they are returning to Earth under Chinese guard. The details of Grabowski's death make for scandalsheet copy all over human space.

The best-informed news sources — including Cori Heisler and the satisfactory-intelligence construct that serves as Warren Shaw (the real McCoy died five years ago) — are aware that the experiments were illegal, involved bioware and may have had human subjects. These agencies sit on the story, however, until conclusive proof can be found. There's no sense in starting a panic without having all of the details.

best angle. Clinic dignitaries — including Zweidler and Monahan — stand to the side, looking uncomfortable at the whole maelstrom and ducking interview requests from the likes of the redoubtable Cori Heisler. Clinic security, augmented by a contingent of elite Black Company guards, is scattered across the plasticrete landing pad, providing a subtle but unmistakable presence. The entire Black Company detachment, incidentally, looks bored beyond belief. Also present is a gaggle of dignitaries from Basel's city government, as well as assorted tourist-friendly entertainers and hangers-on. (The traditional brass band in lederhosen adds just the right touch of lunacy to what is already a madhouse.)

When the characters' hopper descends, the musicians blurt out "Edelweiss," the locals cheer and the media-types jockey for position near the landing pad. One overenthusiastic reporter is nearly incinerated by the hopper's landing thrusters, and is removed unceremoniously by security. The rest wait for the characters like hyenas stalking prey.

When the ship lands and the doors open, the psions must exit and face the music. Security keeps the reporters away from the characters. Basel's mayor (Clement Huber, a young and amiable fellow) and the clinic's representative (Pierce Monahan) make short speeches welcoming the characters. Zweidler hovers in the background saying "no comment" whenever the press gets near. There are a few poses for the holovids, and then the reporters descend like locusts.

Security is poised to escort the characters through Montressor's massive front doors after the clinic bigwigs enter. The press is sure to pelt them with questions as they go. Although Æon encouraged the characters to keep a low profile and the Æsculapians desire the same, it's likely that at least one of the characters wants to chat. Most of the media reps are fairly harmless; Cori Heisler of *The Painful Truth* fame cuts through them like a shark scenting blood. Heisler's charisma and persistence make her a focal point almost immediately. She starts soft by pumping the characters' egos, congratulating them on their recent defeat of the Aberrant Anders Nash over Mars, and on their new roles as goodwill ambassadors. (If the characters didn't go through the events of **Descent into Darkness**, have Heisler mention something that one of

the more public characters has accomplished.) Heisler doesn't do fluff, though. Her next battery of questions includes:

• Can you describe the chase through *Freya*, and what it was like in Summit Center when it was falling?

• What was your connection to the events on Luna and Olympus Mons?

• Is it true that you found evidence of Aberrants being detained on Luna?

• How do you respond to allegations of corruption among the orders? Do recent events correspond to the Chitra Bhanu situation?

• You were among the last people to see Beaulac Clinic Director Jerzy Grabowski alive. Do you think he was guilty of allegations leveled against his stewardship of Beaulac Clinic, and do you really think an Aberrant killed him?

• Have you seen any experimental bioware, and if so, could you describe its operation? (This is a shot in the dark; Heisler is fishing for a reaction.)

Other reporters chime in as well, each hoping that the characters will slip up and say something juicy. If the characters are wise, they deflect the questions or respond with "No comment." Attempts to actually address the media end up with the characters digging an increasingly deeper hole for themselves. Clinic security only does so much; it's loyal to Zweidler, not the characters. Once the psions are grilled to an appropriately embarrassing degree, Neihaus gives the signal to get the guests away from the media and through the doors.

Even if Ramirez doesn't catch the characters' performance when it first airs, he is certainly forwarded a copy. He's sure to have strong words for the characters about what "keeping a low profile" means if they blab to Cori Heisler in a public interview.

The Guided Tour

Once inside the clinic, the characters meet Jakob Neihaus, Montressor's head of security (Zweidler and Monahan slip off too quickly to allow personal introductions). An honor guard and two Black Guard troopers flank him. Neihaus explains that the characters will be escorted (read: watched) by security throughout their visit, and that their requests will be taken care of by the escorts.

Neihaus fades and Dr. Atul Mundassery steps forward, introducing himself as an assistant to Administrative Director Monahan. He offers to give the characters the grand tour. Assuming they accept, they are whisked through an introduction to Montressor. A few select (read: tame) journalists are pulled "randomly" from the crowd outside and allowed to tag along. Mundassery has no connection to anything important, but is a loudmouth who likes to show off. As such, he's a great means to disseminate information to the characters if they ask him the right questions — what he thinks of Drs. Huang and Marr, his experiences with Zweidler, or anything based on Mundassery's impressions of Montressor.

(If anyone asks, the characters' luggage is taken off the hopper and to guest quarters in the Black Company dormitory. It is professionally but politely searched. Nothing is taken and no effort is made to hide the search. Instead, the individuals responsible "unpack" for the characters.)

Some sites of interest on the tour include:

• **The Free Clinic and Emergency Room:** This area was cleaned up significantly for purposes of the visit. Extra staff was assigned to speed patients through, the place was freshly scrubbed and generally looks a lot nicer than it usually does. Patients, if questioned, are full of glowing praise for the clinic, the service it provides, and for the friendly and helpful doctors. Most even tell the truth; the coaching of the rest isn't glaringly obvious. Observant psions note security armed with webguns, tasers and the occasional carbine.

• **Operating theaters:** Each operating theater, from neurosurgery to cosmetic surgery, has a seating area behind plexiglass, located over the main room. Mundassery invites the characters to watch a procedure in progress — the party arrives just as a team of heroic rexs are in the midst of saving an accident victim's life. Prominent uses of Vitakinesis, operating-room melodrama and all sorts of expensive-looking medical equipment convey the feeling that *this is important medical work*. Anyone questioning the use of all of the gadgets is shushed immediately as an ungrateful cynic — after all, the doctors are saving a woman's life down there.

This scene should provide an object lesson: The Æsculapians are doctors, dedicated to the preservation of life. All order psions have medical training in addition to their psionic abilities; most are full MDs, RNs or PhDs. They rely on their medical training as much as they do their psionic powers, and are damned good at what they do. The team should appreciate the importance of the institution that it might well be destabilizing.

• **Outpatient and GP Offices:** The characters arrive here in time to see a friendly, helpful Æsculapian giving an adorable little child a checkup while the boy's mother waits, visibly nervous. It's a scene right out of Norman Rockwell, or would be if Rockwell had been Swiss. The doctor, a young Æsculapian named Thorah Eimundsdottir, gives the child (Joachim Puhl; his mother is Anna) a clean bill of health and a lollipop, then sends them on their way. Thorah is Icelandic and looks like she belongs on a recruitment poster. She's more than happy to talk about her work, how much she loves Montressor and the order.

• **Wards:** There are rows and rows of hospital beds in the clinic, most of which are located in the oldest parts of the building. While the tour does not go through Critical or Intensive Care, it does stop in one of the regular wards. The place bustles with helpful nurses (of both genders), attentive rexs and normal doctors, and orderlies. Patients seem gener-

A Peek Behind the Curtain

Mundassery is currently a junior assistant, and intends to rise higher in the clinic hierarchy. He's therefore more than happy to lead the pre-planned tour. He knows he's doing something important and overplays his hand. The whole tour comes across as a little too contrived, a little too plastic.

There are some clever aspects to it, though. Æsculapian staffers are constantly moving throughout the building during the tour, prepping rooms that are about to receive visits and tidying up messes. In addition, areas that might raise questions (research labs, the morgue) are avoided, as the purpose of this tour is to show Montressor as a well-oiled machine, with no reason to look further than the obvious.

ally cheerful and well-tended to. The occasional visitor shows up with flowers.

• **Administration:** With any luck, this part of the tour bores the characters to tears. Mundassery waxes rhapsodic about the incredibly detailed records that Montressor keeps on everything, drowning the characters in minutiae while an obviously embarrassed desk clerk tries to look stoic. The idea is, of course, to get the characters out of there without allowing them to actually look at anything important, and to give them little desire to go back.

• **The Prometheus Chamber:** After going through a half-dozen complex and involved security checks that take the characters into the main building's first sublevel, Mundassery displays the heart of the Æsculapian Order — its Prometheus chamber. Six Black Company psions stand at strategic points around the room, supplemented by regular security. The raised control booth is empty as no one is scheduled to undergo the process today, but Mundassery takes great delight in demonstrating to the media the way the procedure works. It's all old hat, but the holovid folks eat it up anyway.

As any docs on the team know, this chamber is a sham, set up for visitors and camera crews. The actual Prometheus chamber is tucked much further underneath Montressor, behind real security checks and in a vault. There's enough armor around the real chamber to protect it from anything short of Divis Mal's return. The true Prometheus chamber is far too valuable and fragile to expose to tourists.

While this bit of deception is understandable, and the characters may well agree with it, the fact that the order has no problem with lying to protect its own interests should raise questions about where the lies stop.

Audience with Zweidler

The tour ends in the office of Herr Doktor Zweidler himself (the proxy is just finishing business with Monahan, Black Company head Glück, and another man whom docs on the team may recognize as Delemont, the Special Projects Director). Monahan and Delemont leave, but Glück remains, casting a cool professional eye over the characters. The office is large and furnished elegantly and simply; bookshelves cover most of the

walls and Zweidler's medical-school diploma is displayed prominently, along with a number of plaques and awards. Mundassery whisks away the reporters and regular security at this point.

Zweidler gives the characters a pleasant but somewhat distracted welcome, introducing Glück in the process. He apologizes for the showy reception, especially since the characters are here on such grim business. Zweidler further conveys his regrets about the recent discoveries made offworld, and about his sadness about the fate of Dr. Grabowski (a personal friend who walked a doomed path), and offers his full cooperation to the psions. "Of course," he says, "I am sure you will find nothing here of what the wolves might wish. This is a hospital, a place of healing."

Zweidler warns the characters that they may unfortunately face hostility from some members of the staff. If the characters went through **Descent into Darkness**, he explains it's a result of professional or personal loyalty to those whom the characters have implicated in their investigation. If the characters are new, Zweidler says the people at the clinic consider this visit an attempt to do the same "hatchet job" here as occurred at Beaulac. The proxy apologizes formally for any tensions, and assures that the characters' security escorts will assist in whatever ways they can.

Meeting Zweidler should be an eye-opener. He virtually radiates power, unconsciously using Mentatis to calm everyone around him. The sheer strength of Zweidler's psionic abilities is awe-inspiring; most people fall under his spell without even knowing it. It must be emphasized that the proxy does not consciously try to affect people; the power just radiates from him. It's as if Zweidler has a very soothing bedside manner, and most people in his presence find him quite charming and reasonable. It takes real effort to disagree with or get angry at Zweidler face to face. (See page 50 for further details on Proxy Zweidler.)

You may call for standard **Willpower** rolls. Success means a character can shake off Zweidler's presence enough to focus on tough or argumentative questions. Failure means the character allows the proxy to take the lead during the entire interview. A botch turns the character into a sheep who hangs on Zweidler's every word.

With perseverance, the characters can get a few answers out of the proxy:

• Zweidler and Grabowski stopped speaking about work long before the latter went to Luna. Their friendship suffered as a result, which Zweidler now regrets. The proxy seems genuinely surprised that Grabowski was involved in any sort of immoral research.

• The notion of working with taint is repugnant to Zweidler. He shares the view that if we can find a way to combat it, we should not hesitate to do so. Indeed, the rise of taint-based illnesses such as D or GCS (Genemorphic Compression Syndrome) mandate that we should destroy the taint immediately.

• Zweidler has no knowledge of the biorg project or who might be involved in it aside from the individuals whom the characters have already implicated.

• Zweidler has authorized an internal investigation, being run by Special Projects Director Delemont. The proxy would have introduced the characters to him, but Delemont was just on his way to Luna to personally investigate the staffs of Beaulac and Covenants Clinics. (Delemont is in no way involved in the biorg project, but his name should serve to shock players who have read the introductory story in **Trinity**. If need be, Ramirez quashes attempts to go after Delemont. The characters are to investigate Montressor.)

• Zweidler has absolutely no compunctions about getting rid of anyone who threatens to compromise his order, his clinic or his ethical standards. This is perhaps the only topic that rouses the proxy's passion, as he is married to his work and his goal.

• The glasses Zweidler wears are "old friends," and he doesn't feel comfortable without them. He does, however, recommend eye surgery for anyone else with correctable vision problems.

• Zweidler simply doesn't know anything (about "Minerva's" identity, Orgotek's involvement, Mangels' current whereabouts) that isn't described here. However, any information the characters offer will certainly help the order's own investigation....

All discussion must be verbal; Zweidler easily registers any attempt to use **Telepathy** on him. Doing so ends the interview immediately, with Zweidler unleashing a tirade that the characters would try such a thing. Offending psions are shown to their dormitories and the proxy sends an official complaint to Ramirez. While the characters aren't taken off the case, they are reprimanded. Furthermore, story of the investigators' effrontery against Zweidler spreads like wildfire throughout Montressor, making the rest of their stay that much more difficult.

Dorm Sweet Dorm

Zweilder ends the meeting by inviting the characters to a reception that night in their honor at the nearby Mittenza building. Glück ushers them out of the office almost before they can accept. The characters' security escort awaits outside. It leads the way to the rooms that have been set aside for the characters.

The Black Company apartments are luxurious. Each is a suite with a private bath, two rooms, a full set of furnishings, and entertainment and communications hookups — there's even a fully stocked bar. The suites are all on the fourth, highest floor of the dormitory, which sprawls out in a rough L-shape. None of the characters' rooms are contiguous.

Each character gets her own suite, and finds the contents of her luggage neatly put away in drawers and the closet. Any non-clothing items are laid out on the suite's desk. Complaints about this are routed to Neihaus (who's not happy to get them, as Glück authorized the rummaging). He explains the incident as a routine security precaution, and notes that any complaints about the service provided by the housekeeping staff should be routed to Monahan. He then logs off before a character can say anything else.

Terse treatment of the characters is a deliberate attempt to keep them off-balance and uncomfortable in ways that seem ridiculous to complain about, hopefully hastening their departure. Aside from these minor inconveniences, Æsculapian security has taken some more subtle steps. Room computer terminals are restricted in what materials they can call up (though much more subtly than "ACCESS DENIED" — there's a whole system of false menus and links designed to confuse and misdirect anyone going after sensitive data). Any requests made are logged, noted and analyzed. The characters can bypass the dumbed-down terminals by hooking their own minicomps to the ground line. However, Glück has that and the communications hookups tapped to record any conversations or research the characters perform.

The Reception

On their first evening at Montressor, the characters are invited to a formal reception celebrating the Æon representatives' arrival. Along with the team, the guest list includes high-ranking clinic personnel, a few Basel dignitaries and a very few members of the press. Most of the last are there to do "Lifestyles of the Rich and Psionically Active"-style puff pieces — Dazyl Grenich is the 22nd century's answer to Robin Leach — but Cori Heisler has managed to weasel an invitation and lurks in the background, waiting for someone to make a slip of the tongue....

The reception is not actually held on the clinic grounds, but rather at the nearby Mittenza building which formerly hosted Muttenz's municipal functions. A small plaque by the front door notes that the remodeling was made possible by a donation from the Zweidler Foundation. Inside, a string quartet plays in the background. Tuxedoed waiters cruise silently through the crowd, serving drinks and making empty glasses vanish without a trace. The entire atmosphere hearkens back to times long past — indeed, if it weren't for the modern cuts of the tuxedos and formal gowns, the characters might well be at a 20th- or even 19th-century affair.

Outside the mix of dignitaries, Zweidler stands at the back of the main reception room. He's flanked by two bodyguards (one normal, one Black Company) and chats with his assis-

Paranoid Yet?

Neither Glück nor Neihaus has any connection to the Huang-Marr Project. Instead, both are fiercely loyal to the order, to Montressor and to Zweidler himself. They consider the characters a malign threat intent on indiscriminately tearing down the clinic and all it stands for. Neither of the security heads — well, not Neihaus, anyway — has any intent of doing the characters harm; the investigators are not going to be assaulted in their sleep by Black Company psions in ninja outfits who swing in through the windows. Instead, the idea is to make the characters want to get out as quickly as possible, having found nothing and not wishing to endure uncomfortable circumstances any longer than necessary.

tant Elaine Hightower. Zweidler has no interest in talking to the team beyond polite inconsequentialities. Hightower is very protective of the proxy's privacy and takes it upon herself to lead the characters away from him if need be. (Contrary to clinic gossip, the two are not an item. In fact, Hightower and Neihaus have been secretly engaged for over four years.) Doctor Zweidler and his assistant do have an extremely close working relationship, though.

The other prominent clinic employees attending the party are more inclined to chat. While Organ Banks Director Roland Stoltzfus is currently assisting with an overhaul of banks in Beijing, other Æsculapian directors are on hand (Administrative Director Pierce Monahan, Clinic Network Director Dr. Gemma Fiosi, and Research Director Dr. Karen Dietrich — for more information on these individuals, see **Hidden Agendas** and **Shattered Europe**). Monahan does his best to interpose himself unobtrusively between the characters and anyone whom they wish to talk to, under the guise of "showing them around." Monahan intends to cut short any conversations that might result in embarrassing revelations. If the team allows Monahan to tag along, its discussions with other guests are sure to be quick and unsatisfactory. However, characters can frustrate his interference through a number of methods: Splitting up works well, as does leading Monahan into Heisler's net.

The Toast

A few minutes after the characters arrive (enough time to get an idea of the people in attendance but before having a chance to talk to anyone), Monahan gets the crowd's attention. Raising a glass of champagne, he proposes a smoothly flattering toast of Montressor's "most-honored guests," wishes the characters a happy and illuminating stay, and then cracks a few lame jokes about them finding out why the air conditioning in his office never works. (Actually, it's because the clinic physical staff dislikes Monahan and toys regularly with the room's climate control.)

The effect of this toast, beyond a round of polite applause, is to make sure that everyone on the reception floor knows exactly who the characters are and what they're doing there.

Dr. Karen Dietrich

Being the director of research, Dietrich is probably the doc with whom the characters are most interested in talking. While she has no connection to Huang-Marr, Dietrich can be persuaded to discuss her recollections of anyone the characters are investigating (Huang, Marr, Mangels, Grabowski) and the work they did before they went illicit. If the characters haven't heard, Dietrich tells them that Dr. Abel Marr died in an accident a few days back. In accordance with his request, Marr's parts were donated to the Organ Banks.

Dietrich notes that Huang and Marr were very methodical, each a superior student (they went through clinic training two years apart). Huang was more practical; Marr was the theorist. In fact, Huang did a semester's internship directly under Dietrich, working on research into GCS (Genemorphic Compression Syndrome), a taint disorder. Both filed a steady stream of grant proposals and progress reports that stopped about three years ago. Dietrich didn't follow up with them; she assumed that Huang and Marr moved into private-industry research (there were rumors a year ago that Marr worked on the North American Blight Project). Besides, Dietrich had a lot more pressing matters on her plate than pursuing the whereabouts of a couple of former students.

Dietrich gives Mangels a harsher review. She claims Mangels was a single-minded student, quite skilled but overly proud of his talent. Dietrich recalls that he turned in some project proposals that were borderline unethical. Mangels' fascination for all things tainted was well-known, and in a couple of Medical Ethics seminars he'd expressed an "ends-justifies-the-means" position on working with the stuff. Dietrich personally approved Mangels' transfer to Luna to get him out of Basel. She hasn't seen him since, and says frankly that she won't lose any sleep if she never runs across him again.

The biorg project is a new rumor that Dietrich has heard of, but knows nothing about. If the team explains the research to her, Dietrich looks grim but not surprised. She expresses her outrage at the concept of cooperating with Aberrants, and comments that she would never allow such acts on her watch.

Dr. Gemma Fiosi

Fiosi is the clinic network director, and theoretically oversees personnel transfers throughout the order. However, Fiosi is the first to admit that she's more interested in the big picture — establishing entire clinics — than she is with the minor details; which security guard just went from Rochester to Minneapolis, for example. Fiosi has a vague memory of seeing transfers for Huang and Mangels recently, but that's about all. If the characters make a reasonably good impression on her, Fiosi later sends them messages that Huang was transferred to "Records," but Huang's file was tampered with to delete her current location.

Mangels' record has him transferring out of Luna but not *to* anywhere else (in **Descent into Darkness**, Grabowski's email has Mangels headed for Basel, but Fiosi has no record of Mangels arriving). The characters may persuade Fiosi to investigate further, but she does so only when she has spare time and adds that, following policy, she'll share her findings with Delemont. Fiosi tracks Dr. Ella Huang to Minnesota by recompiling her file. However, this data comes to light only after the characters have tied up events here in Basel, serving as another lead to the next episode, *Signals and Flares*.

Other Luminaries

There are other movers and shakers at the party whom the characters can meet. Figures such as Mayor Clement Huber or media maven Cori Heisler have no plot relevance, although they're useful for local color or any subplots you may wish to pursue. Also, there are a few clinic psions with whom the characters should have some brushes.

Chief among them is Dr. Gustaf Beitz, a quiet, self-effacing doc who spends most of his time at the party listening to the string quartet and commenting on the music (he assesses the cellist's ability as less-than-inspired — within earshot of the musician). As noted earlier, Beitz is the enigmatic "Minerva"; he's interested in meeting the team to "size up the opposition." Any attempts to draw Beitz into extended conversation are futile. Even if a character figures out a way to use **Telepathy** without other psions at the reception noticing, Beitz has a t-blocker hidden in his vocoder like those used by Grabowski and the Willoms. It's enough to prevent an overly energetic telepath from getting a peek at his memories (plus, the signal doesn't register as a bioapp and isn't illegal should the characters somehow discover it).

Beitz surreptitiously takes the measure of each member of the team, noting their interactions with others. Beitz excuses himself from the reception relatively early (but after The News Flash, below), claiming that the music isn't up to his standards. In reality, Beitz decides discretion is the better part of valor. He's off to scrub certain files from his minicomp and office, and then it's off to the safety of *Eyrie* Station.

Assistant Organ Banks Director Dr. Tomas Catalanotto is also present, going on to all and sundry about how complex and stress-filled work is down in the banks (a view other docs at the reception are quick to correct should the characters inquire). Even a casual glance shows that other guests do their best to avoid staying around Catalanotto for more than a few seconds. The man has an unpleasant personality, and a strange slightly smoky scent clings to him. Eavesdropping reveals that Catalanotto is pissed off at a new transfer named Tuten, who (according to the assistant director) is trying to score points with the Powers That Be by filing all manner of regs violations on other hard-working Organ Banks staffers. The prevailing opinion on Catalanotto is that he's a weasel with an overdeveloped sense of his own importance; everyone tunes him out as white noise.

The team should meet the ebullient Jeroen Mitterwaald before the night is out. The man is already half-drunk when the characters walk in the door, and has no love for anyone trying to air the clinic's dirty laundry. Sic Mitterwaald on the characters if they get dangerously close to throwing the story off-track; if they behave, bring him by during a lull in events. A huge, mustachioed walrus of a man, Mitterwaald spots the characters from across the reception and storms his way over to point out (at high volume) "what an *ungrateful* lot of *bastards* they are, trying to bite the hand that's healed them," and other drunken ramblings. After a few short but colorful moments, Monahan intercedes and helps security haul Mitterwaald away. If the characters don't haul off and slug Mitterwaald, he approaches them, shamefacedly, the next day and offers to help in their investigation in what small ways he can.

The News Flash

There's a balcony off the reception hall where the characters can go to enjoy the crisp night air (and escape the smoky haze inside — Zweidler doesn't ban smoking at his parties; presumably rexs can heal themselves easily enough that tobacco has little affect). If they venture outside, characters may see a flash of light in the sky that looks like a shooting star (if the characters are indoors, have them stand near a cracked-open door and overhear someone outside exclaim as much). It's an incoming ship, one of several that pass on approach to Zurich or Basel during the course of the reception. This particular ship, however, has an interesting passenger.

Within an hour of the sighting, a susurrus of rumor sweeps through the room. A Luna-to-Earth ship was supposedly attacked by an Aberrant while on final approach to Basel spaceport. According to the news report quoted — and re-quoted and distorted as you see fit — the crew tricked the Aberrant into the cargo bay and blew the hatch a few hundred meters above the ground, along with packing material and a portion of the cargo. The wreckage was recovered, but the Aberrant's body wasn't. Sixth Legion patrols are already on the job. There were, thankfully, no casualties, and no further details are available at the moment.

A character looking for the straight scoop who has brought her minicomp (a bit bulky and unsightly for a formal affair) can find a ground data hookup. Otherwise, she can check with one of the guards equipped with a HUDset. With some finagling, the character can even get patched through to the Basel Legion post, whereupon she's told that everything is under control. However, if the Aberrant is sighted, the character will certainly be contacted. This sounds like a thinly veiled effort to placate a zealous Aberrant-hunter (unless the character calling is actually a Legionnaire, in which case the offer is genuine). Cori Heisler vanishes as soon as the story breaks.

Winding Down

Zweidler takes off shortly after Beitz does. Perhaps one or two others leave early as well, but most people stay until midnight, when the music stops (recordings replaced the live quartet an hour earlier). The two pairs of regular security and Black Company psions appear once again to escort the characters to the skimmer that returns them to their rooms. The attendees drift off in leisurely fashion to their own vehicles. Mitterwaald is the last to leave, and security needs to remind him rather emphatically that the bar is closed.

Nocturnal Activities

There is a variety of things that the characters can do after the reception ends. Following up with specific individuals is difficult unless a specific assignation was scheduled earlier; most attendees either head to bed or are on call. However, that doesn't mean that the evening's investigation is over.

The Falling Star

The team may wish to follow up on the story that broke during the reception. Neihaus hasn't blocked access to any newsfeeds, so the characters can hop on the OpNet. A standard **Engineering** roll tracks down the latest update on the incident. The crew of the *Lysander* was interviewed, and its accounts are available for download. The crewmembers explain that, during approach, an Aberrant came out of the cargo hold, roaring something unintelligible and making threatening gestures. The crew managed to trick it back into the hold. ("We just sorta waved and pointed, and in it went. Damndest thing I ever saw. Then we blew the seal and dumped the creature." — Capt. Jamie Donohoe)

Attached to the newsfeed is the ship's internal-security-camera log of the incident. The footage is eerily reminiscent of that of Grabowski's cell in **Descent into Darkness** — it shows the transformed Dr. Malachi Ross, former doc and biorg test subject. The phrase he chants can be deciphered with some effort (**Linguistics** [English] at +1 difficulty): "Take me to the bastard Mangels."

The characters can do several things with this information. They can race off into the countryside on their own, looking for Ross (and they likely meet with one of the well-armed squads of grim Sixth Legionnaires that also searches for him). The characters can report to Ramirez immediately, enabling Æon to assist officially in search efforts. Or the characters can sit tight and prepare — after all, Ross is quite probably headed for Montressor to pursue his vengeful agenda.

Night Flight

Characters with insomnia note a takeoff from the clinic's landing pad around 3:15 AM. A check of the flight plan reveals that Dr. Gustaf Beitz, a senior Æsculapian staffer has left for São Paulo, site of a new Æsculapian clinic. If the characters follow up on this after six hours (enough time for a craft to make it from Switzerland to Brazil and presumably after they discover that Beitz is "Minerva"), they learn there's no record of Beitz's ship landing anywhere in South America. However, a global check of the craft's registry (extended **Engineering** roll, requiring a total of seven successes due to the amount of data to sift through),

shows it landed in *North* America — Hopkins, Minnesota to be exact. This provides another link to the events of *Signals and Flares*.

Personnel

If the characters wish to follow up on anyone they met at the reception, they have limited access to the files of almost anyone in whom they're interested (except for Delemont and anyone else in the Special Projects Division, to whom they have no access). You can share tidbits from the Dramatis Personae section in this book or from those of **Hidden Agendas** or **Shattered Europe** to simulate the brief data files for which the team scrounges. Beitz's file certainly contains no mention of his Huang-Marr links or of "Minerva." An **Intrusion** roll (+2 difficulty) reveals that the file on Reinhardt Tuten is a well-done forgery. Tuten's file links devolve into dead ends. His service postings are confirmed at other sites, but he has no evaluations or project reports on record.

Night Doings at the Clinic

The team can wander around certain parts of the clinic without too much trouble. Neihaus' security personnel take their work seriously, maintaining a sharp eye whenever they're on the job. However, Glück's Black Company psions have drawn night watch. Although by no means incompetent, the pair of Black Company security guards are prepared to underestimate the characters (once, at least). They don't expect that the characters are up for rooting around in the middle of the night (they may be right; if the characters sack out, advance to the Investigations section). The guards use the apartment at the corner of the "L" as their "watchpost" — meaning they sit inside chatting and leave the door open, poking a head out occasionally to see if anyone's cavorting in the halls. As long as the characters are quiet about it (standard **Stealth** rolls), they can slip out either exit.

The 24-hour emergency room is the only area that the characters can investigate. The rest of Montressor follows traditional hours, with few departments operating night shifts. Security patrols roam the entire clinic during off times; the characters are bound to run across Neihaus' security if they try to access any closed building sites. Such contact shouldn't devolve into violence. Security simply leads the characters politely but firmly back to the dorms (looking rather smug when they turn the characters over to the chagrined Black Company guards).

A steady stream of people flows through the ER. The waiting room is subdued but packed with the injured and ailing, and the rest of the place is full of docs and nurses working busily. Dr. Atul Mundassery is on call and working — hard — when the characters arrive. People's lives hang in the balance; there's no time for shoptalk or gossip. The characters are uniformly unsuccessful at any attempts to interfere or pull someone away from duty. A first attempt makes the characters look bad; a second gets them ushered out of there forthwith. Future interactions at Montressor are that much more difficult, since word of the team's skewed priorities spreads quickly. (What kind of people are more interested in asking questions than helping the injured?)

The characters do overhear something interesting while looking around: A doctor in a trauma room screams on a phone that she needs a kidney up here, *right now*, and that by God if she doesn't see a nice shiny kidney in front of her ASAP, *every* Organ Banks staffer is going to be an organ donor, starting with their apparently unused brains. If the characters attempt to interfere, they get the cold shoulder as the rex tells them, "It's an internal matter."

Investigations

There is no specific timeline for the characters' investigation of Montressor. The only (living) conspirator left there is Mangels, and he stays off-stage until Ross arrives (see below). Even so, there are some sites and scenes of interest that the team should check out.

Allow the characters to make their own agenda, offering the information detailed in the appropriate sections below. If the characters stray from their agenda, an overheard comment between their guards or a half-glimpsed media report may be all you need to steer them back on track.

The Organ Banks

Astute characters recall that Mangels was initially listed as transferring to Montressor's Organ Banks directorate. He never arrived; another doc was assigned to the division instead. That obviously looks fishy — to the staff it's merely more office politics, but the characters should pursue every lead.

The exterior of the Organ Banks directorate is unassuming, with an intermittently busy loading dock out back. Ambulances roll in and out at a steady pace, urgent but unhurried. Most of the building is below ground, but the part that's visible is done in mock-historical style that matches downtown Muttenz. There are plenty of windows on the building's face, and the main entrance is framed in a broad stone archway.

The first obstacle the characters encounter is the smell of the nutrient baths; the acrid emissions are noticeable even in the reception area. The Organ Banks are not a pleasant place to be or to work, and the place is thick with fumes and negative vibes. The staff, with a few notable exceptions, is slow-moving and surly, rightly seeing the intruders as a threat to their comfortable existence.

The reception desk is manned by Elisa Gruber, an officiously pleasant, plodding woman with standing orders from Dr. Catalanotto to stall anyone who asks questions. Assuming the team checks in at the front desk, it spends a half-hour cooling its heels in a rather odoriferous front room. Catalanotto hopes that the characters get tired and go away, but that's not likely. If they stick around, they're eventually shuffled into Catalanotto's office.

Catalanotto wields power in Stoltzfus' absence. Organ Banks Director Stoltzfus is generally a good man, but is much more interested in the politics of his position than in working in the trenches. Stoltzfus seldom spends time in the directorate, preferring to meet with various dignitaries and corporations to garner funding and support for the Æsculapian Order. Running the day-to-day falls to Catalanotto; he likes power, but not the work that goes with it. The Organ Banks is a pet that Catalanotto likes to play with, but he doesn't care about it.

He knows how precarious his position is, and the characters' arrival throws him into a barely concealed panic. Catalanotto, by turns wheedling and bullying, tries to talk the characters into agreeing that they have no reason to investigate the Organ Banks. Of course, his rapid speech and nervous movements are likely to make the characters even more suspicious of illicit goings-on. While there are a lot of shady dealings at the Organ Banks, there's nothing related to the biorg project — besides Mangels. Catalanotto doesn't know the true identity of his most aggravating employee. As far as Catalanotto is concerned, "Tuten" is just another pain in the ass who transferred in recently. If Catalanotto is hiding anything, it's inefficiency and brutality, petty corruption rather than grand treachery.

The characters don't have to push very hard to get Catalanotto to give in and show them around

Asking About Tuten

Organ Banks staffers are relatively closemouthed about fellow employees, even new hires. However, there is one transfer that they gripe about with relish: Reinhardt Tuten. Nobody likes him. He's a busybody, a know-it-all, and he's had members of the old gang fined, fired or suspended. Tuten has a superior, snotty attitude and seems to think he has some sort of special deal going. He also gets on people about their work habits, and Ledee caught him snooping around, double-checking other people's work.

The best guess around the banks is that Tuten is Zweidler's spy, sent in to see what needs cleaning up. No one talks to him, knows where he lives or gives a rat's ass if he lives or dies.

The two pertinent details the characters can get about Tuten are a description (which matches any images the team has of Mangels) and the fact that Tuten started without any fanfare three days after Mangels left Luna. Workers might even drop the fact that Tuten walked like a short-timer in from off-planet (a look at the transcript from the color setting section confirms this).

Tuten is off-shift when the characters come through. No one has any idea where he lives (nor do they care, and make a point to say so). The address listed in his personnel file is, of course, incorrect. Ledee confirms that Tuten is scheduled to come on for the graveyard shift tonight. If the characters really want to talk to Mangels, their best bet is to wait until he comes back to work.

However, by digging around in the Organ Banks subsystem (an 8 Fail-safe, like the rest of Montressor's systems), the characters can find Mangels' diary (as presented in the color setting section; withhold that material until now).

the facility. However, Catalanotto doesn't give the tour himself; that honor is reserved for a slow and not terribly informative technician named Ledee. Ledee is a normal whose mind is a sieve of various crimes and misdemeanors committed at the banks (none of which has any bearing on Huang-Marr). Each room that he takes the team through has a central tank filled with nutrient bath. Each tank is subdivided into layers of shelving and compartments, with preserved organs resting in most of the compartments. Each organ is labeled, and there are easily accessible temperature, pH and other monitoring controls nearby. Ledee checks on a few organ tanks in an overly serious manner that reveals to even the least medically inclined character that Ledee has little idea of what he's doing. Workers whom the characters encounter during the tour are sullen, ignore the passing visitors and give monosyllabic answers if questioned. They don't know anything about conspiracies and are irritated at being asked.

Despite general attitude problems in the Organ Banks, the characters don't encounter any difficulties until the tour hits the back room. This is the operating theater where cadavers are carved up for parts. In fact, a dissection proceeds as the psions enter. Ledee sees this, thinks it's a great way to gross out the guests, and motions the team forward.

Unfortunately, the body being dissected is a local strongarm's "mistake" — the remains were dumped in the Organ Banks as a coverup. The docs performing the autopsy are hip-deep in the "chop-shop" scam and try to shoo the characters out before they get a good look at the body. It's unlikely that the characters can be shunted aside so easily. The banks cutters are smart enough to realize that investigators will connect the face of a missing judge (which is posted on that evening's news) with the face of the cadaver currently being dismembered. However, they're not clever enough to bluff until the characters leave. Instead, the two rexs panic, diving for the far exit and the steam-tunnel access beyond. The startled Ledee is left behind, realizing too late that he has just exposed illegal organ dissection to Æon Trinity investigators.

The team is probably surprised by the sudden flight, and has the option of chasing or calling security. (This altercation is designed to give the characters a passing familiarity with Knossos, knowledge that becomes important when Ross slips into Montressor that evening. However, don't force the characters into the tunnels if they choose not to go.)

If the characters give chase, the players need to make standard **Awareness** or **Intrusion** checks to hunt down the fleeing men. The quarry know the tunnel system much better than the characters do, but they split up, leaving one doc with the longer of two escape routes — enough time for the characters to catch up with him. Barring that, characters who hang onto Ledee can question him. (If they leave him behind while they pursue the two docs, Ledee runs in the other direction and looks for a new line of work elsewhere.)

A captured conspirator gladly rats out the others if offered protection (the characters have no legal authority in such matters, but they don't have to tell their captive that). The characters learn nothing about the biorg project, but do uncover a racket involving a number of local crime syndicates who bring in bodies for disposal. You can involve as much criminal element as you like if you wish to expand this lead into future stories. Otherwise, the doc doesn't know many names and the matter is handed off to clinic security and the authorities. If the characters themselves follow up on this racket — perhaps by discussing it with Glück, Neihaus or Mundassery — they learn that reports were made by other Æsculapians, but the order's labyrinthine bureaucracy hindered commissioning an investigation.

Data Trails

Characters are sure to pursue electronic leads in their investigation. Beitz wiped all information relating even vaguely to Huang-Marr from his files before he left. The characters find nothing in Montressor's system — even "Minerva" is a dead end. However, checking into such things as the Blight Project, equipment transfers or previous posting assignments of known conspirators all turn up a common connection: a local Swiss company known as Schilltronix.

Researching those leads requires digging into Montressor's system (an 8 Fail-safe). Once the Schilltronix link is established, the characters can tap into the corporation's system (a 6 Fail-safe) through the OpNet. (See **Trinity**, page 236, for details on hacking, and page 270, for handling fail-safes. The **Trinity Technology Manual** also has expanded information on both hacking and fail-safes). Each piece of information below requires a separate, appropriately modified **Engineering** roll to acquire.

• A single extra success reveals that Schilltronix signed an agreement with Orgotek to pursue research on the Blight Zone (as indicated by the excerpt from the color setting material).

• One extra success confirms that an Orgotek senior researcher, Horace Meeks, was involved closely with Schilltronix's representative Ilse Wanamaker in coordinating the Blight Zone contract.

• With two extra successes, the characters reveal the ownership link between Schilltronix and the Æsculapian Order.

• Two extra successes calls up Schilltronix shipments of materials and work orders to Blight Zone sites as well as off-planet — to Olympus, Boltzmann and Wanjing. A single additional success confirms that Ilse Wanamaker authorized these shipments.

• Three extra successes are needed to uncover the names of the two key people in the Schilltronix-Æsculapian relationship: Dr. Gustaf Beitz and Ilse Wanamaker.

The characters find this information by piecing together disparate bits of emails, memos and requisitions in Schilltronix's files. Compiled together, it's certainly impressive evidence. However, the characters must still find witnesses to confirm it (after all, data can be faked). Right now, Wanamaker looks like the best lead.

Schilltronix

If the characters find the Schilltronix link, they probably want to speak to Wanamaker. If the characters don't find the tie to Schilltronix, they can still do so by tracing the equipment that was transferred from Luna back to Basel in **Descent**. It's easy to determine that the gear Grabowski sent back never arrived at Montressor; the transports were sent to the public Basel spaceport. The characters can use their status as Æon investigators to finagle access to the spaceport's manifests (standard **Subterfuge** roll — after all, the Trinity doesn't really have the legal right to dig through anyone's files). After some tedious but relatively easy backtracking, the characters learn that the transports sent from Beaulac Clinic in January offloaded their cargo to Schilltronix trucks. Again, the next step seems to be to look in on Schilltronix.

Any investigations the characters undertake off Montressor's grounds are done without security shadowing them. The characters can rent ground transportation to Schilltronix (the corporate offices and warehouses are at the same location). If they're relatively polite and well-groomed (slummers waving about weapons find themselves in the local jail for disturbing the peace), the characters can meet with Ilse Wanamaker, Vice President of New Projects. Wanamaker authorized all the equipment transfers in the first place, so talks to them no matter whom the characters ask for. Unfortunately for her, Wanamaker's been busy with other new projects, and Beitz never bothered to keep her informed of the Huang-Marr Project's status, so she has no idea what the characters really want.

Wanamaker has her minicomp set to record even before the characters enter her office (standard procedure for her). She's out for herself, and that initially means stonewalling them on what projects she's accepted. Eventually, however, proper application of **Command**, **Interrogation**, **Intimidation** or **Subterfuge** (or just plain old roleplaying) may get her to break and reveal some of what she's been up to. The characters have an advantage over Wanamaker in that she doesn't know what information they're trying to uncover; she toes the corporate line out of habit.

Once Wanamaker realizes what the characters ask after, she clams up and tries to get rid of the them (summoning security and planning a call to Beitz for help). The characters have only a few minutes to impress upon Wanamaker that she's better off telling them what they need to know; otherwise the Trinity could make life very difficult for her. Wanamaker is savvy enough to know that's true, but she still demands some kind of immunity before she tells all. While the characters don't necessarily have the authority to confer such a thing, Ramirez supports them as far as he can legally.

After Wanamaker gets the characters to agree, she shoos away security and tells what she knows. She confirms that she worked with Beitz and Meeks to set Schilltronix up as a third-party conduit of materials and finances to selected sites (at Olympus, Boltzmann, Wanjing, Hopkins and a half-dozen other places of your choosing — some may even remain active if you wish to pursue the conspiracy further). Wanamaker checked around enough to determine that Beitz and Meeks were developing some kind of secret project under the radar of their respective orders. Since the deal channeled a respectable amount of money into Schilltronix, Wanamaker didn't ask any questions. She doesn't know anything important beyond that.

Wanamaker takes the characters to the storage facility if they demand it. If they're hoping to find more illegal bioware, they're disappointed. The canisters in storage are filled with junk; it's obvious at a glance that the odds and ends have nothing to do with bioware research. Unknown to anyone but Grabowski, Beitz and the transport pilot, the craft stopped *en route* from Luna to Earth and unloaded the actual equipment on *Eyrie* Station. This private orbital platform shortly becomes the direct focus of the characters' attention. First, however, they must get through the remainder of *Friends in High Places*.

"Minerva" (a.k.a. Dr. Gustaf Beitz)

The characters should suspect by now that "Minerva" is actually Dr. Gustaf Beitz — only he, with his position in the Æsculapian Order, could have forged the connections between Schilltronix and the Huang-Marr Project. If they've somehow missed this fact in their investigation, move on to Ross Returns, below (they'll just have to find out by backtracking from Mangels or Schilltronix).

The characters are sure to call for Beitz's head. They should remember to report the break to Ramirez first; he authorizes pursuing further leads on Beitz at Montressor, but reminds the characters that there may still be other conspirators there. By now Ramirez has also heard the reports of Ross in the area, and urges the characters to keep an eye out for him.

Only after contacting Ramirez can the characters ransack Beitz's office (Æon brings Zweidler up to speed, who allows the characters to proceed with security monitoring their progress). There's no hard evidence of corruption laying around, but there are significant chunks of information simply wiped from Beitz's system. Anything dealing with Huang-Marr, biorgs, bioapps, Schilltronix, Mangels, Tuten, Meeks, Luna, Grabowski, Boltzmann or the Blight Project is gone. The electronic gaps are obvious, ragged and telltale. Standard **Psychometry** use shows Beitz the same night he left, deleting files and shredding or packing papers.

If the characters decide to chase Beitz, Ramirez stops them and reminds them that Mangels is as important, and probably closer at hand. They must find as many witnesses as possible to corroborate the data they've uncovered. Only in this way can they trace the extent of Huang-Marr's corruption. That, after all, is exactly what Ramirez — and the Æon Trinity — wants.

Should the characters chase Beitz to North American anyway, he has moved on before they arrive. Proceed directly into *Signals and Flares* at this point. Mangels can still be killed by Ross in the characters' absence, as occurs in this story. You can even have Ross travel to North America, in pursuit of his next conspirator victim, if you want characters to confront him once and for all.

Ross Returns

The characters can investigate with little further interference from the media after the first night. Throughout their stay, the characters see media updates on the continuing search for the "Aberrant" that plummeted to Earth. (Note: Clairsentients who search for an Aberrant don't find anything; Ross isn't one. Even after the characters determine that the creature is Ross, there's still a lot of ground to scan, and Ross doesn't exactly sit still waiting to be found.) Neihaus and Glück step up patrols around Montressor, but they have no idea what they're looking for unless the characters reveal what they know of Ross (which, admittedly, isn't much).

Security doesn't give the characters' input much weight until they turn up the wealth of evidence described above. As night falls, things are jumpy at Montressor. Security establishes a firm defensive perimeter, nonessential personnel are sent home, some patients are airlifted to other clinic sites and a siege mentality takes hold. Glück insists that her people can handle one Aberrant or enhanced psion — whatever the creature is. She's probably right, but Ross isn't playing by her rules. The vaunted Black Company ops — and Neihaus' security force — never get the chance to show their worth.

The characters aren't much use to Neihaus or Glück, and both make sarcastic noises that the characters should go off and continue digging up dirt on the Æsculapians. This is a perfect time for the characters to remember that one of their prime suspects, Dr. Mangels, is due in for the night shift in a few hours. With all the hubbub, it's not difficult to slip away from security escorts (the guards are more interested

in getting a piece of an Aberrant than in baby-sitting the characters, anyway).

Mangels (as "Tuten") is scheduled for the night shift at the Organ Banks. He's completely out of the loop at this point. Although he knows Æon sent investigators to Montressor, he knows nothing of the characters' breakthroughs, Beitz's recent retreat or of Ross' impending arrival. As far as Mangels knows, there's an actual Aberrant out there somewhere. He's acutely familiar with the danger such beings represent and is quite pleased to be working tonight. Mangels figures the safest place to be in case of an Aberrant attack is in the bowels of the Organ Banks, with rank upon rank of security and Black Company ops blocking any way in.

As the sun sets, the team and Mangels head for the Organ Banks, Glück and Neihaus deploy their troops, and the rest of the clinic bolts its doors. And the "Aberrant," biorg-modified Malachi Ross? He's already inside the clinic compound, having burrowed his way in earlier, through the solid Alpine rock. He perfected his tunneling technique on Luna, after all.

Meeting Mangels

Mangels doesn't hesitate to head for the protection of Montressor; he's a few hours early for his shift. As he has a reputation as a snitch, this causes no more comment among his coworkers than normal — and the other banks staffers have enough to talk about with the "chop-shop" scam exposed and an Aberrant watch going on, all in one day. Mangels has enough time to overhear his coworkers' discussion of the day's events before the characters track him down. He is clever enough to realize that Æon investigators searching the Organ Banks were looking for more than the body-dumping scam. He dials for "Minerva," but Beitz disabled their shielded connection when he left. That's all Mangels needs to know that he's on his own. He heads for Knossos immediately, hoping to lose himself in the steam tunnels and leave Montressor completely.

Ross tunnels up into a Knossos section about then. His grand entrance cuts through power cables, water pipes and steam conduits, rendering the entire underground complex dark except for emergency lighting, and filling the place with the sounds of hissing steam and gurgling water. Characters moving through the lower sections of the tunnels find themselves ankle-deep in murky water.

If the characters are serious about catching Mangels, they have to track him in the tunnels (when the characters arrive at the banks, "Tuten's" co-workers happily point out that the snitch went dashing for the basement). The characters may not initially realize that Ross is down there, but the former test subject is not quiet. He bellows Mangels' name intermittently (as well as Huang's, Marr's, Grabowski's, Meeks' and "Minerva's"); that should clue people in quickly. Ross is also fusing shut every door that he comes to in order to deprive anyone of escape routes. Ross is operating on instinct at this point. He's not sure where he's going, but (thanks to his biorg-enhanced **Clairsentience**) he comes ever closer to Mangels.

Although Ross' voice is distorted through rage, pain and echoes, Mangels recognizes his former colleague. Mangels knew about Ross, but didn't think the man would come here. Mangels now has more to worry about than Æon investigators.

The situation becomes a deadly game of cat and mouse. Mangels does not want to be captured or killed. He flees from both the characters and Ross, looking for a way up near one of the landing areas, but fear and the flickering lights conspire to make him lost. Ross is drawing ever closer to Mangels, vengeance the only thing on his mind. He has no compunctions about killing anyone who keeps him from exacting retribution, and that includes the team. For their part, the characters stumble around in a foreign environment in less than ideal conditions, Ross' reverberating screams and Mangels' involuntary yelps drawing them inevitably into a final confrontation.

The Showdown

The chase through the tunnels should be nerve-wracking, with the characters never knowing if they're the hunters or the hunted. Footfalls in water, distant screams and crashes, and the occasional near-miss with Mangels or Ross should keep tensions high. The team can call for help, but it doesn't arrive until an appropriately dramatic moment. Knossos is big — where's the fun in showing up in time to see the Storyteller's characters bag the big monster, leaving the "heroes" nothing to do but applaud?

The team finally comes upon Mangels — just as Ross bursts through a tunnel wall! Ross looks even worse than he did before, and obviously has murderous intent for his former colleague. The characters hopefully feel duty-bound to save Mangels from a horrible and messy death. Mangels' death is inevitable, though; Ross crushes the doctor's head with his bare hands. The characters' efforts to save Mangels only bring them into direct conflict with Ross, who fights to kill. He doesn't think at all at this point; he's little more than a titanically powerful animal that must be put down.

Doing so, however, is difficult. Ross' implants enable him to take Lethal Damage as Bashing Damage; he heals rapidly as a result. A single turn in which Ross takes a full 16 Health Levels of damage — twice what a normal human can take — is finally enough to overload the Huang-Marr bioapps. Ross collapses like a ton of bricks due to a combination of bioware overload and massive physical trauma.

Conclusions

In the cinematic tradition, Ross is lucid for a few moments before he expires. A quick-thinking character who sets his minicomp to record can get Ross' confession, confirming from yet another source the involvement of Grabowski, Mangels and the rest in illicit taint-influenced bioware research. Ross dies with a peaceful look on his face, his last tortured days finally at an end.

Beitz, of course, fled some time ago. Although he destroyed data under his direct control, there were enough leads in other areas to provide damning evidence against him. "Minerva," the head of the entire Huang-Marr conspiracy, is exposed. It remains to be seen if Beitz is clever enough to continue avoiding capture or if the characters have what it takes to bring him to justice.

Even without Beitz's capture, the characters reveal the breadth and depth of Huang-Marr's operations in Basel. Yet another conspirator is dead, "Minerva" is flushed into the open, and the legacy of Huang-Marr's worst excesses seems to be laid to rest.

Aftermath

Once Ross is put down, the team probably needs a few days to recover from the battle. And, since the final confrontation with Ross under the clinic is rather destructive, Montressor needs some recovery time, too. The Æsculapians react quickly to recent events, though, in an attempt at spin control.

Director Stoltzfus, in conjunction with Neihaus, purges and reorganizes the Basel Organ Banks. Catalanotto and a number of Organ Banks staffers are fired and brought up on legal charges.

Glück pursues the capture of minor Huang-Marr personnel hidden in Basel, after reconstructing some of the files from Beitz' system from backups. That same process also offers even more proof that Beitz is "Minerva."

Zweidler makes a public statement (written by Monahan) apologizing to humanity at large for the trouble "a few zealots" have caused, and promises to root out the trouble immediately. The proxy also declares the opening of three more clinic sites.

That announcement does little to redirect the public's attention from the rumors of corruption. Too much was exposed within Montressor to allow for simple hand-waving and apologies. Not only do the characters finally have irrefutable proof of immoral research — with links to Orgotek — but they've exposed a body-dumping ring in the Organ Banks. Even within the normally close-mouthed Æsculapian Order, tongues start wagging and the nearby media is on hand to record what's said.

Æon wasn't interested in a witch-hunt; it just wanted to gather Aberrant conspirators. Zweidler is of a similar mind; he considers his order a monument to ethical purity and wants any smirches wiped clean, quickly and quietly. With the media involved, it's impossible to keep things silent. The public, other orders and even a number of Æsculapians call for an official investigation. True, the Trinity was looking into matters, but it's not an actual legal body. The United Nations gets involved in the aftermath, commissioning an official third-party study to look into the situation that Æon (led by the characters' efforts) has already uncovered.

Now that the conspiracy is exposed, Æon is in a race against time. It knows full well that, without proper handling, this could quickly escalate into another Chitra Bhanu-style purge. It's now more important than ever that the characters capture the remaining Huang-Marr conspirators and present the entire plot to the UN, all wrapped up neatly. Otherwise, there are sure to be rough times ahead for the Æsculapians, Orgotek and quite possibly psions as a whole.

Luckily, the characters have strong leads. Beitz's flight and records of shipments from Schilltronix all point directly to North America and the Blight Zone. The characters grow ever closer to apprehending the major players in the Huang-Marr conspiracy.

Other Endings

This story does not have to end as described above. There are a number of alternate directions that it can take.

• **Mangels escapes:** You may decide Mangels keeps his head well enough to slip out of Knossos while Ross and the characters still search for him. He flees Montressor, leading the characters on a chase across the European countryside (or perhaps even farther, if you want to extend the cat-and-mouse scenario).

• **Mangels is captured:** Alternatively, you could reward the characters for all that they've accomplished and allow them to catch Mangels in the climactic fight under Montressor. This still leaves Beitz's flight and records of shipments to Hopkins for the characters to pursue.

• **Beitz is captured:** Gustaf Beitz is quite sharp (he'd have to be to coordinate the Huang-Marr Project). However, you may decide he was too confident in his own abilities and thought he could safely endure the characters' scrutiny. The characters prove too clever for Beitz and, upon discovering his identity as "Minerva," they burst into the senior researcher's office and catch him with incriminating data still on his computer. While other conspirators remain on the loose, the characters have the ringleader. This way, the Æsculapian Order suffers much less public scrutiny. Beitz can be trotted out as the mastermind and other leads can be tied up rather neatly by looking through his files.

• **Following the body-dumping ring:** You want to wrap up the conspiracy with Beitz's capture and have the characters become involved in the gritty European underworld. Various criminal organizations were using Montressor's Organ Banks to dispose of victims. The characters have exposed the body-dumping ring, but that doesn't stop the criminals from killing. The characters might decide to take matters into their own hands and track down leads provided by captured Organ Banks staffers.

• **Schilltronix had a greater role:** As it stands, Schilltronix provided a convenient third-party conduit for transporting personnel and materials for the Huang-Marr conspirators. Wanamaker and her staff had no idea of the project's true extent. However, you may decide that Schilltronix was more closely involved in the conspiracy, even to the point of swiping research and starting its own independent studies. The characters must investigate the company and discover how many new sites Schilltronix established on its own. It may even have its own biorgs up and running, unleashed to take care of nosy investigators.

• **The hydra grows another head:** Just because the characters have the ringleaders on the run doesn't mean Huang-Marr has to be shut down. There could be any number of sites still pursuing taint research. As with the Schilltronix story idea, these locations may have functional biorgs that terrorize the characters.

Dr. Matthieu Zweidler

Shattered Europe describes the good doctor Zweidler in detail; the following is simply a brief overview. It should help you to roleplay the proxy well in his interactions with the characters during the events of this book.

Matthieu Zweidler is extremely reserved in his bearing, completely dedicated to the clinic and the order, and resolutely devoted to the betterment of humanity. He's also micromanagerial, dislikes conflict intensely and is not above using his powers to soothe disagreeable visitors. If the characters present Zweidler with evidence of wrongdoing, he thanks them politely and passes it on to the investigation that Delemont runs. If the characters come to him with demands, he digs in his heels, and the characters learn that he can push a lot harder than they can.

Characters who (for whatever reason) take aggressive action against Zweidler regret their decision immediately. He has a standard security and Black Company operative tagging along most of the time, and Neihaus and Glück are often around as well. Furthermore, his assistant Elaine Hightower is skilled in close-combat techniques. As if all that weren't enough, Zweidler is a proxy. He's more than capable of taking care of himself through Mentatis or Algesis. If he waits for security to deal with an assailant, it's because he feels that it is the polite thing to do.

Dr. Zweidler is a very busy man, and the characters' contact with him should be at a minimum. Familiarity can lead to contempt, or at least to taking someone for granted, and having the characters become "comfortable" with Zweidler diminishes the considerable power he represents.

Dramatis Personae

The following are profiles and statistics for important individuals in *Friends in High Places*. There are a number of people with whom the characters can interact, not only in their official investigation but in any other stories that you wish to run in Basel.

Æsculapians

Dr. Tomas Catalanotto

Catalanotto is the Organ Banks' second in command, handling the day-to-day operations while Director Stoltzfus oversees the Organ Banks program as a whole. Catalanotto is a powermongering ogre who is despised uniformly by both his staff and his peers. He's also at least mildly corrupt and not too picky about what goes on in his purview, but gets defensive when anyone pokes their noses into his business. Catalanotto has no problem with theft, brutality, hiding evidence or turning accidents into donations. He's just lousy at the paperwork that goes along with it.

Elaine Hightower

Hightower is Zweidler's administrative assistant-cum-major-domo, and the clinic would be chaos without her. Hightower is rarely seen, but she's the one who keeps Zweidler's schedule manageable, smoothes over disputes between departments and generally keeps total chaos at bay. Hightower plays the lowly administrative type until the characters get bored and go away. Earning her friendship can go a long way toward making life easy for the team; earning her enmity gets the characters in a great deal of trouble.

Dr. Jeroen Mitterwaald

A crony of Zweidler's from their medical-school days, Mitterwaald is of Dutch extraction and is probably the most conservative member of Zweidler's inner circle. He doesn't trust women, people younger than he is, people older than he is, non-Dutch — really, he doubts that anyone other than himself can do things properly. The fact that Mitterwaald tolerates Zweidler's authority is a subject of much office humor. Mitterwaald is all for throwing the characters out on their asses, and maintains a siege mentality that has been heightened to near paranoia by the events at Beaulac and Covenants Clinics. Amusingly enough, the Huang-Marr conspirators considered approaching Mitterwaald but decided against it — he's an outspoken proponent of doing whatever it takes to get rid of Aberrants, but he holds staunchly to scientific ethics. Even so, his loudmouthed "get the job done any way you can" rantings — whether reported to characters from other docs or overheard at the reception — are sure to make him a prime suspect.

If the characters approach Mitterwaald with an adversarial attitude, he becomes a very powerful enemy, working to hinder them at every turn on general principle. On the other hand, if they show Mitterwaald professional respect, he is certain to be outraged at the mere thought of Huang-Marr. Mitterwaald acts like a bloodhound thereafter, assisting agreeable characters in tracking down information about the conspirators. He is a useful ally if the characters hit a brick wall in their investigation.

Dr. Atul Mundassery

Mundassery regards himself as one of the order's shining lights — an opinion shared by few others. Most in the clinic regard him as a suckup, a tightass and a loser (not necessarily in that order). Convinced that he's in line for a top promotion, Mundassery makes a big show of ordering "inferiors" around and demonstrating how much he knows. The latter can be a useful trait for the characters, enabling them to learn much about Montressor's bureaucratic process and behind-the-scenes activities through some judicious ego-stroking.

Mundassery knows nothing about Huang-Marr, the Organ Banks' body-dumping or really much of anything else. He does, however, have a lot of opinions and he loves to talk. Mundassery is desperate for friends and allies, so is likely to be chummy with investigators, telling them what he knows in exchange for the "prestige" of being their point of contact. Beitz and Zweidler are happy enough, for their own reasons, to let Mundassery serve that purpose. After all, Mundassery knows little that's useful and nothing that's incriminating.

Mundassery therefore makes a superb voice with which to pass information to the characters. Don't let him know too much, but if the team is at a dead end, Mundassery can share some gossip and get the characters moving again.

Huang-Marr Conspirators

Dr. Gustaf Beitz

See Beitz's full description in the Dramatis Personae of *Signals and Flares*, page 112.

Drs. Huang and Marr

Only one of the doctors originating the biorg research remains in residence at the clinic. Unfortunately, he does so in about nine different pieces, scattered across two levels of the Organ Banks. Dr. Abel Marr was killed in a traffic accident in Muttenz a few days before the characters arrive in Basel, and his remains have been rendered into spare parts for the greater good. Surprisingly, if the characters investigate, they learn that the accident was exactly what it seemed to be — Marr was simply a victim of bad luck.

Dr. Ella Huang, on the other hand, received a transfer to a special project two days before Marr's demise. Where exactly that project is located is a matter of conjecture. It looks like there's been some fudging of the files. (A successful **Engineering** or **Investigation** roll at +1 difficulty indicates file tampering has occurred, and another standard roll proves that Huang is nowhere to be found in Basel.)

Huang left quickly after getting her posting (and Marr's office was rather hurriedly packed up), so poking around in their leftovers produces some interesting but frustratingly incomplete data. Chief among this is a partial record of the DNA sequences involved in the Huang-Marr bioapps' construction; astute psions remember it from the wall in Dr. Grabowski's office in **Descent into Darkness**. Other tidbits remain as well: experimental protocols, lists of experiment subjects and results, and requests for equipment (much of it on Schilltronix corporate letterhead). This information can provide characters with the Schilltronix link if they haven't pursued computer research. Otherwise, this data provides even more confirmation of the Huang-Marr conspiracy.

Ilse Wanamaker

Wanamaker is forceful, ambitious and quite protective of her own skin. Right now, the Huang-Marr Project looks like it will be her best bet for wealth and power, but once the characters give her the full details of what she's involved in, Wanamaker turns on a dime to save herself. Still, Ilse's been battle-hardened by a hundred board- and project meetings. It's unlikely that a ragtag bunch of psions can bully her into spilling the beans.

Wanamaker is out to protect herself and Schilltronix, in that order. She sells out Huang-Marr (and gives a decent description of Beitz if asked sufficiently probing questions about "Minerva") for Schilltronix, and Schilltronix for herself. However, Wanamaker is sure to get a good deal (anonymity regarding any official investigations, for starters) before she reveals what she knows.

Dr. Malachi Ross

Dr. Ross was brilliant, dedicated and not a little bit ambitious. From the moment he was pegged as an Æsculapian, he had a single goal: being named Zweidler's eventual successor. During his hospital internship, Ross garnered a reputation for being cold and impersonal. He had the medical and psionic skills down pat, but failed at his interactions with others.

Try as he would, Ross remained apart; even his connection to subquantum resonance left him feeling distant from others. He went with his strength, then, throwing himself wholeheartedly into research,. His ambition led him right into the arms of Huang-Marr. Ross worked feverishly on the project, certain that his role would cement his place among the upper echelon of rexs. Then, Ross' humanity finally got the best of him. He began having moral qualms about the nature of the experiments. He brought his concerns to Grabowski in late 2119, and Grabowski made him "disappear."

Used as a doped-up guinea pig for the project, Ross was accidentally left behind when the Beaulac site was shut down. Augmented by his biorg implants, Ross freed himself from confinement and went in pursuit of the man who brought him to his state — Dr. Jerzy Grabowski. The Huang-Marr bioware had already unhinged Ross' mind by the time he found and killed Grabowski. The murder put Ross the rest of the way over the edge. He's now determined to find and destroy all of his other colleagues on the project. It doesn't matter how long it takes him; with what Huang-Marr has done to him, Ross doesn't have anything else for which to live.

Image: Ross is a twisted, misshapen hulk, a rough parody of a human. His skin crackles with yellowish bolts of energy, while strange subcutaneous bulges twitch and squirm along his arms, legs and back. His body is hairless and smooth, and only the rags of a Brazilian-cut suit now drape him. Anyone unlucky enough to meet Ross' eyes recognizes that he is quite mad.

Roleplaying Hints: You *will* find the other conspirators. You *will* make them feel your pain. You *know* where they are; they are at Montressor. You *will* go there and make them suffer. Nothing else matters. Nothing.

Nature: Bravo
Allegiance: None

Physical Attributes
Strength 5
Dexterity 4
Stamina 4

Abilities
Brawl 5, Might 5
Athletics 5, Melee 4, Stealth 2
Endurance 5, Resistance 4

Mental Attributes
Perception 3
Intelligence 5 (when lucid) 1 (most of the time)
Wits 4

Abilities
Awareness 3
Bueaucracy 4, Medicine 5, Science 5, Survival 4

Social Attributes
Appearance 1
Manipulation 1
Charisma 4

Abilities
Intimidation 5

Aptitude: [Vitakinesis] Iatrosis 4, Mentatis 5, Algesis 5; [Psychokinesis] Pyrokinesis 5, Telekinesis 4; [Clairsentience] Psychonavigation 5, Telesthesia 3
Willpower: 10
Psi: 6
Backgrounds: Contacts (Huang-Marr Conspirators) 5
Gear: Ratty clothes, Huang-Marr bioware; nothing else to speak of

Note: The latest-model Huang-Marr bioapps grafted into Ross' body, resulting in severe physiological and psionic modifications. Most of his mental capacity is gone, except for brief flare-ups of intellect. The bioapps are killing him slowly — his body simply can't maintain the pace the bioware sets.

However, Ross has gained significant advantages as a result of the experiment. All damage is considered Bashing for purposes of applying defenses and determining healing time. The bioapps boost his own Vitakinesis abilities and channel Psychokinesis and Clairsentience effects. They also give Ross a Psi pool of 20 points that he can use to generate effects, and normal power costs are one point less than listed in **Trinity** (although rolls must still be made for effects). Ross' powers function almost of their own volition; he can take a separate physical and psionic action each turn (and he may further split his physical action into multiple attacks). Finally, Ross heals two Health Levels each turn, separate from any active use of Iatrosis.

In other words, Ross is a very scary man with very scary powers, and most of the time he's a single-minded killing machine hellbent on clawing his way to Montressor. Use him carefully.

Doctor Heinrich Mangels

As a youngster, Heinrich was fascinated by all things Aberrant. He collected news clippings on them, studied books about them and generally became a walking, talking encyclopedia on taint and its carriers. This led to an interest in the body and medicine, and eventually to the Æsculapian Order.

While Mangels' prowess as both psion and doctor was unquestioned, his bedside manner was described as "unnerving" or even "terrifying." It wasn't long before he found himself in the clinic's research wing, working on nerve-regrowth techniques that Zweidler himself had created. Mangels' academic interest in taint became known to his colleagues, some of whom were already laying the groundwork for what would become the Huang-Marr Project. Offered a chance to indulge his passion, engage in challenging research and do something for the betterment of humanity, Mangels leapt at the opportunity. Since then, he's been one of the pillars of the project — going wherever he's needed and doing whatever needs to be done — all in the firm belief that he is working in humanity's best interests.

Image: Mangels is small and wiry, with close-cropped sandy hair. His features are sharp and narrow, and he has piercing dark eyes. Odds are that if you find Mangels at all, he's wearing a lab coat; the lab is where he's the most comfortable. Even when exiled to the Organ Banks, Mangels likes to keep up that sort of appearance. He takes tremendous pride in his abilities as a scientist, and the coat is another way for him to demonstrate those talents.

Roleplaying Hints: You are strictly ethical and moral in your behavior — it's just a question of what you consider moral. Firm in your belief that the Huang-Marr bioware offers humanity its best chance to defeat the Aberrant menace, you work tirelessly toward that end. You know, better than almost anyone else alive, how powerful taint is, and you are convinced that the war will be lost unless drastic measures are taken. Hence your dedication to Huang-Marr. Hence your willingness to do whatever necessary. Inside the lab, you're all business and extremely competent, it's just outside, when you have to deal with people, that you're lost.

Nature: Analyst
Allegiance: Huang-Marr Conspirators

Physical Attributes	Abilities
Strength 2	
Dexterity 3	Drive 1, Legerdemain 2, Martial Arts 1, Stealth 2
Stamina 3	
Mental Attributes	**Abilities**
Perception 4	Awareness 3, Investigation 2
Intelligence 4	Academics 4, Bureaucracy 4, Engineering 2, Linguistics (English, German, French) 3, Medicine 5, Science 4
Wits 3	Meditation 2, Rapport 1
Social Attributes	**Abilities**
Appearance 2	
Manipulation 3	Command 2, Interrogation 1
Charisma 3	Subterfuge 4, Savvy 1

Aptitude: [Vitakinesis] Iatrosis 3, Mentatis 2, Algesis 1
Willpower: 7
Psi: 3
Backgrounds: Allies (Jerzy Grabowski) 3, Contacts (Huang-Marr Conspirators) 4, Resources 3, Status (Huang-Marr) 4
Gear: Work clothes, lab coat, Steinhardt VirtuX minicomp (Chris agent), vocoder (Portuguese, Chinese)

Aprille Glück

Zurich born and bred, Glück was plucked from her schooling by Zweidler to undergo the Prometheus Effect at an early age. Zweidler recognized her enormous psionic potential, although he was a little blind to her personality. Simply put, Glück was and is a bully, and once she got her head around Algesis, it took direct intervention by Zweidler himself to rein her in.

Rather than waste such talent, however, the proxy decided to put it to best use. Black Company had been on the drawing board for a while; with some minor modifications it became the perfect stage for Glück's talents. A devastatingly effective recruiter and a superb field tactician, she's taken Zweidler's mandate and created one of the most elite and feared fighting forces on the planet.

Image: Glück is handsome, not beautiful. With high cheekbones, a hawk nose and sharply angled eyebrows, she reminds observers of a bird of prey waiting to spot a meal. Well under two meters in height, Aprille keeps herself in fighting trim and can probably take any other member of the company in hand-to-hand combat. Her black hair is cropped short. She prefers black or gray fighting togs to any other form of clothing.

Roleplaying Hints: You take orders from one person, and one person only: Zweidler. Neihaus and his squad of normals are beneath contempt — let them handle the menial stuff. Anyone you meet is either a threat, an annoyance or an obstacle — make your call and treat them accordingly. You know how to handle yourself in debate as well as in combat, and have as much fun shutting idiots down with a well-placed barb as you do with a spinning kick to the jaw. In the end, it's results that matter, and you get them any way you can.

Nature: Leader
Allegiance: Black Company

Physical Attributes   **Abilities**
Strength 4   Might 3
Dexterity 5   Athletics 5, Drive 3, Firearms 5, Martial Arts 5, Melee 5, Pilot 3, Stealth 3
Stamina 5   Endurance 4, Resistance 4

Mental Attributes   **Abilities**
Perception 3   Awareness 3, Investigation 3
Intelligence 3   Bureaucracy 2, Engineering 2, Intrusion 3, Medicine 1, Survival 4
Wits 4

Social Attributes   **Abilities**
Appearance 4   Intimidation 5, Style 2
Manipulation 4   Command 4, Interrogation 4, Subterfuge 3
Charisma 4   Savvy 2

Aptitude: [Vitakinesis] Iatrosis 3, Algesis 4
Willpower: 8
Psi: 6
Backgrounds: Allies (Zweidler) 5, Contacts 5, Followers (Black Company) 5, Influence 3, Mentor (Zweidler) 5, Resources 3, Status (Æsculapians) 5
Gear: Voss 33K laser pistol, Orgotek Electric Eel taser pistol, Black Company uniform (reinforced), Wazukana 300E minicomp (Bill v5.0 agent), vocoder (English, Portuguese, French), handcuffs, cell uplink

Black Company Guard

The characters probably don't come into direct confrontation with Black Company. Assume that each guard has four dots in one of his Aptitude Modes, and a single dot in each of the remaining two.

Jakob Neihaus

A street punk from Vienna who managed to make something of himself through military service, Neihaus is tough as nails and half as personable. At least, that's as far as outsiders are concerned. Orphaned and bounced from relative to relative, Neihaus found a family with only a gang of street thugs who specialized in beating up immigrants and, when they were feeling bold, tourists.

The latter acts caught the attention of the city police, who cracked down on Jakob and his friends. Given a choice between prison or military service, they chose service; Neihaus never looked back. Winning multiple commendations, he found himself transferred to Special Forces, was given a command of his own — and then mustered out.

Psions took over the division and there wasn't much room for an uppity normal like Neihaus, no matter how talented. Ironically, Zweidler made the first offer to the now-unemployed soldier. Wanting someone in place to balance Glück, Zweidler handed Neihaus enough power and authority to compensate for the man's issues with working for a psion, and set him up as head of security. Neihaus in turn recruited his old buddies, and the core of the security team was in place. Now Neihaus stays at Basel unless events in the field demand his presence. His disciplined, frighteningly effective troops provide protection for every Æsculapian clinic out there.

Image: Neihaus is stocky and solid, with a graying crew cut. His square jaw, broad face and heavily wrinkled brow make him look something like an ill-humored dwarf from a particularly unpleasant fairy tale, though Jakob keeps his beard trimmed relatively short. Rarely found out of uniform, Jakob hauls out his entire supply of medals — and there are quite a few — for formal dress occasions. He and Glück are of equal height, making for an amusing image when they flank the half-meter-taller proxy.

Roleplaying Hints: You are all business, with little time for anyone you don't trust implicitly. Those few know you as gruff, uncommunicative and standoffish. You have the respect of many, but the friendship of few. Your people love you because you treat them well, and because you foster a real us-against-the-world mentality among them. So far, that attitude has served you — and the clinic — well.

Nature: Traditionalist
Allegiance: Æsculapians
Physical Attributes
Strength 5
Dexterity 4
Stamina 5
Mental Attributes
Perception 4
Intelligence 3
Wits 4
Social Attributes
Appearance 2
Manipulation 3
Charisma 2
Willpower: 9
Psi: 1
Abilities
Brawl 5, Might 3
Athletics 5, Drive 4, Firearms 5, Melee 4, Pilot 2, Stealth 3
Endurance 3, Resistance 3
Abilities
Awareness 4
Bureaucracy 3, Engineering 3, Intrusion 4, Linguistics (English, French) 2, Survival 4
Arts 1
Abilities
Intimidation 4
Command 5, Interrogation 4, Subterfuge 3
Etiquette 2, Savvy 4

Backgrounds: Allies (Zweidler) 5, Contacts 5, Followers (Security Staff) 5, Influence 3, Mentor (Zweidler) 5, Resources 3, Status (Æsculapians) 5
Gear: Security uniform (reinforced), armor vest, L-K Avenger 11 mm autopistol, Voss 63K laser carbine, Wazukana DX70 minicomp (Lt. Bushido agent), vocoder (Arabic, Portuguese, Russian), handcuffs, cell uplink

Normal Guard

Treat Neihaus' guards as police officers (see the Police Officer Template, **Trinity**, page 306).

REPORT TO FIELD OPERATIVES

ÆON TRINITY TRANSMISSION [NEPTUNE DIVISION]

North American Terrestrial Office, Deputy Office Director Marilyn Koziana
Fellow Æon Members —

You have performed beyond our greatest expectations in the resolute pursuit of matters far more complex than they first appeared. Frankly, had we known at the outset what an altogether dangerous and far-reaching case this would be, we would have assigned it to senior operatives. However, you rose to the challenge as well as — and in some instances better than — anyone could have hoped.

Unfortunately, events have progressed beyond the Trinity's control to contain them from public awareness. The Æon Council hoped that an investigation into psi-order corruption could be handled with secrecy and discretion. We wanted to avoid the spread of panic and fear among the populace. Unfortunately, that is exactly what is happening now that news of illegal bioware research — the Huang-Marr Project — has come to light.

Even though the entire Æsculapian and Orgotek Orders are being implicated publicly in illicit (and if I may say, immoral) pursuits, we must maintain perspective. Apprehending the primary Huang-Marr conspirators must remain our goal for the moment. The single most responsible individual in this matter has thus far proven to be Dr. Gustaf Beitz, a high-ranking Æsculapian and contemporary of Proxy Zweidler himself.

BLIGHT PROJECT FACILITY >>> TRINITY FILE IMAGE

Beitz's last known location was in the Federated States' Great Lakes District. The Swiss company Schilltronix is associated with Orgotek on the Blight Project, which is based in this region. It seems that neither company is involved directly in the Huang-Marr conspiracy. However, apparently Beitz and his associates — most notably Horace Meeks of Orgotek — used both organizations' resources and personnel for their own ends. There's no guarantee that Beitz went to a Blight site (or that he remains there if he had), but it seems a viable place to pick up his trail.

While other Æon operatives follow related leads on the Huang-Marr Project, you are directed to continue your pursuit of the primary conspirators. Special Agent Hector Ramirez will keep you apprised of any breakthroughs made on other fronts. In turn, be sure to communicate with him as you make progress.

I must also inform you that the proxies demanded that they meet with the Æon Council to discuss recent events in detail. The group discussed the Huang-Marr situation via secure broadcast link. Although we feel confident that most of the information remains secure from the orders as a whole, it's possible that you may be contacted by representatives of one or more of the proxies. Proxy Cassel is sure to take a personal interest in matters. He showed an apparently genuine anger and remorse at the conspiracy being linked to his order. Orgotek may well offer you assistance, may exchange information, or may propose other negotiations in the course of your investigation.

We recommend that you accept any such offers. Still, be aware that while the electrokinesis order — and its proxy — may be interested in achieving the same goals as the Æon Trinity, it may well have its own reasons for doing so. Take advantage of any assistance offered, but accept nothing blindly. Your insights and discretion have been vital in the past. Maintain your vigilance, and we are confident that this entire sordid affair will be resolved quickly and quietly.

Best of luck to you,
Koziana
North American Terrestrial Office, 15:00:33 5.6.2120
Hope Sacrifice Unity

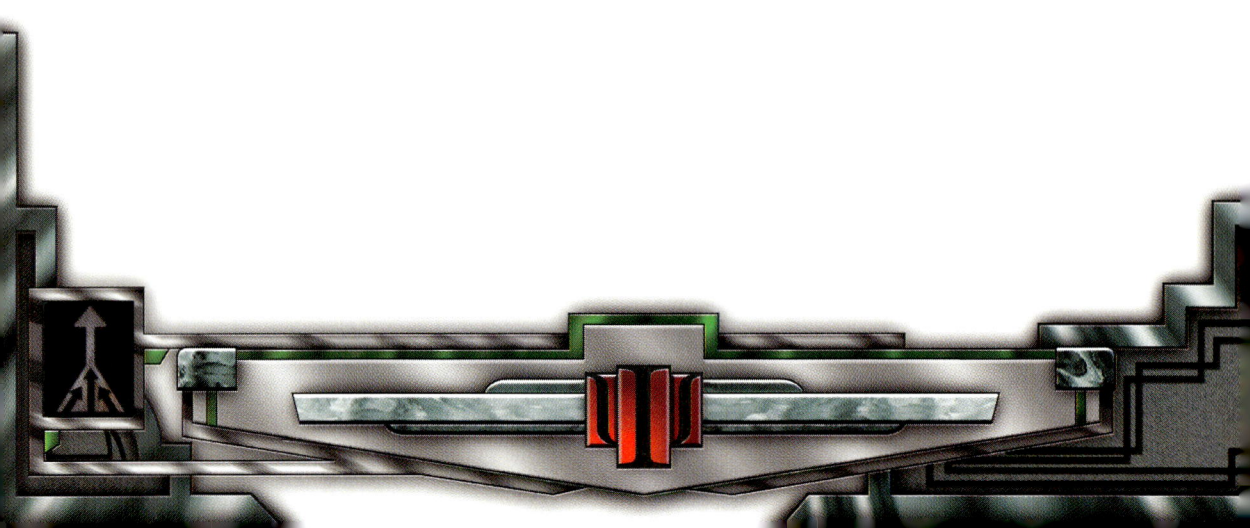

WORLD ENTERPRISES PRESENTS: WORLD LEADERS
PREXY ON PSI ORDERS IN SOCIETY

— **Rebecca Spriggs, exclusive to World Enterprises, Inc.**
[Hold for airing 18:00:00 4.23.2120]

Prexy Cassel spoke with reporters this afternoon in an informal but extended session, addressing what he calls a "crisis of values" within the psi orders: "Collectively, the orders are in late adolescence. We're at the end of our big growth phase and are looking for our adult identity. But just like teenagers, we don't always handle things as well as we could or should."

The Prexy's record on matters of interorder cooperation is well-known to all Americans, and is available for perusal by those unfamiliar with it. So when he issues criticisms, we in the media listen carefully.

Cassel's immediate concern was the recent reports of corruption within Æsculapian-related facilities, both here in America and in Europe. "I don't think anyone has gone wrong here but a few isolated nut cases," he assured us. "*No* organization with more than about five members is safe from that. Sometimes," he noted with a chuckle, "it doesn't take *that* many. Wherever people see a chance for power, unreliable ones congregate. Despite our best screening efforts, some fringe elements are bound to slip into the orders. Unfortunately, the Prometheus Effect doesn't make us saner, smarter or wiser than a normal person."

But, he added, the orders have a special responsibility in such a regard. Since

ALEX CASSEL>>> TRINITY FILE HOLOGRAM

the orders wield unique powers, they are accountable, to earn humanity's trust. "The public can make us all go away just like the quantakinetics. We have to show them why we're worth keeping around. This is a difficult time for all of us, as we figure out how psions fit into the fabric of society, and we're doing it all in the public spotlight. That generates a lot of pressure to get it right the first time."

The Prexy praised the role the Æon Trinity has played in mediating between the orders and the rest of society. "Æon's our bridge. It's been close to us for so long that we can trust it, but it's distinct enough from the orders that the public can trust the Trinity, too."

He explained that Æon's work makes it easier for the orders to become *part of* society, rather than be outsiders. "So when an order starts hassling Trinity operatives the way it looks like the Æsculapians have, that's a warning sign to me. If there's a problem, the orders need to deal with it. Shooting the messenger never works."

The Prexy reminded us of Orgotek's long and varied partnership with Æon, from the very early days of the psions, to large-scale ventures like the Blight Project, to local assistance efforts like the Arco-San Francisco Domestic Violence Unit.

"The Trinity isn't always right. We all make mistakes. But we should always listen, and I think the other orders need to listen more than they do. Our common future depends on the Æon ideals: hope, sacrifice and unity. Now, as we decide where to go from here, is a time for unity, not dissension."

PREXY TO INVESTIGATE ALLEGED CORRUPTION

— **Rebecca Spriggs, exclusive to World Enterprises, Inc.**
[Hold for airing 18:00:00 5.6.2120]

Alex Cassel announced today that he will personally investigate the rumors of psion malfeasance directed at his order. "Orgotek is dedicated to promoting progress," the Prexy said, "and I will not tolerate any people in my employ using my company for their own selfish ends. While I hope that this investigation proves my people to be innocent of any wrongdoing, I promise that any transgressors will be punished to the full extent of the law."

Mr. Cassel knows that the independent foundation known as the Æon Trinity is conducting its own investigation into the matter: "I welcome any Trinity investigators to my facilities — although they'll have to go through normal clearance procedures just like the rest of us!" Growing more serious, the Prexy stated, "Nobody can stand apart from the rest of the society — we all need checks and balances. If Æon can help keep us on the straight and narrow, more power to them."

Mr. Cassel will first take a tour of the Blight Project, the series of North American research sites where unscrupulous psions reportedly conspired to violate Orgotek and Æon Trinity standards for biological research safety. (See the recent WEI special "Profiles of the New Future" for more about this project.)

Once again, the Prexy expressed his confidence that these are isolated problems, and promised swift justice to any guilty parties. "Joe and Jane Hologram need to know that they can trust us. So we need to be worth trusting. I hope that this investigation provides the reassurance people need."

With a grin, he added, "Besides, I need a vacation! Any excuse to get out of the office will do."

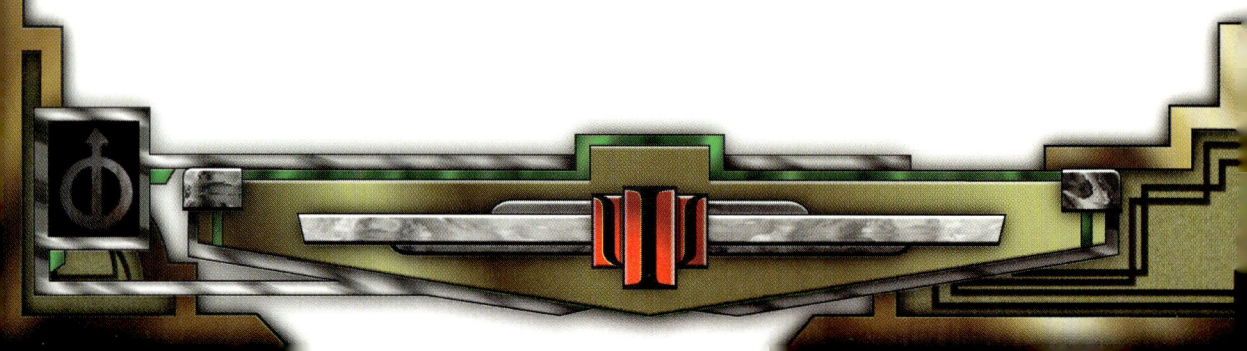

ÆON TRINITY LIAISON MAXIMUM-SECURITY PROTOCOLS

THE PROXY PROTOCOL

>>> **This document not for distribution. Access is monitored.** <<<

1. Context and Rationale. It is a regrettable fact of life, given mathematical rigor through semiotic analysis, that publicity often impairs truthful exchange of information. But information theory demonstrates that truthfulness is less energy-intensive and more reliable than concealment or deception, since both of the latter require the successful transmission of data layers beyond those involving facts. In short, secrets cost energy and are vulnerable to entropy. Since it is necessary to keep secrets — so that we may avoid the chaos that would follow the release of sensitive information — we seek to reduce secrets' entropic and social costs.

The Æon Trinity's role as coordinator of constructive social engagement often required operatives to speak frankly with leaders in social and political groups. These parties' personnel and resources were often as badly taxed as our own. Æon needed a system whereby those wishing to contact our organization could convey the degree of secrecy and scope of the issue at hand.

2. The Protocol. The "Proxy Protocol" functions as a partial solution to this problem. The Æon Trinity's regular communications protocols cover all but the most urgent crises. The Proxy Protocol is the final link in the chain of security.

The Proxy Protocol combines hardware and software elements. Those authorized to use it are issued special interface chips protected by Æon's maximum-security tamper-proofing mechanisms. On this platform, users run a customized agent that interfaces between them and their normal communications software, recognizing identity through genetic and neurological processes and providing on-the-fly encryption via Gruborsy N-Layer coding. The specialized encryption subroutines access Trinity software that the Æon operative installed in his communications system upon joining the organization.

With the protocol in place, a proxy — or an Æon director or council member — can signal any Æon computer with an alert that indicates an emergency. The ranking individual can thus communicate with a field operative on a priority beamed-transmission channel, with the highest level of secure transmission.

>>> full documentation schematics enclosed <<<

Profiles of the New Future, Part 4

The Blight Project
— WEI Special Features Staff © 2115 WEI/SF

"The Blight." Two words that mean the same thing to all Americans: a dustbowl, a wasteland, the symbol and source of our troubles, the definition of the Aberrant menace. We have all seen the images of our sterilized heartland, and worse, of the twisted abnormal life there. It's a hole in the center of North America, and in the center of our lives.

So the first serious effort to address the Blight is important to all Americans. But Orgotek's Blight Project has received very little attention since it began in 2111.

Project Director Patrick Burmeister says that's at least partly by design: "No offense to the orders — they pay our bills — but psions tend to do things very publicly. Even research groups like Lumen and the Haiti Group work in the limelight. They have to devote precious resources to managing the public. By working within the 'danger zone' of the Blight and not attracting attention, we get more done."

And what, exactly, *is* the Blight Project? Let's start at the beginning.

The Choice to Restore

The psi orders' proxies have gathered for regular meetings since they went public back in 2106. In the fall of 2111, they gathered at a free-zone Pacific resort. (The meeting was originally scheduled to be in Hawaii, in the Federated States' Pacific District, but the FSA government made it clear that psions who hadn't pledge oaths of loyalty weren't welcome.) ISRA Proxy Otha Herzog turned discussion to the most prominent symbols of the world's tragic past, and guided debate about which would be amenable to psions' healing hand.

The Blight was quickly raised. After intense discussion, the proxies agreed that they might be able to repair the damage done to the region. Thus, the Blight Project was born. The following spring, the proxies involved as-

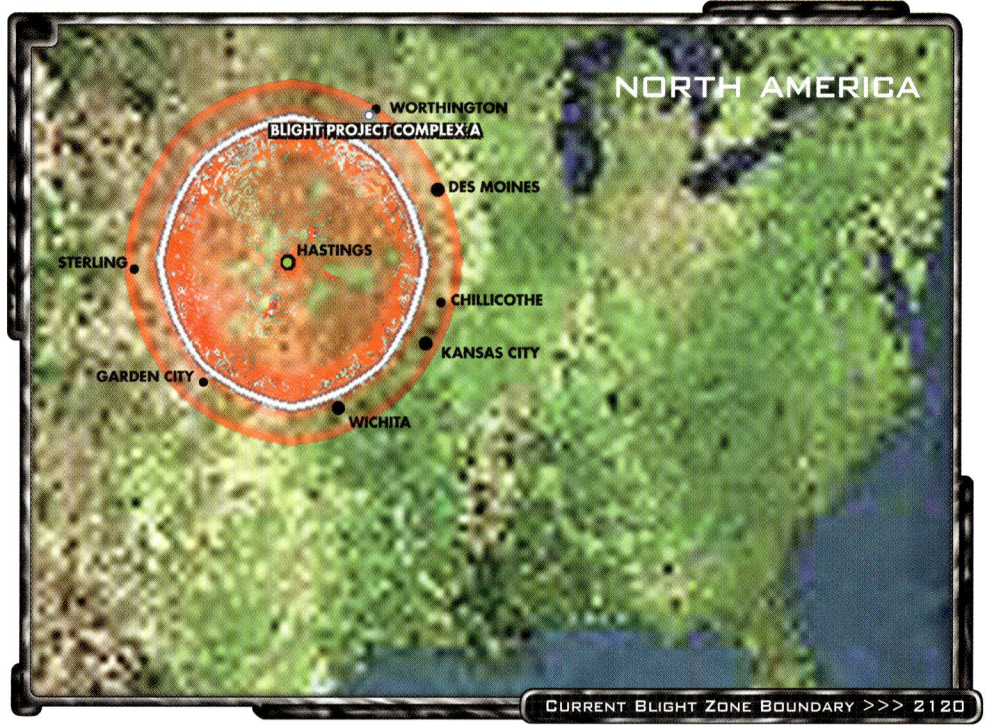

22ND-CENTURY EARTH

Blight Project Facility >>> File Image

signed delegates to work out operational details.

We spoke with Lisa Bogman, Special Executive Assistant to Jeff Kenyatta, of Orgotek's Operations Division. "Well, the first thing we did was sort out who had what to contribute," Ms. Bogman explained. "There were already a number of studies being conducted on the Blight Zone. Still, we were confident that psions would add an important wrinkle to Blight research. Specifically, Orgotek's presence was a given. It's our turf, insofar as we have such a thing, and while biology isn't our strong point, we're very good at designing tools that others use.

"We knew right off that we wanted the Æsculapians and Norça involved. Although a few biokinetics assist on the project, we never did get the degree of Norça involvement that we hoped for. They just don't seem to like operating on others' turf. But Zweidler was great. The Æsculapians are known for being healers, but what a lot of people don't know is that the docs are terrific researchers. After all, before the Chitra Bhanu were corrupted, the two orders did a lot of groundbreaking exploration into noetics.

"In some ways this is Herzog's baby, but the way ISRA works hard to get a lot of them involved. The clairsentients are very independent, and often go chasing after their latest visions. I'm not saying they're flighty, mind you. They just operate on a different level. We get by just fine with the clears who've joined Orgotek. Any others who want to help out are more than welcome!

"The Legions have worked something out with the Federated States government to patrol the central Blight Zone. It's called the 'Legion Aberrant Search Territory' or something. Having Legionnaires patrolling for Aberrants takes a load off our minds. It allows us to focus on our research.

We don't seem to need telepaths here. Still, I understand the Prexy keeps the Ministry apprised of our progress. I must admit we miss the quantakinetics, corrupt or no. They were *useful*, at least to us. Someday somebody's gonna get

BLIGHT ZONE > AFFECTED GENE SEQUENCES > GRAINS >>> BLIGHT PROJECT ARCHIVE

that order going again and do it right this time."

After *Esperanza*

The disappearance of the Upeo wa Macho was a significant blow to the Blight Project. Data Management Chief Rayef Forkis told us, "We didn't really realize just how much we'd come to depend on the teleporters. Once we had the general mapping done, they could get in, gather specimens or probes, and get out. They could check out anomalies easier than any probe can, and they could bring noetic sensitivity to bear.

"Even years later, I find myself looking around for the Lehman triplets, or Ting and Eng. Not to underplay the big losses, mind. What we've got here is nothing compared to what Europe's going through. But when the loss is up close and personal, it's hard to see past it. I hope we someday find out where the teleporters went."

The First Steps

By the end of 2112, research into the Blight Zone and construction of the main Blight Project facility were underway. Early labs were set up in temporary quarantine structures airlifted from Minneapolis, Chicago and Dallas.

Geoffrey David Watt, the project's first chief operations officer, recalls his work: "We had to fight for every concession from the FSA from the very beginning. Their idea of dealing with the Blight was to throw up a few thousand klicks of fence, shoot trespassers and ignore it until a miracle made it go away. They talked as though they expected anyone going in there to turn into a ravening monster, or to unleash a swarm of giant crickets or something.

"But we had good intentions, and my bosses the proxies and their staffs are pretty sharp. So eventually we cleared enough hurdles to convince the FSA that we weren't going to be a problem. I think it helped that the Legions were working out their own arrangement to patrol the region. Things have been even easier since some executive orders in 2113 gave us a (very conditional) seal of approval.

"Do you realize that until we came along, nobody had even drawn a precise map of the different areas of the Blight? *Fifty years*, and they'd simply ignored the mess — out of sight, out of mind, yeh? We spent a year-and-a-half on satellites, fly-overs, ground teams, clairsentients and other means of defining the problem."

The Blight Project at Work

By the end of 2113, the Blight Project was in full swing. Its researchers had detailed baseline data on the zone's condition, identified different degrees of Blight effect, and began long-term monitoring. The full complement of orders involved — and non-psion scientists, as well — was present.

Since then — well, according to Bogman — "Not a lot of drama has occurred. In the past two years, we've disposed of a lot of easy generalizations, ruled out many simplistic theories. Knowing what doesn't work is a very important element of knowing what does."

Only when we asked about the Legions' "shooting gallery" in the central Blight region (in the "LAST Zone") did we find reluctance on the part of those we interviewed. Bogman simply said, "That's their project. Go ask them about it. We're here to fix things, not blow them up."

What does the future hold? Agronomy Section Chief Calvin Watts had this to say: "We're taking lots of little steps that add up to a big distance. For instance, in my section we've isolated six specific gene sequences affected by whatever it is that Wycoff unleashed. If we make some fairly simple corrections, we get grains that... well, they're still sterile, but they lack 85% of the nutritional deficiencies that afflict the parent strains. By itself, that's not enough. But it adds up with whatever they're doing over in soil chemistry, meteorology and everywhere else around here, composing a more complete picture of how to fix the zone."

The Final Word: Lisa Bogman

"Someday the Blight will be a 'was,' not an 'is.' I'm damn glad to be here, doing my part to make that happen."

• TRITON ARCHIVE •

BLIGHT PROJECT: STRATEGIC CONCERNS

— Evaluation: Ian Marsh, Triton Division, 02.09.2112

The first conclusion is the most fundamental: We believe that the Blight Project deserves Æon Trinity support, and formally recommend that we commit ourselves accordingly. The work here seems valuable and well-conducted. This is not another Farsearch or Holmes fiasco in the making.

However, there is some grounds for concern regarding the mixture of motives behind the project. We see potential for unauthorized, unsupervised and unethical biomedical experimentation, given the environment's necessarily remote and sometimes dangerous nature. (This wouldn't be an issue if the Blight were safe — but then the project wouldn't need to exist if the region was safe.) We recommend that Proteus Division make regular surveillance sweeps; Triton will periodically monitor the project's research advancements.

Triton feels that the available evidence warrants a stance of guarded optimism. The nature of the project requires regular updates, with evaluations at appropriate intervals. The Blight Project should contribute to the continued rehabilitation of Earth, and is unlikely to generate serious moral, social or scientific problems.

— Addendum: 4.12.2120 (unattributed)

Well, they were half-right, anyway.

On Wings of Ether: *Eyrie* Station

— Mason White, 2118 Science News Network (a division of Global News)

One: What it Is

You can see it from the ground when the angle and lighting are just right: a yellow-silver dot zipping from north to south, or vice versa, faster than anything else in the sky. More details present themselves through high-powered binoculars: Four main solar panels expand to form a circular shield around the station's "midsection," the twin slabs of the main hulls hidden beneath temporary work sites or "bladders" — white bubbles that shelter greenhouses and transparent bubbles that house equipment. Approaching and departing transfer craft provide scale, proving the station to be almost a kilometer long, the solar panels five kilometers in diameter. Only with a telescope can the ground observer see the station's 20-kilometer-long tether arrays that enable maneuverability.

Eyrie Station is the "road less taken" in space-colony design. As an aerospace engineer in the days after the Exodus said, the rule of the day was "Let a hundred rockets launch, let a hundred platforms contend." Countless experiments shot up, testing a huge variety of theories about the best use of then-current technology in space settlement. Most failed, of course; where there were once 100 schools of design, there are now only a handful. But experiments crop up now and again. *Eyrie* Station is one of them.

• TRITON ARCHIVE •

21st-Century Biotechnology

Most Earth governments outlawed biotechnological research in the early days of the Aberrant War. Reports from a number of sources suggested that bio- and nanotechnology were to blame for the creation of Aberrants in the first place. Even though Aberrant Syndrome was later agreed to be genetic, fear already caused the dismantling of most development programs. Operatives do well to never underestimate the power of mass opinion; it's a primary reason why Æon operates largely outside of public awareness.

Before psions reinstated full-fledged biotech research, organizations that pursued such development did so outside the purview of Earth governments. JaDe Associates was one of a handful of private concerns that built upon what remained of biotechnology. The company launched *Menagerie* Station in the early 2070s, using the unclaimed space in Lunar orbit to pursue its research.

It appears that 21st-century biotechnology, at least that pursued by groups like JaDe Associates, was a dead end. The key problem with large-scale bioware was its dependency on a complex chemical regimen for growth and maintenance. A failure in any component halted the whole process, and the bioware shriveled and rotted. Maintaining stability was fairly easy in microgravity and vacuum, but almost impossible at the bottom of an atmospheric gravity well. Furthermore, JaDe's biomaterials had narrow applications: They performed their designed tasks well, but could do no more. JaDe's attempt to contain and support biotech within hardtech exostructures, as evidenced in *Eyrie* Station, expanded biotechnology's usefulness. In the end, though, it still proved to be inferior to the advances made by Orgotek and the Norça in the early 22nd century.

SPACE

EYRIE STATION >>> SCIENCE NEWS NETWORK

In the late 2080s, JaDe Associates worked out a plan for a combined biotech/hardtech approach to space-colony development. They intended *Eyrie* to be proof of the concept. Unfortunately, while *Eyrie* proved a viable orbital-station design, it also proved to be too expensive and required too much ongoing control effort to compete with other, more straightforward approaches. It also became clear that very few orbital installations had any use for some of *Eyrie*'s most impressive products.

Eyrie is in a tight polar orbit, 300 to 400 kilometers above sea level, circling the Earth from pole to pole once every two hours. (Once every 112 minutes in its standard orbit, to be precise.) Polar orbits are effective for observing the whole planet on a regular basis; spy satellites have used them since the mid-20th century, and scientific platforms have used them almost as long. They're not good if an installation is supposed to remain in constant communication with a particular point on the ground; that's the domain of geosynchronous orbits. So *Eyrie* was designed with global observation capabilities in mind.

Despite the discovery of hyper-fusion as a relatively cheap and abundant power source, JaDe Associates was determined to continue down the road less traveled. *Eyrie's* primary power source is microcrystal solar cells woven throughout the station's collapsible solar sail. The cells are not as efficient as somewhat bulkier solar matrix units. Yet the cells' low mass allows the sails to be more than large enough to provide power for all of the station's needs. *Eyrie* also draws power from magnetic and tidal differentials along cables extending the length of the station. Readers interested in consulting the mathematical systems used in this power system may refer to the linked site >>> space science database <<<.

Eyrie's abundant power enables the station to maneuver in orbit. Adjusting a typical satellite's orbit is a complicated and energy-intensive process involving careful calculations — not unlike steering a supertanker into one of Earth's ocean harbors. By comparison, shifting *Eyrie's* orbit is like sailing a yacht. Ion engines and solar winds make orbital changes fast and smooth, and the continuous energy available via solar sail means that adjustments take as long as needed. *Eyrie* can maintain a continuous sequence of orbital shifts over a period of days.

But as the JaDe consortium learned, there just isn't that much demand for continuous sequences of orbital shifts. It's easier and generally cheaper to put up small

SPACE

EYRIE STATION

— Update: Iris Ouest, Neptune Division, 06.10.2119

My evaluation of *Eyrie* Station hasn't changed from previous reports. We find it an interesting social experiment — not the sort of society the Trinity hopes to build, but instructive. It's especially interesting to note the social dynamics of talented but not necessarily socially skilled communities. I do feel that specific points warrant adoption as Æon policy >>> file enclosed <<<.

On a more immediate level, *Eyrie* remains useful to Æon. Its observation capabilities are effective, able as they are to gather important scientific and geographic data. Recent discoveries include Mid-Atlantic Ridge 20, the North Seattle Unauthorized Urban Area, and Tel Bekha. Yet these are only the tip of the iceberg. I propose that Neptune refer to the benefits gained from these discoveries when budgeting for the coming fiscal period >>> file enclosed <<<.

However, observation is not all that *Eyrie* provides. Æon is among the regular customers of its covert and valuable surveillance capabilities. The Cheltenham operation >>> file enclosed <<< provides a clear example of a mission whose success depended on *Eyrie's* intelligence. As with the general research, I recommend that Neptune reconsider these benefits to covert efforts when planning the next fiscal period. I believe a 20% increase may be warranted, considering the variables >>> file enclosed <<<.

dedicated satellites or to use powered units on existing platforms. *Eyrie* pays for itself, but there is simply no demand for other stations of its kind.

Two: What it Does

Eyrie's primary mission is planetology. Like other polar-orbiting facilities, it studies weather, maps ocean currents, and evaluates ground conditions. It works on a contract basis with archeological ventures to apply long-wave radar and other methods of scanning — its alterable orbit makes it particularly useful for this sort of task. Popular rumor also credits *Eyrie* with providing contract espionage. Certainly the world's more repressive governments routinely denounce it for doing so. Hard proof, however, has yet to materialize. Optimists claim that this is because *Eyrie* does not host spies; cynics claim that this is because the denouncers themselves use it for such purposes.

Eyrie also hosts microgravity research and development, with particular emphasis on providing changing conditions for experimental apparatus or organisms. *Eyrie's* wanderings take it into regions of very diverse magnetic potential, particle flux, microatmosphere and other environmental factors. Such variations are disruptive to most specialized processes in which every factor is calculated and simulated in advance. But for those whose subject of concern is variation itself, *Eyrie* is a wonderful base of operations.

Finally, *Eyrie* is a repository of offbeat ideas and their advocates. Most orbital installations aim for homogeneity or at least strong mutual compatibility among their residents. Since the late 2090s, *Eyrie* policy has been to disregard compatibility except within each working group. In 2097, then-station manager Cervaise Simon explained the point in a press release: "We seek intellectual and cultural hybrid vigor. So long as the work is not endangered, we welcome engagement between diverse views, even vigorous engagement. Out of this ongoing synthesis we shall build the new dialectic of orbital activity."

Simon's grander vision has not come to pass. At least, one may search long and hard for any sign that what happens at *Eyrie* strongly influences developments on other installations, except perhaps as a cautionary tale. Nonetheless, *Eyrie's* engineer/poets, mechanic/historians and agronomist/artists have generated a steady flow of intriguing ideas to much critical acclaim, if not to great financial reward. Three Nobel Prizes in the humanistic undertakings, four Calvin Awards, eight Kodiak Citations and eleven Alpha Rho Gamma Prizes form the capstone of a pyramid of honors awarded to *Eyrie* dwellers.

SPACE

Eyrie inhabitants (or "Eagles" as they refer to themselves) contrast their "evolving perspective" with the "spatiotemporal fixity" that prevails among those who maintain a constant gravitational and cosmological condition. "We see things differently" is the unofficial motto of the 1000 residents.

Three: Life on *Eyrie*

From the outside, *Eyrie* is a typical hardtech construct, not particularly different — apart from the solar sail — than countless other orbital installations. Inside, *Eyrie* is a riotous kaleidoscope, both visually and socially. From the moment you board *Eyrie*, you are surrounded by rainbows and panoramas: *Eyrie* is crisscrossed throughout by an elaborate network of fiber optics. One never escapes views of the surrounding universe — some "raw," others processed with varying degrees of sophistication — unless one deliberately turns them all off.

Planetologists and their families comprise the single largest percentage of *Eyrie's* population, along with those who support them and those who keep the research infrastructure operating. This includes about 700 people at any given moment. Five hundred are permanent residents; the remainder stay for stints ranging from a day to years.

The other 300 Eagles on board handle duties related closely to *Eyrie* itself. These include management, operating the docking and transfer facilities and providing liaison services with other installations and Earth. However, almost all staffers regard their jobs as "what they do" rather than "who they are." The Eagles consider themselves a collection of creators, a new generation of universe-changing geniuses gathered together in their unique lair.

• TRITON ARCHIVE •

FSA CONDEMNS ORBITAL TERRORISTS

Office of Public Relations, 10.09.2118

The Federated States of America issued an explicit condemnation of efforts by hostile foreign powers to exploit low-Earth orbits for purposes of illicit surveillance. "We particularly condemn espionage done under the guise of scientific research," the notice reads. "Other nations threaten our ability to protect our citizens by properly exploiting knowledge about the physical conditions of our sovereign territory. Further, even independent orbital facilities like *New Horizon* and *Eyrie* Stations are guilty of these transgressions."

The notice links this manner of surveillance directly to terrorist attacks by unidentified hostile nations on FSA infrastructure. "The Federated States declines to participate in a useless exchange of accusation and denial. The guilty parties know who they are. All citizens and potential citizens of good will have confidence in the reliability of our threat assessment modality."

At the present time, the FSA has not committed itself to a particular strategy of threat response. It reiterated its commitment to protect its airspace by "whatever means are most likely to promote the well-being of our human, biological and technological intellectual resources."

SPACE

Eyrie Station and Specialized Manufacturing

Imagination at Work

Eyrie Station offers fabrication services without peer anywhere in human space. Our scientists have spent decades developing unique environments and the proper tools to use in them. From the comfort of *Eyrie's* remote-control research and manufacturing facilities, you can supervise chemical and mechanical processes with three key variable conditions:

- **Gravity.** From standard orbital microgravity up to two gees, courtesy of our advanced gravcrystal arrays.
- **Temperature.** From 0.0001º Celsius (colder than orbital space!) to 500,000º Celsius for days at a time. Higher temperatures are possible for short periods.
- **Pressure.** From 0.0000001 atmosphere (less dense than orbital space) to 40,000 atmospheres, indefinitely — and even higher pressures for short periods.

Eyrie can create every scientific condition imaginable — the crushing gravity of Jupiter's atmosphere, the searing heat of the Sun's corona, the pressure of the ocean bottom. All can be found in low-Earth orbit on *Eyrie* Station.

Eyrie Clients

Here are just a few of the products and services *Eyrie* provides, and the prestigious clients who use them:

- **Elemental iron** [in kilogram quantities] to New Copernicus Electronics for use in a superconducting relay system on the far side of the Moon.
- **Million-atom carbon nanotubes** [in gram quantities] to FangTech (for research into biotech deep-sea submersibles), to Amalgamated Business Interests (for experiments in post-OpNet networking technologies) and to Jensen Enterprises (for currently undisclosed purposes).
- **Metallic hydrogen clathrates** [in gram quantities] to Beaulac and Covenants Clinics, Luna, for use in multi-fluid treatments for Total Allergy Syndrome.
- **Metallic helium film** [in kilogram quantities] to Tau Ceti Development Corporation, for experimental radiation shielding and telepathy-amplification systems.
- **Synthetic nucleic acids** [in gram quantities] to Wazukana, for biotech computing experiments.

Eyrie provides licensing contracts for any of the processes and compounds developed by our talented independent researchers. Furthermore, there is space available for you to perform your own private research. Contact us today to see how *Eyrie* Station may benefit you!

• TRITON ARCHIVE •

ANALYSIS: *EYRIE'S* SPECIALIZED MATERIALS PRODUCTION
—Dr. Cletus Skinner, Triton Division

It took us a while to even identify some of the things that *Eyrie* folks produce.

Elemental iron, truly free of impurities, is a high-conductivity, soft, white metal. Carbon nanotubes are lattices of carbon molecules forming a hollow tube; they usually enclose highly reactive chemicals that can't be transported otherwise without loss of integrity. Metallic hydrogen and helium are incredibly dense superconducting elements found in extremely high-pressure environments. Clathrate is a matrix with water ice (also metallic under these conditions) that can hold some gases.

Now, there's nothing unusual about most of this — except the quantities being made. Nobody's made these things on a commercially viable scale before. Although *Eyrie* produces relatively small quantities itself, they fetch top yuan from some powerful companies.

We're less concerned for what's being produced than who's using it. It's quite possible that Wazukana's using the synthetic nucleic acids to construct biotech simulations of the human brain with faster "nerve" transmission rates. Alternatively, they could be making mobile biotech chassis — androids or "dolls," if you will — to house conventional hardtech processors. I don't begin to understand why they'd let *Eyrie* use such sensitive information in a publicity packet, though.

Similarly, preliminary analysis indicates that Jensen Enterprises is an orbital front for Huang-Marr research. If this information is accurate, it helps explain where the recently discovered biorg project got some of its specialized equipment.

SPACE

EARTH ORBIT TRAFFIC

LOW-EARTH ORBIT TRAFFIC INTERCEPT

Target: *Eyrie* Station / **Date:** 15:23:10 5.6.2120

Note: Subject Jon Galin Reese identified as 28-year-old citizen of FSA West District, employed as telecomm research/PVU operator for *Eyrie* since 11.18.2119.

FTC Six: >>> disrupted transmission <<< Far Tether Crew Six to *Eyrie*, some… messing with the reliability… normal comm. I'm kicking in fiber backup and crank… broadcast power— >>> transmission clears <<< *Eyrie*, this is Jon Galin Reese. I want to file a preliminary claim. There's something weird out here, and if there's money in it, I want my piece.

***Eyrie* Station:** Claim noted. What d'you have out there, Reese?

FTC Six: Hang on; lemme turn this pod around so you get a view. Are you getting an optical feed? Looks the size of a cargo hauler. Big whale of a thing…. I can't place the make, and I'm *sure* it wasn't there a minute ago.

***Eyrie* Station:** You sure you didn't just overlook it? Ships just don't appear unless — you picking up taint disruption?! Check now, Reese!

FTC Six: Hey, settle down, *Eyrie*! Jesus. I'm blank, y'know? I read the tech journals — unlike some nervous comm operators I could mention. This close to Earth, there should be a couple thousand psions able to pick up an Aberrant warp that could bring in a transport this size — plus, there's supposed to be funky shimmers beforehand or so—

FTC Six >>> Eyrie Station

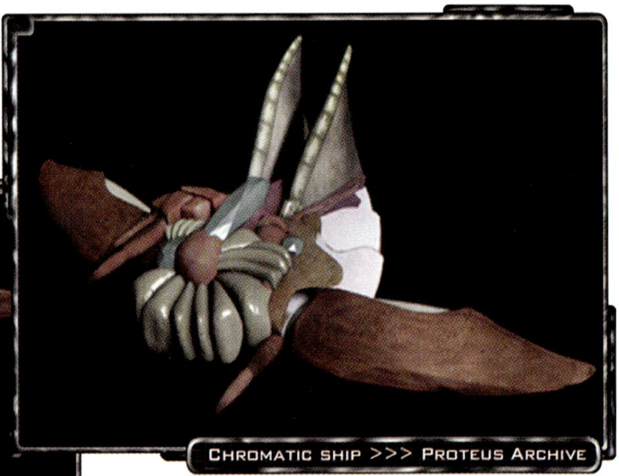

Earth Orbit Traffic

Chromatic ship >>> Proteus Archive

Um, hey, *Eyrie*? The thing's coming right this way.

Eyrie Station: Checking… no reported Aberrant incidents or derelicts in near space, Reese. Adjust optical to give us a better view.

FTC Six: Sure, sure. My PVU's drifting; gimme a sec. Wild; the body is almost as dark as space, but it's got these irregular bright spots. Can't figure out the pattern, but it's not random.

Whoa. A bunch of the lights detached. One is headed this way! Y'know what, it looks a bit like a—

Christ! The thing fired on me! I'm leaking! Oh, Hell! Son of a bitch—

>>> communication terminated <<<

Target: *Eyrie* Station / **Date:** 15:25:55 5.6.2120
Note: Speaker not identified.

Eyrie Station: —matic distress beacon on? Are we transmitting? Help! This is *Eyrie* Station. We're under attack! I can't tell what it is, but something has blasted big holes in the sail and now it's pounding on the hull! Four lab bladders have already been blown loose. All we've got is small arms. We need help — fast!

Again, this is *Eyrie* Sta—

>>> communication terminated <<<

[END TRANSMISSION]

EPISODE TWO: SIGNALS AND FLARES

This story is the second episode in **Passage Through Shadow**. The preceding color pages should be shared with players at the outset of this story or when appropriate documents are found throughout.

Signals and Flares is a turning point for the characters and for the Trinity Universe. The characters decisively crush the Huang-Marr Project conspirators, but the characters also face a surprising new complication. Only through quick thinking and decisive action can they triumph.

Overview

As *Signals and Flares* opens, the Æsculapian Order is rent by scandal. Public attention turns to Orgotek due to the rumored corrupt ties between the two psi orders. As the United Nations responds to demands for a public investigation into events, Special Agent Hector Ramirez orders the characters out of Basel to avoid the political mess developing there. Æon has Neptune Division operatives (like Ramirez himself) to deal with that sort of thing. Instead, the characters are to pursue the fleeing Huang-Marr ringleader, Gustaf Beitz, to North America.

A number of fingers point directly to an Orgotek Blight Project facility in Minnesota. These leads — materials and personnel shipped there via the Swiss Schilltronix corporation, Doctors Huang and Marr's involvement in the site at separate points in time, and Beitz's flight record from Basel to Minnesota shortly before the characters learned of his identity as the cryptic "Minerva" — were outlined to Alex Cassel by the characters' Æon Trinity superiors.

The characters meet the Prexy upon their arrival in North America, and they all enter the Blight Project. Cassel informs the investigators that he's already acted on the information given to him by Æon and is rounding up suspected accomplices. After interrogating the suspects — a collection of mid-level conspirators — the characters also apprehend a final one, Rita Disbray (Horace Meeks' senior partner among the Orgotek confederates). Amassing the intelligence they've gathered, the characters not only confirm the scope of Orgotek involvement in the Huang-Marr Project, but also determine the location of its master control center — on *Eyrie* Station.

As with the Æsculapians, the Orgotek personnel on the project claim they were working outside official channels. Even the Option-8 teams dispatched in **Descent into Darkness** were sent by a high-ranking Huang-Marr conspirator — the electrokinetic Horace Meeks. There have also been numerous communications with orbital-station *Eyrie* — and recently significant materials and personnel transferred there. The captured conspirators were to round up the remaining data in North America (which ironically compiles it all neatly for the characters to use as evidence), and then take a transport to *Eyrie*. Coincidentally — ominously so — as the characters (with Cassel still in attendance) prepare to leave for *Eyrie*, they learn the orbital station is under attack from unknown extraterrestrial assailants!

Cassel mobilizes Orgotek forces with the characters in tow. The investigators have the dubious honor of taking part in the first battle against aliens in Earth space. As the battle rages first between fighters and then through the halls and chambers of the devastated *Eyrie* itself, the characters learn that their opponents are none other than Chromatics. During the battle, the characters witness — or even participate in — the destruction of the Huang-Marr Project's central archives and the death or capture of the last surviving conspirators: Gustaf Beitz, Ella Huang and Horace Meeks.

Although the Chromatics struck at Olympus and Earth as well, the characters learn the aliens attacked *Eyrie* with a purpose. Aside from being a haven for the Huang-Marr conspirators, the orbital station was home to one Argente Essem, a clairsentient who came in contact with an alien intelligence when he performed extrasolar exploration with the Upeo. This same intelligence (which the characters learn is something called "the Doyen") contacted the Chromatics and told the aliens where to find important data on humans (and psions) that Essem was collecting. Just as surprising is that Alex Cassel — and possibly the other proxies — know of the Doyen but have kept the information secret for years!

The characters solve the mystery of Huang-Marr, but now they find themselves in the middle of an even larger mystery: How did the Chromatics get to our Solar System, and will they do it again? Who are the Doyen, and have those aliens contacted others as they did Argente Essem? The answers to these questions are unveiled in **Ascent into Light**, the final installment of the **Darkness Revealed** adventure trilogy.

Theme

Signals and Flares focuses on heroism and depravity — opposing factors of the human soul. The characters see individuals and the orders at their best and worst. While exacting justice on those whom they pursue, the characters themselves have the potential to rise to the heights of heroism, or to fall victim to their base instincts. In their recent investigations, the characters have looked into many dark shadows and seen horrible things; now they encounter brighter images. The evils the characters dealt with in **Descent into Darkness** and the previous episode are not truly representative of all groups or individuals in the Trinity Universe. There is hope for humanity. The characters should conclude their investigation of the Huang-Marr conspiracy with a sense of real accomplishment, and should be poised to answer greater questions. Indeed, they should feel that they have truly passed through shadow.

Mood

This is an exciting episode. Threads set in motion in the first book weave into a coherent whole in *Signals and Flares*. Those with action-oriented talents get to exercise them to their fullest, while much room remains for thoughtful planning. This episode should be fast-paced and energetic. While dramatic and challenging, it should also be *fun*.

The Setting

The first part of *Signals and Flares* takes place in the Minnesota site of a network of research facilities spread around the Blight Zone. The locale is one of the intellectual great-grandchildren of field-research projects performed by such organizations as the 20th century's Centers for Disease Control. The second half of the story takes place in space, in a doubly unusual environment. *Eyrie* Station is a collection of strange ideas and peculiar people. The surprise Chromatic attack adds chaos to the mix.

The Blight Zone

The Federated States of America thrives on order: "The FSA has a procedure for everything," the saying goes. The Blight Zone represents the ultimate in disorder, a whole landscape that refuses to follow guidelines or directives. In typical fashion, what the FSA can't micromanage relating to the Blight, it tries to foist off on someone else and summarily ignore.

Worthington, Minnesota, became a "research town" in the 2090s — the equivalent of a college town, except scientists rather than students flocked to the city. By the mid-2110s, Worthington and other middle-sized "Blight-fringe" cities, such as Sterling, Garden City and Chillicothe, soon joined the larger urban centers of Des Moines, Kansas City, Wichita and Sioux Falls as Blight research centers. These areas were all devastated, less by Wycoff's second-wave taint effect than by the public panic that followed it. The burgeoning taint-oriented research efforts of the end of the 21st century gave the cities a second chance.

Life in the Northern Blight

In 2120, Worthington's economy is based on supplying equipment and services to various research projects. The single largest labor employer is Worthington Municipal Airport, which has specialized cargo bays and handling facilities that rival the largest arcologies' — even though total volume is a tiny fraction of what passes through New York or San Francisco. The facilities are designed to handle all manner of scientific shipments, from microscopes to dangerous live specimens. The majority of the town's employable citizens who don't work at the airport have jobs in research projects or in the service industries that support them.

The public often thinks of scientists as soulless white-coated robots or crazed lunatics tampering with secrets that humanity was not meant to know. The men and women who work in the Worthington Research Corridor fit neither image. They work hard, dealing constantly with stressful matters. When they are off-duty, most of these scientists take relaxation very seriously. On weekends, Worthington looks much like any college town near Fraternity Row. The local contracted FSM division faces special challenges; the drunk and disorderly aren't mere students, but often highly trained and experienced staff. The authorities handle their drunks with care.

Orgotek's Blight Project Complex A lies five kilometers southwest of Worthington, on farmland that fell into disuse in 2055. Orgotek claimed the site for research purposes when the Blight Project formed, and constructed access roads, lab facilities and administrative complexes.

The Geography of the Blight

Worthington is 400 kilometers northeast of Hastings, Nebraska, close to the Minnesota-Iowa border. This puts it in a transitional region: still influenced by the Blight, but not afflicted by the oddities near Hastings.

The outer portion of the Blight circle (see **Trinity**, page 103) has recovered to a great degree, looking somewhat more desolate but otherwise little different than it did half a century ago. No giant mutated plants or monsters lurk in the shadows.

The inner regions of the Blight are still affected — enough so to keep hundreds of scientists busy studying them. The Blight Project is the biggest research venture in North America, but scientists are not alone there. The Blight Zone is home to a significant concentration of Legionnaires who patrol the area and take part in specialized training exercises. The Legions and Orgotek test new technology and techniques here, in one of the very few amicable agreements between the FSA and psi orders. The Federated States Military is also known to maintain some level of involvement in the area, despite — or perhaps because of — the country's politicians turning a blind eye to the Blight.

Within 50 kilometers of Hastings, the Blight Zone environment becomes extremely bizarre. Legion patrols have found a few Aberrants sheltered in eroded valleys and ruined buildings. Some areas stretch lifeless for entire counties; others harbor evolutionary regressions, mutations and mysterious symbiotic combinations. The entire environment, from earth to sky, has an unnerving otherworldly quality to it.

Manufacturing Under the Gun

The FSA actually wants the (relatively) safe Blight fringe to be used, but by handpicked corporations and industries, not by regular citizens. The Federated States Board supports extensive tax breaks for businesses willing to do business inside the Designated Safety Zone Terminator (see The Blight Defenses, page 86).

The FSA also supervises scientific research indirectly through the Blight Zone Special Administrative Unit. (The BZSAU fights constant jurisdictional battles with the Great Lakes, Central, Southwest and Tex-Mex District governments, all of which want federal funding.) The roster of major contributors to the Worthington-area economy — besides the many scientists — reads like a list of Who's Who in the All-American Media's Big 40, the continent's largest and most loyal corporations.

Test facilities that work on new manufacturing techniques without regard for pollution concerns dot the landscape; the BZSAU prefers to ignore most environmental processes regarding the Blight. After all, the place can't get any worse, right? Of course, environmentalists argue that it's that very attitude that contributes to the region's slow return to normalcy.

The Blight Zone: Public Reaction

In the beginning, public reaction to the FSA's handling (or dismissal) of the Blight was simple: unanimous approval. However, the more time that passes, the more complicated things get. People want to return home or to use apparently safe land that nobody claims anymore. Those who live on the Blight fringe know that FSA propaganda exaggerates the region's condition.

While citizens far removed from the area have no reason to doubt the government's sincerity, the clash between claim and reality feeds Midwestern distrust of the FSA. This sentiment seldom manifests as active rebellion — it's mainly a quiet refusal to do more than the minimum that the government requires of citizens, and a willingness to grab whatever the FSA won't miss.

Eyrie Station

The unique orbital station was created as a testament to scientific ingenuity. Ever since it came online, *Eyrie* Station has promoted this ideal. The facility is home to scientists and crackpots, theorists and poets, engineers and artisans and has stimulated all manner of intellectual and spiritual creativity — and on occasion, harbored misguided and downright immoral pursuits as well.

Industries

Eyrie pays its bills through an ever-changing mosaic of revenue generators. Besides works of art, scientific discoveries (and the patents attributed to them) and other intellectual properties, *Eyrie* supplies near space with unique manufactured goods. Breakthroughs in small-scale manufacturing are explored on *Eyrie* until the systems are optimized, when they're licensed to the highest bidder.

The station dominates a very small but highly lucrative industry: microgravity manufacturing in high-atmospheric-pressure and extreme-temperature environments. Small "bubbles" or "bladders" with rigid hulls are attached to the station, and have interiors comparable to the depths of Jupiter or the Sun... except that the bubbles have almost no gravity. These scientific marvels also contain mills that produce exotic metals, complex organic molecules, and synthetic materials that combine biological properties with those of metallic hydrogen and other strange substances. There's seldom high-volume demand for this sort of material (but those who need it pay premium prices for it).

Orgotek contracts out some of its biotech development to *Eyrie* groups, which focus on development efforts between the initial-research and large-scale-manufacture stages. Alchemy Computer Corporation also uses *Eyrie* facilities for its own purposes, much to Alex Cassel's annoyance. The Prexy can't prove theft of concepts or materials, but Alchemy produces a number of small devices that resemble Orgotek prototypes. Orgotek Operations now provides special security services for the order's groups on *Eyrie*.

Intelligence

With its polar orbit and maneuvering capabilities, *Eyrie* can examine any point on Earth in close detail. Once a destination is determined, the station is repositioned within two to six hours. Legitimate public reasons for close approaches include:

• **Resource evaluation.** Low-orbit cameras in visual and other spectra, magnetometers, gravimeters and other instruments can probe a strip of ground (or ocean) 10 kilometers wide in exacting detail. Two complete orbits generate enough information to permit highly accurate resource and commercial-value estimates on such things as mineral veins, ground water, geological conditions and the local ecosystem.

• **Census work.** It's difficult for authorities to gather accurate information about people in parts of the world that recover from calamities (the Blight, *Esperanza* impact areas, Florida's collapse, Middle East strife). Infrared imaging, sometimes supported by psionic scans, generates reliable census data.

• **Archeology.** Archeologists have depended on aerial surveys since the introduction of the balloon. Station probes allow for the study of structures and geography. In addition, long-wavelength radar can probe beneath the surface to identify underground archeological information (buried walls, old river channels, subterranean complexes).

Eyrie doesn't focus entirely on Earth, though. The North Hull supports a wide array of visual, radio and other telescopes that supplement the work of other near-space observatories.

This End Up

Direction is relative in space. "Up" and "down" are artificial designations. However, they help avoid confusion for humans. The invention of gravcrystals has helped define "up" and "down"; the source of artificial gravity is "down." Simple. Of course, grids can be installed almost anywhere, making one room's "up" another room's "down."

Like many old-time stations, *Eyrie* has its own arbitrary conventions. The station's engines occupy the "north pole," making that half the North Hull. The half with the quartered solar sail is the South Hull.

No bureaucracy can object legitimately to *Eyrie's* survey work. Governments have little say over who can take orbital views of geographic conditions or ancient structures. More serious legal struggles surround information gathered by means other than the purely visual, such as radar probing. *Eyrie's* six-person legal corps does a lot of traveling between orbit and surface to handle disputes.

But *Eyrie* does perform covert work. Three small bubbles on the South Hull hold "special clients" who generally spend days or at most weeks on the station, never discussing their work with others. These secretive individuals — *Eyrie* has a "don't ask, don't tell" policy that keeps any information on such users to a minimum — move equipment in sealed containers, assisted by cargo robots rather than human beings. Payment to *Eyrie* comes in the form of well-worn and difficult-to-trace hard currencies or in credit drawn from anonymous accounts. Eagles who persist in making unwanted inquiries suffer mysterious accidents or simply disappear. *Eyrie* management bears no responsibility for such events, and makes sure all residents and visitors are aware of this when they first arrive.

The vast majority of Eagles learn not to ask questions; they generally have a good idea of whom visitors are anyway. Most "special clients" work for terrestrial governments, though corporations, psi orders, the Æon Trinity and other groups also seek information that targets won't give up voluntarily. These agencies pursue their own covert channels, but *Eyrie* provides an extremely useful neutral vantage point.

Additionally, a portion of *Eyrie's* computing facilities works exclusively on data-gathering and interpretation for espionage clients. The residential levels closest to the South Hull's spy bubbles are isolated from the rest, with independent food services, life support and maintenance. These facilities allow spies to mingle with Eagles — and one another — only if "special clients" choose to.

In the Bubbles

JaDe Associates intended *Eyrie* to adapt to changing circumstances. The station's twin hulls provide all the fixed facilities necessary to support the station. The bubbles (or bladders, as they're also known) handle everything else. *Eyrie's* hulls offer a dozen or more access ports on each deck, and countless brackets to hold securing cables. Bubbles range in size from a few meters to 100 meters in diameter. The largest ones don't typically attach directly to the hull, but connect via reinforced access tubes. The station's metallic main hulls literally disappear beneath a swarm of bladders of all sizes, small ones nestling beneath large ones.

Six 70-meter bubbles — three on each hull — house most of *Eyrie's* food supply. Crops genetically engineered for compact size and maximal yield grow in nutrient troughs supported by collapsible tiers not unlike grandstand seats. The station's orbit around Earth provides natural daylight, but agronomists can adjust bladder walls to filter, intensify or dim incoming light and radiation.

Each of *Eyrie's* hulls also supports a park bubble that is 100 meters in diameter and mounted 150 meters away from the hull. Genetic designers, breeding researchers, bonsai fanciers and even residents who produce unusual plants display their handiwork for the public to enjoy. The park bubbles enjoy a reputation as the *Eyrie's* best places to rendezvous for quiet liaisons, with many niches and byways offering privacy.

Large bladders tend to be used for extended periods. Occupants of small bubbles come and go with particular contract jobs. *Eyrie* offers a wide variety of modular furniture, electronics and other room furnishings ready to be installed in a newly erected bladder. Most bubbles have opaque shells; transparency is handy for only agriculture, observational equipment and windows.

Running *Signals and Flares*

If your series follows the events of **Descent into Darkness** and *Friends in High Places*, then events lead quite naturally into this story. Some modification is necessary if the characters come into things late or bypass previous episodes.

Bypassing *Descent into Darkness*

Luckily, you did all the hard work in getting the characters together in *Friends in High Places*. The pursuit of Beitz leads to the Blight Project, and the Chromatic attack proceeds regardless of the characters' personal backgrounds.

Bypassing *Friends in High Places*

Characters who only now return to Earth from the Moon and/or Mars (depending on whether you used some or all three of the adventures in **Descent into Darkness**) may begin at the Blight Project, following the lead about Horace Meeks mentioned at the end of **Descent**. Some other group, probably Triton Division, pursues the leads in Basel. Once Beitz's identity is discovered, Ramirez forwards the information to the characters. (You could have Cori Heisler try to get the scoop on the team when it arrives in Minnesota, or you can have Malachi Ross land here and make an attempt on Disbray's life, if you want to inject those scenes into this episode).

Otherwise, the characters could be recuperating or pursuing personal affairs when Special Agent Ramirez contacts them about the events of *Friends in High Places*. He provides the news of Ross' demise and "Minerva's" true identity. The characters are still among the most knowledgeable regarding the Huang-Marr Project; once Cassel is informed of how things stand, he asks for the characters' involvement to learn about their experiences directly.

Behind the Scenes

The public knows of corruption within one, possibly more psi orders. The characters are in a race against time, urged by Æon to tie up the Huang-Marr conspiracy quickly so that public-relations damage is minimal. The characters are not the only ones moving quickly, though. Conspirators, psi orders and even approaching aliens have agendas.

Huang-Marr Conspirators

The Huang-Marr conspirators' major concern at this point is survival. Of the ringleaders, only Beitz ("Minerva"), Meeks and Huang remain at liberty. Subordinates in various locations evade capture for the moment, but the project is doomed. The only question for the remaining conspirators is "Will I escape"?

The Blight Project holds the last notable concentration of Huang-Marr researchers outside of *Eyrie* Station. As the characters arrive from Basel, the conspirators flee capture. Little do they realize that their escape route takes them into the middle of a multi-species war.

Orgotek

Orgotek has done a much better job of keeping the Huang-Marr Project under wraps than the Æsculapians have. Still, the electrokinesis order is linked very closely. If the teks can set up scapegoats quickly and decisively, they hope that Orgotek can come out of this relatively unscathed, with the Æsculapians bearing the brunt of public (and private Æon Trinity) scrutiny.

Alex Cassel

The Prexy knew of Huang-Marr from the very beginning, at least in a general sense. Cassel has people researching the taint (just look at the Blight Project); Huang-Marr was just one minor venture among many, running some risks in the hopes of a long-shot payoff. He expected that, like the vast majority of other ventures he's approved, it might achieve some minor breakthroughs, but would otherwise fade away and be filed quietly in the most classified Orgotek archives. On the chance of success, Cassel's eminently capable PR staff would bury issues of questionable legality and morality and focus on positive, sound-byte-friendly aspects — par for the course in the corporate world.

However, the Huang-Marr Project became a kind of Frankenstein-meets-Mengele horror; something Cassel didn't condone in the slightest. The Prexy never expected a noisy, messy, disturbing failure — just as he didn't expect to find his staff dealing with Aberrants, or to have investigators materializing out of nowhere and making trouble all over the Solar System. Cassel knows that explaining his side of things wouldn't sit well with the masses, so the situation calls for some serious cleanup.

Luckily, Cassel has done this sort of spin control before. He has initiated a three-pronged attack on the problem:

- **Public-Relations Blitz:** Orgotek press organs downplay the scope of corruption, point out that any scapegoats are loose cannons, aim a few pointed jabs at the Æsculapians, and praise Æon's vigorous efforts to apprehend the conspirators.
- **Mobilize Option-8:** Orgotek's covert security force has orders to uncover any and all Huang-Marr conspirators, who serve as patsies to draw attention from Orgotek itself. Those conspirators determined to be a risk to Orgotek integrity disappear or suffer accidents or suicides (with the deaths pointing to exposed conspirators). Any equipment of obviously Orgotek make devoted to the project is hidden, moved or destroyed.
- **Personal Intervention:** Cassel steps into the spotlight to show outside investigators (the characters) the results of Orgotek's own housecleaning. Option-8's efforts aren't alluded to, of course. The characters simply see vigorous, though conventional and sincere, internal-affairs activity on Orgotek's part. This step unwittingly puts Cassel in the front lines when the Chromatics descend on *Eyrie*.

Option-8

Option-8 has received advance notice from Cassel to clean up the order (although it did not receive direct word; the Prexy always maintains a safe level of deniability). The covert force has had a few weeks to perform its tasks before the characters arrive. The Option-8 force called into Boltzmann Station in **Descent into Darkness** had little information from which to work; the covert group has more complete data. Option-8 has discovered other Huang-Marr facilities that involve Orgotek, and rounds up personnel and materials.

Due to Option-8's skilled efforts, the characters find only the conspirators and data that Cassel allows them to. The investigators don't uncover even a scrap of information clearly indicating Orgotek's knowledge of or complicity in the biorg project. Even so, what's left is more than enough to put the final nail in the coffin of the Huang-Marr conspiracy.

The men and women of Option-8 are trained to do whatever is necessary to preserve Orgotek's security and integrity. Usually, though, the crises they face are small — a rogue individual within the order, an obstinate outside individual or office. The Huang-Marr cleanup is a larger operation than normal. Nonetheless, Option-8 operatives are loyal in the extreme, and they devote themselves entirely to fulfilling their directive.

Cassel hates wasting human resources. "Minds are the first tools," he once said in a motto emphasized repeatedly in Orgotek indoctrination. Option-8 operatives therefore determine if Huang-Marr personnel are worth rehabilitating. Conspirators who seem misguided but not fanatical to the cause are smuggled out. As with the Blight Project facility in Worthington, too much sudden migration would draw notice, so Option-8 concerns itself only with "reliable" conspirators.

People who remain committed to the biorg project don't enjoy Cassel's mercy. He calls for their capture. This ensures that those lacking moral fiber face the consequences of their actions, provides investigators with convenient victims, and shows that Orgotek is fully committed to stopping the secret experiments.

Huang-Marr zealots who know that Cassel approved Orgotek's involvement in the project must be eliminated. Option-8 has no particular moral compunctions about this (and, apparently, neither does the Prexy). The good of the order directly advances the good of humanity as a whole, and sometimes sacrifices must be made. For that matter, some Option-8 agents probably consider the Huang-Marr Project as abhorrent as the characters do, and consider this justice of sorts. Option-8 must be pragmatic, though; too many suspicious accidents or deaths would attract too much attention. Only individuals who can assuredly implicate Orgotek are killed, and the deaths are made to look like they were accomplished by other conspirators.

There is an alternative saved for conspirators who have yet to be exposed in Æon's investigation: mindwipe. Cassel has skilled telepaths in his employ, and bioware that can actually store mental thoughts and images. However, deleting memories is a tricky business. Despite the Prexy's command to induce only selective and temporary memory loss, there's always the chance that something will go awry; the wrong thoughts could be destroyed, additional memories could be deleted, the subject's personality could be distorted, or complete portions of thought could be lost permanently. Option-8's few telepaths are also savvy enough to know that powerful Æon Trinity telepaths could detect such psionic tampering. Option-8 thus mindwipes only those individuals on whom it knows the investigators have no information. (Since Æon itself recently told Cassel what the characters have learned, Option-8 has very accurate data.) If there's any doubt about a conspirator, that person is smuggled out or terminated.

Option-8 has similar orders regarding any incriminating hardware and data it finds. When possible, operatives move vital equipment to private storage facilities not associated with Orgotek. A storage site must be distant enough that investigators are unlikely to discover it, but near enough if emergency access is required.

Gear that Option-8 can't smuggle out, but that is too important to be destroyed, is concealed. Operatives construct innocuous-looking shells around critical equipment, hide small pieces in secret compartments, and alter labels and documen-

A Plethora of Psions

Like all orders, Orgotek has psions whose powers were triggered in other orders' Prometheus chambers. Since Orgotek cannot create telepaths — not to mention clairsentients, psychokinetics, vitakinetics or biokinetics — the company hires them. Orgotek offers psions lucrative salary packages and attractive perks to join the electrokinesis order.

Orgotek is by no means alone in this practice. Every psi order employs psions from other orders to varying degrees. The Æon Trinity also draws psions into its ranks as consultants, associates or full members. The orders devote a respectable amount of time and resources to luring in other orders' psions. This headhunting between groups has gone on since the psi orders' earliest days.

tation to disguise the identity of items remaining in view. Invariably, these disguises are designed to make the equipment look like just another coolant tank or subsystem not worthy of a closer look. Once attention is directed elsewhere (hopefully back toward the Æsculapians), Option-8 can remove the equipment under the guise of renovation or refitting procedures.

What cannot be removed or hidden is destroyed. Option-8 knows that anything indicating direct Orgotek involvement in Huang-Marr must be disposed of. Electronic data is not only wiped, the hard drive is dismantled and reduced to slag. Other devices are rendered into their component parts and put on the scrap heap. Organic parts are returned for recycling in the Orgosoft matrix arrays.

Aliens

Chromatics

To the very spiritual Chromatics, the universe holds two kinds of living beings: pure souls (like the Chromatics themselves) and corrupt ones (those that carry taint). When beings came down to the Chromatics' world from the great darkness beyond, the Chromatics received them warmly. These new souls were welcome to join the fellowship the Chromatics shared, but the visitors did not want to share anything. Instead, they brought the Chromatics suffering and death.

This massacre angered the Chromatics' gods. The beings of light appeared before the frightened and angry race, offering tools and guidance on how to repel their corrupt attackers. The gods named the Chromatics' adversaries — "Aberrants" — and explained that there were entire worlds teeming with their corruption. Unless the Chromatics were strong enough to drive this corruption away, their world would fall to it as well.

Chromatics, though not technologically advanced, are not stupid. They did not know at first if they could trust these "gods of light," but the gods showed them miracles and provided them with tools which proved effective against the invaders. Although the Aberrants were driven back, the Chromatics were assured of their enemy's return.

Valuing heroism in the face of great odds, the Chromatics leapt into action. They trained themselves how to use the gifts their patrons gave them, striking at their enemy's outposts. Although the gods of light seemed to know a great deal about Aberrants, the beings did not differentiate between Aberrants and humans. Thus, neither did the Chromatics.

Now the Chromatics are prepared to strike at the heart of their enemy — which the Chromatics and their gods consider to be Earth, the Aberrants' birthplace. But the gods of light require one last task. Around the Aberrants' homeworld is a "chariot" similar to what the Chromatics ride. That vessel contains important tools that the Aberrants took from the gods of light. The Chromatics need these tools to be certain their assault succeeds.

The Chromatics know what to do. They must venture into enemy territory to recover the lost tools of their gods. And death to all Aberrants who stand in their way.

The Doyen

Cassel and the other proxies have kept a secret since the very beginning of their new existence. One of the first alien races humans encountered is one whose presence has never been made public. The proxies, in the very first days of their newfound psionic awareness, learned of beings they came to call "the Doyen."

The proxies decided to keep the aliens' existence a secret. These soon-to-be influential leaders were still exploring the full extent of their abilities and were hard at work finding others with similar potential. The proxies knew that humanity would have enough to cope with when psions revealed themselves. Explaining that psions had already encountered aliens would likely be too much for everyone to accept.

For their part, the Doyen don't interfere directly in human affairs. As long as that continues, the proxies don't feel the need to reveal the aliens. What the proxies don't know is how much the Doyen have learned about humanity and its past.

The Doyen (and humanity) regard Aberrants as a grave menace to all untainted life in the universe. But the aliens seem divided on whether all of humanity is destined to become corrupt like the Aberrants. Doyen nature does not encourage direct action; they spend significant time arguing the ramifications of humanity and Aberrants.

Some Doyen, however, finally decided to take steps. These aliens came to the Chromatics and warned them of the Aberrant menace. These Doyen also manipulated humans and psions to provide information and materials that the aliens then gave to the Chromatics. One such unwitting individual was Argente Essem. He recorded data on human exploration and military efforts which he transmitted to the Doyen. The transmitter malfunctioned recently though, and the Doyen now receive incomplete information. Yet they're confident that Essem's recordings are intact. If the Chromatic invasion is to succeed, the aliens must first get accurate details on how humanity's defenses are arrayed — details stored in the alien data device Essem has secreted on *Eyrie* Station. The Chromatics thus stage a raid on *Eyrie* now in anticipation of a full-scale invasion of Earth.

Mr. Cassel Goes to Minnesota

Signals and Flares begins with the characters still at the Black Company dorms in Montressor. They rest after the exertions of *Friends in High Places*, presumably discussing recent events and future options. The Æsculapians want them out of there posthaste, but Æon wants the characters to stay put until it figures out where to send them next.

Tensions run high when the characters receive a call. Ramirez gives them the green light to pro-

Pressing On

The characters may decide to not wait for orders from Æon. They can head to North America after Beitz on their own, but they find the going difficult once they arrive.

The characters arrive at the Worthington Blight Project site (Schilltronix's records list that location as its primary shipping destination). However, despite representing the Æon Trinity, the best the characters can hope for is to be allowed access as visitors. This greatly restricts their investigative abilities; they're assigned a chaperone who keeps the characters on a tight leash.

The characters quickly discover that they can look only at a fraction of the facility, and its records are off limits. Once frustration sets in, have Cassel arrive. He gives the characters the spiel outlined in "You Can Call Me Alex." Set the scene in a Blight Project office instead of in Orgotek's Hopkins location.

ceed to North America — something the characters have likely bugged Æon about in the hours that they've cooled their heels. (If the characters bypassed the previous episode, Ramirez contacts them wherever they are and sends them to Minnesota). During the flight, one of the characters receives a cellular transmission (the psion with a cellular uplink; if more than one character has one, use the team leader or the one tied most closely to Orgotek). Cell calls are pretty rare, so it's bound to be important.

The transmission is via the Orgotek standard computer agent (described in **America Offline**) and uses the Proxy Protocol as covered in this episode's setting section (page 59). The agent represents none other than Alex Cassel, who invites the characters to meet him upon their arrival in Minneapolis-St. Paul to "discuss our mutual concerns about trouble among the orders." Suspicious (or inquisitive) characters can study the signal to confirm its validity. Players may roll **Intrusion** (+1 difficulty) or **Engineering** (+2 difficulty), or perform a standard **Interface** roll. Success confirms that the signal is what it appears to be.

Cassel has a car waiting upon the characters' arrival (a plush Reed Rosen limousine), ready to whisk them off to Orgotek's small regional headquarters in the arcology's Hopkins Sector. The office is nothing elaborate, but it is in an aboveground level with a view of the peaceful Midwest countryside.

"You Can Call Me Alex"

As always, Alex Cassel calculates his initial appearance very, very carefully. He knows that the characters have the potential to create a great deal of trouble. He therefore wants to create as little friction as possible (not that Cassel's afraid, mind you; just very thorough).

He dresses tidily, but not very formally, in a simple suit that would have been as fashionable in 2020 as it is in 2120. Characters making a standard **Style** test know that the suit may look simple and unassuming, but it's of high quality and probably costs more than a mid-sized sedan. It is apparent that the Prexy looks much younger than he is. If not for his bearing and the context of the situation, it would be easy to mistake Cassel for a recent college graduate.

The first thing Cassel does is get everyone on a first-name basis, and he makes sure the characters are relaxed and receptive. After inquiring after the characters' trip and offering refreshments, Cassel gets down to business. This is the second time in a week that the characters meet a proxy. However, the mood is quite different than when they sat with Matthieu Zweidler. Alex Cassel is devastatingly charming, easygoing and approachable. Characters should be surprised that this man is a proxy. He seems more the kind of guy you'd hang out with in a bar; "just one of the gang." Only characters with antisocial dispositions or those with Allegiances to groups opposed to Orgotek aren't won over completely. (Especially paranoid characters who sense with **Attunement** to check if the Prexy is using psi manipulation are disappointed — Cassel's just a naturally charismatic fellow.)

Alex Cassel certainly has ulterior motives in meeting with the characters (ensuring that they find only what he wants them to), but he bears them no ill will. The Prexy wants the characters to agree to work closely with him, rather than perform an independent inquiry. Cassel covers the following points:

• He is appalled at the Huang-Marr conspiracy. The Prexy abhors the Aberrants. His first and most

important task is protecting humanity from Aberrants; he's shocked that people would work *with* the creatures.

• He had no idea that biorg researchers used the Comm Restoration Initiative (see **Descent into Darkness**) as a cover for their illicit endeavors. Cassel has taken steps to closely monitor other projects in which Orgotek is involved. He hopes to negate the potential for corruption and wants to discuss these steps with the characters.

• He plans on inspecting Orgotek's Blight Project sites and invites the characters along. Joining the Prexy, the characters have full security clearance instead of being limited to visitor status. This allows for a more thorough investigation and should leave no doubt (Cassel believes) that any conspirators acted with Orgotek's authorization.

• He says that Orgotek security confirms reports of Beitz's arrival in the region, but they haven't found him yet (the same goes for Horace Meeks).

• A character with the effrontery to initiate a telepathic probe of the proxy confirms the truth of all this (or at least that Cassel believes it to be true). The character also finds herself the sudden focus of Cassel's considerable ire (the proxy is very well-attuned to subquantum fluctuations, and picks up any psi use against him). Cassel drops not-so-veiled threats to offending characters; "I'm surprised that you've come this far when you make such painfully foolish errors. Don't do it again."

Cassel also compliments the characters on past accomplishments, not just in the **Darkness Revealed** series but in previous stories, explaining that such initiative and talent will be more effective at this stage if they all work together. Characters may know they're being fed a line, but shouldn't find fault with Cassel's logic or feel that he's being disingenuous in any way. He's a master of interpersonal relationships, he's not some heavy-handed politician. Cassel has no problem if the characters want to check with the Trinity before joining him. Ramirez is surprised at Cassel's offer, but sees nothing wrong with the characters accepting it.

If the characters accept, Cassel provides rooms for them in a nearby hotel (it's comfortable, but not ostentatious). He recommends they spend the rest of the day relaxing and getting used to the time change. Cassel heads to the Worthington Blight Project site the next morning, and has a car pick the characters up to join him. They fly in comfort on Cassel's *Daedalus*, a Cruiser 17 aircraft described under Technology, page 115.

If the characters decide to go it alone, Cassel wishes them luck (remaining cordial the whole time). They go on to Worthington, but run into problems (see Pressing On, above). Cassel gets there first, so he's on hand to re-present his offer after the characters become frustrated.

The Records

On the flight out, Cassel suggests that the characters take the lead in the investigation; he'll be along to give assistance. This aid includes the occasional suggestion as to what step to take next. For the moment, the Prexy offers that the characters peruse the full records gathered by his staff about Huang-Marr research conducted under Orgotek auspices. (Cassel explains that he's had his people tracking down this information since the news first broke; they haven't found everything yet, but they're working on it.)

He provides a series of computer disks, the directories of which show they contain a number of data files. Anyone with experience in constructing databases and queries (three dots or more in **Engineering**, preferably with the Computers Specialty) recognizes that the files were assembled very quickly, even hastily, but with top-notch tools and at great cost. If this is a bluff, it's one backed by the full faith and credit of Orgotek's central administration. Suspicious characters may perform any analyses they desire (leave it up to them to ask "Will this work?") — the end result is that, although incomplete in places, the data appears to be genuine and not tampered with in any way.

Each success at a standard **Investigation** (Quick Search) roll enables a character to retrieve one of the following points from the files immediately (reveal the information in whatever order you wish). A player needs to roll only for efforts to retrieve information *right now*; she's welcome to look through the data at a slower pace later. Working more thoroughly, a character uncovers each point listed below every six hours. This time is reduced by one hour for each dot in **Investigation** (Quick Search) that the character or computer agent performing the search has.

If the characters choose to not poke in the files just yet, Cassel summarizes the data during the hour-long flight. Again, feel free to pick and choose points as you wish, keeping Cassel's priorities and a sense of urgency in mind. If the characters passed on Cassel's offer and are driving to Worthington, set this scene in a conference room in the Blight Project's Building 5, after Cassel presents his offer again (this time, with the files as incentive).

• The project now designated "Huang-Marr" was the offshoot of previous legal research being performed by both Orgotek and the Æsculapians (the Blight Project is another project altogether). The original pursuits were established well within the Æon Trinity guidelines on human experimentation.

• Doctors Ella Huang and Abel Marr were brought together in 2117 by an undisclosed individual within the Æsculapian Order (the file suggests this person was Jerzy Grabowski). The two were commissioned to set up their own group to pursue their previously independent research into expanding the capabilities of bioware, and researching the parameters of taint.

• Orgotek became involved in the biorg project through Horace Meeks, a senior researcher. He set up a complex scheme of aliases and redirection to obscure the order's clear knowledge of the project.

• Meeks was in charge of funneling Orgotek resources (frequently via Schilltronix) to assist in establishing Huang-Marr field-research sites. Meeks accomplished this through various management and accounting tricks.

• In the aftermath of the confrontation on Mars, Cassel ordered a general review of biotech-related research, and began weeding out signs of corruption. The investigations continue, but Orgotek believes that most of the information and conspirators have already been discovered. Many suspects committed suicide or died in struggles to resist capture. Of those taken alive, most are in Orgotek containment facilities, awaiting further questioning. It's quite likely that they'll be turned over to the United Nations when its official inquiry begins.

Arrival at the Blight Project

It's a brisk, crystal-clear day, offering the characters a full view of the subdued strangeness that is the Blight. You may wish to describe this at some length, to express the unique nature of the environment the characters enter.

Specific details of the Blight vary depending on where one looks. Much of the region retains a thin covering of grass and shrubs, enough to forestall the worst of soil erosion. Former farmland around the outer fringe now resembles the western edges of the Great Plains before agriculture (except that few animals move across it). Farther in, the vegetation is sparse enough that erosion has taken a severe toll. Gullies crisscross the land, some dozens of meters deep and hundreds of meters across. Some interior patches, from meters to kilometers in extent, have lost all of their topsoil; bare rock faces the sky in vistas eerily reminiscent of Mars.

If the characters arrive with Cassel, they fly in along a predetermined path and bypass most of the security (it's all handled by the pilot). They see the various zones pass underneath the craft as they approach. Characters traveling on their own get the experience firsthand.

The Blight Defenses, Northeast Sector

Characters encounter varying degrees of security as they approach and enter the Blight Zone. Starting from the Blight's perimeter, defenses include:

- **The Designated Safety Zone Terminator (variable coverage):** A series of sign posts, spaced every 1000 meters, encircles the zone. Each sign declares the interior unsafe. The "safe line's" distance from the TZL1 (below) varies from over 20 kilometers to barely one, depending on how well-recovered the Blight Designation Committee considers the terrain. The FSA reserves the right to deny medical treatment to any injury suffered while the patient was across the DSZT (this threat is meant to "discourage antisocial adventurism").

- **Transition Zone Layer 1 (10 kilometers wide):** FSA security personnel are authorized to use nonlethal force to discourage incursions from the greater FSA territories, and all force necessary to deter anyone or anything attempting to leave the Blight. Main roadways have checkpoints where individuals must provide acceptable reason to enter the zone (surprisingly, this can often be as simple as a persuasive story or moderate bribe). In theory, the TZL1 is subject to constant scrutiny via camera installations and manned airborne patrols every eight hours. The reality almost always involves equipment failures, shift delays, poor personnel coordination and other interruptions. A three-meter-high fence runs along the inner edge of the TZL1, separating it from the TZL2 (below).

- **Transition Zone Layer 2 (two kilometers wide):** FSA personnel use whatever force deemed appropriate to deal with problems within the TZL2. In theory, the region is subject to constant remote surveillance and manned airborne patrols every four hours, but as with Layer 1, reality seldom equals theory. A four-meter-high fence runs along the inner edge of the TZL2, separating it from the "inner Blight."

- **Legion Aberrant Suppression Treaty Zone (350 kilometer radius, centering on Hastings, Nebraska):** Although the Federated States considers everything inside the TZL1 fence "the Blight," this section contains the Blight's still-corrupt core. The LAST Zone is a desolate wasteland, dotted sporadically with strangely mutated vegetation (see **America Offline** for more information on the entire Blight Zone).

As the characters draw closer to Worthington (located just outside the Layer 2 interior fence), the apparently normal countryside transforms gradually. Within a few klicks of crossing the TZL1 line, alert characters notice scattered mutated foliage and strangely discolored patches of ground. The degree of taint influence increases rapidly as

Complex A

The Blight Project isn't limited to one installation. It's a network of 20 complexes spread around the Blight fringe and even at certain points in the interior. Each facility pursues a different research. Complex A in Worthington is the oldest and largest (it was remodeled extensively and expanded recently as part of Orgotek's deal with Schilltronix).

Complex A is, in the typically obscure words of one of its developers, "a probability locus, not a target." Fourteen buildings stand within a one-mile radius, comprising "the Project" in standard usage. There are other facilities scattered farther out, but they are isolated. This basic model differs little with each project site (although Sterling and Wichita are the only ones on a scale approaching Worthington's).

they cross from Layer 1 to Layer 2. From here on in, normal vegetation is a rarity. After covering the last two kilometers to the Blight Project facility, the characters see that the terrain looks as lifeless as the Moon. The LAST Zone beyond is a place of barren desolation, stretching over the horizon. The characters soon learn that it's not all blasted earth; apparently some really serious strangeness occurs within Wycoff's original immolation radius (encompassing the 200 kilometers around Hastings, Nebraska).

Building 5

The Worthington Blight Project site has its own airstrip near the main building cluster of Complex A. The Blight Project can host up to a dozen heavy cargo lifters and about 50 smaller craft (such as Cassel's *Daedalus*). Even casual observers can tell that things are busy in a not-very-planned way. When they disembark after Cassel, the characters are instantly surrounded by a crowd of Orgotek attendants: security, press-management staff, baggage handlers and flunkies of all kinds. Cassel walks through them with calm confidence, letting his subordinates take care of the details. (The characters' luggage is taken to a nearby dorm complex along with Cassel's own.)

Many of the landing spaces are occupied, as are almost all of the ground-vehicle parking spaces. Temporary shelters fill much of the space between the airstrip and the main buildings, and people mill about. Bright Orgotek security uniforms stand out, their wearers stringing bioluminescent cabling to mark "preferred" pathways.

Cassel invites the characters to roam the complex as they wish, but leads them to Building 5 first. This is the current operational center, and it allows the characters speediest access to further stored information. More importantly, it's where Orgotek is holding the half-dozen conspirators taken into custody. Cassel hasn't had a chance to interrogate the subjects yet himself, and wishes to do so before proceeding further.

Building 5 is the largest building in the complex. It's a five-level cylinder dedicated to biological research; each floor bears a higher degree of sterility and isolation. The complex's rapid growth, however, led it to be reassigned as a general research facility, with only individual labs rather than entire floors subject to quarantine. Sensitive research was moved to various outlying structures. Traces of the old containment system remain in Building 5, with heavy pressure-tight seals on doors and deactivated security panels on elevators. Some anonymous mural painter decorated the building's exterior walls with images of prairie fires, and Cassel has allowed them to remain.

Five additional three-story cylinders surround Building 5, connected by enclosed transparent bioglass walkways. Around them sprawl one- and two-story storage vaults, the project administration office, equipment shelters and various other assemblies. Most began as space for some specific project, were never disposed of, and were gradually incorporated into the permanent infrastructure.

The main cylinder's ground floor is now the transfer point for the surrounding labs. It's a single huge room, with alcoves running around the walls, except where passages lead to attached side buildings. No research occurs here; minimal-precautions ("Level One") studies now take place in the attached buildings. The ceiling is very low for what's essentially a large storage space.

The place is full of people performing tasks with feverish intensity. Scientists and security guards disassemble equipment brought in from various labs, searching for concealed Huang-Marr hardware and software. Carts carry in devices too big for laborers to lug in themselves. The gear that comes from high-precautions areas is encased in a multi-layer sterile wrap; disassembling crews use remote manipulators to do their work. There's a man-high stack of bits and pieces of machinery cordoned off with yellow warning tape.

Cassel explains what his people are doing as he leads the characters through. He has no problem if the characters want to stop and look around themselves, although he mentions that the prisoners are being held on the second floor. It takes little insight to realize that these people are searching for the proverbial needle in the haystack; the prisoners are a much better resource. A normal Orgotek guard stands at each of the building's four sets of elevators, each with convenient stairway access next to it. The characters can take either up to the second floor.

The next level is quartered by three-meter wide hallways that terminate near the building exterior at individual elevators, and that converge at the center. Computer monitors arranged on each corner normally display work in progress in the surrounding labs; they've been deactivated for the security sweep. Labs that have already been searched are open to examination, and security seals keep the rest shut. Two rooms, situated kitty-corner to one another off the central intersection, bear hastily printed-out signs identifying them as "Cell A" and "Cell B." A pair of Orgotek guards keeps a watchful eye on the many passersby, inconveniencing the dozens of staff hustling to and fro to arrange gear for examination or to return it to its proper place. *Everyone* recognizes Cassel as he comes down the corridor. Workers simultaneously try to make way for him while still hoping to catch his eye and make a favorable impression. The area is crowded and difficult to move through as a result. The characters push along a few meters behind as best they can.

The Escape Attempt

In some ways more clever (or more paranoid) than his partner Gustaf Beitz, Horace Meeks had a secret assistant — Rita Disbray — who handled many details of the Huang-Marr Project, but whose existence was never revealed to the other conspirators. Meeks wanted an ace in the hole in case things went awry, and Disbray was very good at solving problems.

Although Meeks is already safely on *Eyrie*, he had Disbray remain at the Blight Project to keep an eye on things. Disbray watched as Option-8 quietly captured the mid-level accomplices, and as word came down that the Prexy would arrive soon with Æon investigators.

Disbray relayed this information to *Eyrie*; she was told to try to release the captives and get them out of there as quickly as possible. Since a clean escape was unlikely due to the various monitoring devices placed throughout the Worthington project site, Disbray knew she had to take out the sensors. Not a psion herself, Disbray did extensive reading on noetic theory and the practical application of psi — especially electrokinesis. She was well-aware that a simple electrical short wouldn't do; dozens of teks in the area could fix it psionically. Disbray went for a purely mechanical failure instead.

She had already placed radio-controlled explosives at the main junction box and at critical spots along power conduits leading to the Blight Project's exterior light and perimeter-monitor arrays. One push of the radio trigger would destroy the conduits, blowing the entire lighting and perimeter surveillance network. At that time, the combination of a gas grenade and more well-placed explosives would take out the prisoners' guards and blow the sealed cells.

Disbray knew the project staff had enough technicians and psions to replace and repair the damage within an hour. However, Disbray and the escaped prisoners would be long gone by then, using her skimmer to slip away under cover of darkness and confusion. With everything else in place, Disbray went to evaluate the prison arrangements prior to that evening's planned escape attempt.

She gets to Building 5 when the characters arrive at the project — a full day earlier than Disbray expected. As a result, Disbray is just one of the many people on the scene when the characters reach Building 5's second floor.

She abandons her plan once she sees Cassel with the characters. Disbray realizes that it's pointless to save the prisoners after they've been interrogated. She therefore decides to abandon the breakout and head to *Eyrie*. She runs into a problem, though: Other people push their way forward for a better look at Cassel as Disbray pushes her way back toward one of the other hallways. A character who receives a standard **Awareness** success notices Disbray's movements, but she's not doing anything overtly threatening.

The following sequence of events happens too quickly for even the most paranoid character to do anything about (although if a character noticed Disbray, he gets a good look at her surprised face when things go very wrong). Disbray becomes nervous and shoves a little harder than she should; the technician she bumps pushes back, causing Disbray to reflexively depress the radio trigger she clutches in her jacket pocket. The saboteur's carefully placed charges go off.

Cassel is just a few meters from the first cell; the characters are close behind. Those looking at Cassel see him snap to attention as he senses the radio pulse, and jerk his head to one side (surprised and unsure of what it signifies, the Prexy tracks the signal source — directly to where Disbray stands). The assemblage quiets when Cassel becomes alert. The floor shakes at almost the same instant. Everyone hears Disbray exclaim, "Oh, *shit*."

Oops!

The sounds of the explosions rumble up an instant later, and Building 5 is thrown into chaos for the remainder of the scene (it's best to follow combat turns to maintain some order of events). The structure's power systems fluctuate. Lights

flare, automatic doors slide randomly, sprinkler systems trigger suddenly. (Building 5's sprinklers have fire-suppressing aerogels that aren't poisonous but that cloud vision and stick to everything.) Even though backup systems bring everything under control after a minute, personnel have been thrown into a panic.

As far as anyone knows, Building 5 has been attacked. Half the people on the second floor assume "Aberrant!" and head for the stairs; the other half don't know what's happened, and mill about asking questions and get in the way. Disbray knows what has occurred, but doesn't stick around to explain. She pushes the rest of the way through the crowd, leading a half-dozen people in a charge for the stairs (her flight down the corridor is at a right angle to the characters and Cassel, taking her out of direct sight almost immediately). Cassel isn't certain what has happened, but knows Disbray had something to do with it. The Prexy orders someone to "stop that woman," but with all of the movement, flickering lights and spraying foam, it's pretty hard to tell whom he means (someone who saw Disbray just before the blast has a good idea; otherwise a successful **Awareness** roll at +2 difficulty is required).

As if that weren't enough, the prisoners take this opportunity to escape. They hoped that someone would try to rescue them; after the explosion, their automatic doors spring open like the rest. Six prisoners (a suitable mix of genders and racial types) burst out of each cell. United in purpose but not in direction, they head down and out along the most likely means of escape: the stairs.

The situation is surprisingly simple, although not necessarily easy to resolve. Thirteen people worth apprehending — all but Disbray (who remains a mystery for the moment) already caught as Huang-Marr conspirators — are shoving through a crowded and chaotic mess hoping to escape. Orgotek security would normally blaze away with rifles and psionic powers to drop the escapees quickly, but Orgotek policy frowns on the indiscriminate slaughter of innocent people. Guards try to push through the mob. As Storyteller, wait until the characters make their decisions before announcing the guards' actions. Have security cover whatever angles the characters don't.

Similarly, keep Cassel busy with three prisoners from Cell A (the one closest to him; the hapless escapees tumble out almost directly in front

Force *Majeure*

Cassel's significant powers manifest subconsciously when he is active, energetic or upset. When he slams a fist down, a Static Shield crackles around it. When he points an accusing finger at someone with whom he is angry, low-power Disruption may strike the target. When he raises or lowers his voice, Control Illumination may adjust the lighting of the room.

He doesn't ever actually program his minicomp; he extracts and inputs information directly using Interface. When he wants to illustrate a point while talking, Hologram Creation presents it for his audience. None of this wears him down or requires any concentration; it's as natural as walking. The Storyteller should use these manifestations to convey that electrokinesis is first nature to Cassel.

During the tumult of the prison break, Cassel radiates psionic power and crackling energy on an awesome scale. This provides the crowd with yet another reason to sprint pell-mell for an exit (and adds to the discord).

gested areas (see **Trinity**, page 245, for specifics on cover). Of course, bystanders may be killed if they're used for protection.

- **Chase** — The prisoners seek to put as much distance between themselves and pursuers as possible. They may pass on combat opportunities to run instead. As long as they avoid engaging in actual fights, the fugitives may make extended **Stealth** or **Survival** attempts, pitting their abilities against their pursuers'. A prisoner who accumulates three more successes than his adversaries gets far enough ahead to be out of sight (for the moment, at least). At that point, the escapee heads for a vehicle, or possibly an out-of-the-way place to hide.
- **Hostage-taking** — Taking hostages doesn't help prisoners escape. Orgotek fulfills no demands, the fugitives are vastly outnumbered, and psions are on hand who can drop escapees before they can hurt a captive. But prisoners don't necessarily think logically, so hostages may seem like a good idea.
- **Property Damage** — Fugitives may try the classic maneuver of tossing debris behind them to slow pursuers. It might actually be effective in this case. There are computers, biological specimens (some extremely dangerous, some merely extremely rare), crates, currently unused field equipment and other random objects that can be thrown around to add to the chaos.

Captures

After some intense drama and exciting combat, the characters should have played a key role in capturing the escapees and Disbray. Orgotek security — lots of it — arrives on the scene just as the characters wrap up their various conflicts. They all head back to Building 5's second floor. Cassel is upset — electrical sparks pop and arc from him — although not in any way that implies mental imbalance; he is morally outraged. The Prexy thunders out a review of the Huang-Marr Project's legal and moral transgressions, and the conspirators' general complicity in it.

After a few impressive minutes, his poise returned, Cassel turns to the characters. "Yet again, you folks are on hand to help clean up the mess this trash makes. Do you want to ask anything?" If the characters do, he steps back and lets them go to work. If not, Cassel proceeds with his own interrogation. In either case, the following points emerge under questioning (except with Disbray; see below):

of the Prexy). The characters can go after Disbray or the remaining nine fugitives (who run in roughly equal numbers down the three remaining corridors). The characters must slip past Cassel — and possibly get zapped accidentally in the process — or push through the crowd and back down the stairs the way they came. All **Dexterity**-based rolls are at +2 difficulty. Once the backup systems come online, this penalty drops to +1. Difficulties are ignored if a character catches up to a target on the ground floor or outside.

Pursuit

The situation would be comical if it wasn't deadly. There are a number of scenarios that may arise as the characters try to apprehend the fugitives.

- **Firefight** — The prisoners are unarmed at the moment of their escape, but they may seize weapons from confused guards. Escapees aren't cold-blooded killers, but they are desperate enough to ward off pursuers without heed for people in the way. The crowd provides Light cover to characters and their opponents, increasing to Good cover in especially con-

- Each of the prisoners was recruited sometime in the last year. None of them met their recruiter face to face. He, she or they used the Orgotek Agent and "Minerva" to deliver messages.
- They all had at least one warning in their records for violations of Orgotek's Research Ethics Guidelines. They all presume that this is why they came to the Huang-Marr conspirators' attention.
- The conspiracy apparently isn't well-funded. Most resources they used were misappropriated from participants' "day jobs." There were also infrequent allocations of finances or equipment from an external source — presumably Schilltronix.
- Each of the prisoners knows at least one person who suffered a "mysterious accident" after compromising Huang-Marr security (assign details as you feel appropriate; tying in accidents from earlier episodes in your own series encourages a sense of far-reaching entanglement). This may help explain why so many of the conspirators are so jumpy and closemouthed (and -minded; telepathic probes aren't as effective if a subject is thinking only "Don't kill me!").
- All data they received for their research obviously went through multiple levels of anonymity. Reports came back very carefully stripped of any clues that could identify who did the work or where it was done. They assume that their own data was handled similarly.
- Most are bewildered by questions of morals or ethics. They were advancing knowledge, and don't understand the source of Cassel's (and probably the characters') outrage. They're sorry they got caught, but they expect that the core of the conspiracy will continue to work for the greater enlightenment of noetic science and humanity's benefit.

Orgotek Security and Strike Force Personnel

Orgotek security guards and Strike Force personnel (the order's psion troopers) have the same statistics as normal police (**Trinity**, page 306). They also have the following gear: Orgotek security uniform, Orgotek Shrike sonic pistol, Electric Eel baton, Wazukana DX70 (Orgotek Universal Agent) and short-range transceiver.

Assume that each Strike Force psion has four dots in one of his Aptitude Modes, and a single dot in each of the remaining two Modes. Use your discretion when picking primary Modes.

The Mysterious Saboteur

If the characters didn't go after Disbray for whatever reason, Cassel snatched her up; either way, she is apprehended unconscious and in need of at least minor medical attention (this keeps her out of the way until the characters are done with the other accomplices). Similarly, Cassel "urges" the characters to address the conspirators while the Prexy's own people check out the actual source of the explosions.

Technicians return as the characters finish with the prisoners, but before Disbray regains consciousness. They explain that explosions did extensive damage to the main lighting and perimeter-camera relays, but there are plenty of replacement parts in the facility. Everything should be back online within an hour.

Careful as always, Cassel deploys squads to check the perimeter in case this was part of some kind of invasion. Disbray wakes up then, drawing everyone's attention. Cassel takes over questioning her for the moment. Blue shimmers of electricity crawl over the Prexy, skittering across the floor to spark at Disbray's feet. While not visibly harmful (yet), Cassel's nimbus impresses the hell out of everyone present (characters who receive standard **Willpower** successes refrain from dropping their jaws in envious awe).

Disbray is no coward, but she's certainly not stupid. She's read enough to know that she sees only a fraction of a proxy's power. Disbray is not eager to experience firsthand what other tricks Cassel knows. After another encouraging zap, Disbray admits that she works for Horace Meeks, who himself was closely associated with somebody Disbray heard of only as "Minerva." Disbray has no new information to provide regarding the Huang-Marr Project (in fact, the characters should get the idea that they know more than she does). With some more prodding, Disbray admits that she was supposed to spring the captives and take them up to *Eyrie* Station. From what she understands, Meeks and "Minerva" are hiding up there, making plans for the future.

Alien Attack

As the characters discuss this information, something shatters the subquantum environment overhead. All players roll **Psi** to resist backlash (see **Trinity**, page 192) as a subquantum wave washes over them. Those with sufficiently high

Attunement ratings (9 Psi or the equivalent with Clairsentience Sight) sense a powerful and unfamiliar psionic locus near Earth orbit.

Characters who've been on a jump ship feel like one just forced itself into Earth's space — but Leviathans normally jump away from settled space to avoid the backlash effect. Unlike a jump ship, the thing (actually a Chromatic mother ship) emits a howl that resonates through the subquantum stratum, a scream from both sentient and nonsentient components of some terrible machine forced into endless agonizing exertion. This scream is a subtle but constant sensation that psionic characters feel in the backs of their minds throughout the rest of this episode, until the alien craft is destroyed.

A moment later, a broadcast comes in (the Low-Earth Orbit Traffic Intercept, page 71), which Cassel picks up and transmits into the building's public-address system (he's a proxy; that sort of thing is easy for him).

Flight to *Eyrie*

At this point, all anyone knows is that something big just appeared in near space and it is apparently attacking an orbital station. Cassel is a quick decision-maker; Orgotek owes at least part of its success to his ability to act swiftly in a crisis. This is no exception.

Since *Eyrie* is almost directly overhead, Cassel decides he'd best check out the situation firsthand. The Prexy taps into Complex A's intercom system again and announces a full alert. He directs all combat- and medically trained personnel to the landing field. Cassel extends the offer to the characters as well, acknowledging their competence during the recent escape attempt.

Events move at a rapid pace; Cassel has little time or inclination to wait around while the characters discuss options. If they appear the least bit hesitant, the Prexy points out (while ordering Disbray locked up with the other captives) that the backlash signifies *something* big. It's a psion's duty to protect Earth from all dangers; while he'd be glad to have the characters aboard, Cassel can't afford to wait around while they make up their minds. As always, the characters shouldn't feel railroaded along the plot. At the very least, they've just learned that the ultimate subject of their investigations — the heart of Huang-Marr, if you will — is on *Eyrie*. Even if this new mystery turns out to be nothing, the characters will get a free ride up the gravity well.

The characters may distrust Cassel or be wary of recent events. Let them be, but make sure they're able to at least work with Cassel for the time being. There is time for some discussion of recent events; Cassel is focused on the mystery at hand, but he doesn't just blow the characters off.

The Blight Project has five Orgotek Yellowjacket Interceptors (see Technology, page 115) and pilots to operate them. Cassel brings the characters (and a couple security if there are seats left over) with him to the first, while other Orgotek staffers pile into the rest. A selection of normals joins the electrokinetics, as do psions of other orders. Each Yellowjacket carries enough Orgotek Hornet VI pulse lasers and vac suits for Cassel, the characters and any other individuals present, as well as enough Orgotek Shrike sonic pistols for half the people on board. Characters may have their own weapons, but will probably have to borrow vac suits.

Eyrie is in the midst of low-orbit Blight observations; the station is only 400 kilometers above sea level and almost directly overhead at the time of the attack. Orgotek's contingent of Yellowjackets can get there in about 15 minutes. Blue sky gives way to the black of space in short order. Yellowjackets' sensors register that the strange object radiates intensely in infrared through radio frequencies. An initial analysis of transmissions results in nothing conclusive; they seem to be random spillover. *Eyrie* comes into view soon afterward. It is clear from kilometers away that the ship has suffered heavy damage. Something is ripping huge holes in the station's sail, and there are craft flitting around *Eyrie* that look like bizarre modified bioships.

What the Characters See

The attacking ships are Chromatic fighter vessels; the mother ship they came in approaches slowly; it's still a few kilometers away. The Chromatic craft are primarily a deep-red color. Chromatic biotechnology uses iron-carrying molecules (related to porphyrin, which binds with hemoglobin in human blood to transport iron) for reinforcement and repair purposes. The outermost hull layer is warm to the touch and capable of mending itself to repair light damage. Specifics on the Chromatic vessels are listed in Technology, page 116.

Engines and weapons are mostly silver, as are their mounting brackets. They're based on silicon compounds, somewhat like fossilized bones, which

vent heat extremely effectively (even an immediate examination after capture proves the engines to be surprisingly cool to the touch). Weapons and their mountings are highly reflective and glare in bright light. The ships have small sections in other colors and textures: crystalline blue around airlocks and access hatches, vivid porous green around exhaust ducts, and other colors associated with equipment the function of which isn't immediately apparent.

Characters who've seen some data on Karroo (**Academics** at +1 difficulty) may identify the vessels as Chromatic ships — still, even those characters are disturbed by the alien craft's similarity to human biotech. There's a look of improvisation and jury-rigging about the ships, and of familiar functions mixed with alien purpose. The ships look far too familiar for coincidence. How did the aliens come to build ships that look like derivatives of human designs? Æon asked the same questions after the original Karroo attack.

As the characters draw closer to *Eyrie* (and the Chromatic mother ship), the constant psionic whine grows stronger. Someone or something involved with the transport's propulsion *hurts*, and complains in a way that only the Gifted can detect. Characters within **Attunement** range of it are at risk of being distracted by it. A botched **Psi** roll results in +1 difficulty to all of a character's actions for the remainder of the scene.

The Approach

Chromatic fighters are slower and less maneuverable than Orgotek's Yellowjackets. The alien pilots have far less experience, individually and culturally, with space flight than human pilots do. However, they possess a terrible drive to seek justice for the wrongs that Aberrants have done them. The Chromatics also have a clear plan of attack.

The Orgotek Yellowjackets, while also biotech, are superior craft (mainly due to their hardtech engines and weaponry). The human pilots are quite skilled, and some are even veterans of battles against both humans and Aberrants. They are highly motivated, but they have no idea what's going on. Most of the humans assume this is some new Aberrant scheme, but are baffled when they see Chromatic ships so far from the Crab Nebula.

The Chromatic Plan

The Chromatics' initial attack on Earth consists of the mother ship, 35 fighter craft and a transport. The mother ship teleports in at Earth's L4 point, in the same orbit as the Moon, but 60° ahead of it. Once the subquantum translation — the source of the backlash the characters felt on Earth — is complete, the fighters deploy in two squadrons of 12 ships each and one squad of 11 rounded out by the transport. The first heads for Luna's Mare Ingenii jump-ship base; the second dives through Earth's atmosphere toward Asia; the third goes for *Eyrie*. The first two squadrons are diversions; the Chromatic pilots don't worry about survival, only about causing as much destruction and distraction as possible.

The mother ship closes on *Eyrie* while the last squadron splits into two wings of six craft each. The first wing holds back with the transport, defending the mother ship, while the second attacks the orbital station. The fighters strike the solar sail (most of which survives after an engineer collapses the sail into its four distinct vanes), strafe the outer hull (slicing apart the attached bubbles and leaving a scattered halo of bodies and debris), and disable *Eyrie*'s radiating fins (rendering the station incapable of changing orbit).

Once the station is immobilized, the attacking wing returns to defend the mother ship while the remaining group heads for the station. The Chromatic transport docks while the five fighters take up a protective perimeter around it. The docking ship is crammed with Chromatic soldiers whose task is to find the Doyen device on *Eyrie* and to slay any of the enemy they find along the way. Once successful, the fighters withdraw back to the mother ship and teleport away.

At least, that's how the Chromatics hope it goes….

The Chromatics enjoy a +2 Initiative bonus for three turns due to the humans' surprise and confusion at the aliens' presence around Earth. The Chromatics retain +1 Initiative after that until the first alien fighter is destroyed or disabled. Roll Initiative normally each turn thereafter.

Chromatic ship with boarding troops is already docking at *Eyrie* when Cassel's strike force comes within weapons range. The alien craft attaches (rather clumsily) to a docking hatch in the North Hull hangar. Once inside, the squads use crude tracking devices provided by the Doyen to locate Essem's beacon. The remaining five escort ships advance on the five human craft. The other six Chromatic fighters leave their mother ship and engage the Yellowjackets two turns later.

The Chromatics' top priority is acquiring the Doyen devices, so they concentrate on keeping human craft from firing shots at the boarding ship. The humans' priority is to defend *Eyrie*, so the pilots are unlikely to fire on craft that could blow up and damage the station. Furthermore, both sides recognize the benefit of gaining alien technology (the Chromatics already know of human ships' greater speed and wouldn't mind getting a few, and the humans need to know all they can about the alien ships' capabilities). These factors initially give the battle a cautious, defensive edge.

Cassel orders the Yellowjackets brought close enough to *Eyrie* so that he, the characters and others on board can cross over to the station. The Yellowjackets then drop back to initiate combat. Characters with space-combat experience can stay on board a Yellowjacket (each bioship consists of a pilot and a copilot who currently handles weaponry) and engage the Chromatics in ship-to-ship battle. Others can follow Cassel onto *Eyrie* to protect the station.

The Prexy considers crossing open space to be a reasonable gamble. Enemy fighters should focus on the Yellowjackets long enough for the group to get inside *Eyrie*. The closest approach is directly opposite the Chromatic mother ship; the nearest entry, a maintenance airlock on the upper part of South Hull, is some distance from the attacking Chromatic craft. Crossing from a Yellowjacket requires a successful **Athletics** roll at +2 difficulty — or a standard **Athletics** roll if a character has the Zero-g Specialty — and takes two turns to accomplish.

Gathering Information

So far all the action has been hundreds of meters away from the characters. There are several ways they may gather data on the current situation.

• **Radio broadcasts:** The Chromatic teleportation system generates powerful noetic and electromagnetic disturbances, which disturb most short-range transmissions. Even so, some broadcasts leak through, at least in part. The characters may pick up snippets of the Volunteer Fire Department and other *Eyrie* residents' efforts (see below).

• **Clairsentience:** Psychometry doesn't provide information at the moment, but studying drifting debris (biological or otherwise) and places where combat has already occurred offers images of what has happened. Characters with experience in combat may draw on that knowledge to speculate about Chromatic and defender actions.

Telesthesia certainly has its benefits. Sensory Projection and Remote Sensing allow psions to scout the vicinity (especially *Eyrie's* interior) psionically. Danger Sense is useless, though — after all, the entire area is one big danger zone.

• **Electrokinesis:** *Eyrie* is an open book to teks with skill in Technokinesis. Functioning security monitors, internal communications networks, data lines, pressure sensors and other station apparatus respond to Interface use.

This is first nature to Cassel; he reaches out to touch *Eyrie's* hull and immediately gets a general idea what's happening on board. Where display monitors remain, he can bring up images and data to show others. Cassel can do so subconsciously; the images flicker or vanish only when he concentrates intently on something else (such as shooting or avoiding being shot).

• **Telepathy:** Empathy is possible, but of dubious benefit. Few characters have dealt with the emotions of aliens. Making the attempt involves a +2 difficulty due to the strangeness of the emotions. Success indicates overwhelming sensations of hatred and the desire for revenge.

Mindshare is not particularly dangerous, but it takes some time for the telepath to make sense of data received. Chromatic language is largely visual, both two-dimensional (via patterns of light on their skin) and three-dimensional (via holograms near the "speaker"). Such "communication" is supplemented only infrequently by guttural, clicking and dry barks. A character can at least monitor the aliens' communications as they deal with each other, but doing so is of no direct benefit during combat. Mindshare is useful later, though, as the characters build a mental library of Chromatic associations and meanings.

Revenge virtually drowns out all other thoughts in the Chromatics' minds. They believe themselves holy warriors in a great crusade against the impure. They see themselves doing the will of the spirits of light. The soldiers lack information about any master plan in this war. Nor is it possible to acquire general background information about Chromatic society in the heat of the moment. That requires calm and time, neither of which are available now.

Brainjack, Network and Psychbending do not work on Chromatics. They may after extensive study of the aliens' dual brains, but the powers aren't effective for the time being.

• **Vitakinesis:** Iatrosis and Algesis work on Chromatics only if a vitakinetic has studied Chromatic physiology; even if she has, these Modes' powers are used at +1 difficulty. All Mentatis powers are also at +1 difficulty.

On a botched roll, a character may slam into the hull and suffer a Bashing level of damage. A severe botch might result in the character spiraling away into open space; rescuers have to activate a grappling cable to recover the victim.

Inside Eyrie

Eyrie's plasteel hulls are usually all but completely hidden beneath pressurized bubbles and the unfolded solar sail. This is most certainly not a normal occasion. By the time the characters arrive, the bubbles are perforated or cut loose and the sail is collapsed into its cross-shape, revealing the station's angular hardtech structural core. Remember *Eyrie's* history as a perpetual work in progress. The main hulls have not been altered much since their original construction, but almost everything inside has been. Corridors are a hodgepodge of Lunar-forged metal sheets, synthetics grown in *Eyrie's* own bubble ecologies, hardtech and biotech salvaged from derelict stations, and experiments in recycled packing material. Office furnishings and lab equipment ranges from state-of-the-art technology, bought on the expense accounts of research partners, to scrounged gear of dubious safety.

Some elements of *Eyrie* remain constant, though. The main power system runs lengthwise through both hulls and the connecting strip; conduits link it with the four panes that anchor the solar sail. The service deck, which houses distributing hardware, monitoring computers and related equipment, occupies the station's middle section. Five decks range above and below the service deck in both halves of *Eyrie*. The service deck itself is in vacuum most of the time, to reduce the complications of fire, corrosion and other environmental hazards.

Each main hull's lowest deck holds a hangar. Most spacecraft tie down via standard docking tubes. Cargo that does not require pressurized environments is usually tied down to exterior hulls. In the current state of emergency, it's all been either hauled inside or cut loose.

Most *Eyrie* decks are four meters high, with about a half-meter of between-deck space for ducts, wiring and the like. The North Hull's landing bay is quite large, with a 15-meter-high ceiling, big enough to accommodate small hybrid craft and stacks of ground-to-orbit cargo containers. The ceiling of the service deck is 10 meters high. The station is just slightly less than a kilometer long from one "pole" to the other.

Each half of *Eyrie* has a major observation-instrument cluster. In North Hull, the cluster is spread across the top four decks, within hull segments whose opacity and polarization in various wavelengths are controlled from inside. In South Hull, observation instruments occupy most of the face directly opposite the main engines, thus usually pointing at Earth.

North Hull is devoted primarily to *Eyrie's* support and administrative offices, quarters, mess halls and other apparatus for the people who work there. The bubbles usually attached to it provide most of the station's fresh food. The station's inline manufacturing assemblies are here too, though they're little more than glorified machine shops. Biotechnological development goes on in the exterior bubbles — or at least it did until the Chromatics turned the bladders into debris.

South Hull, on the other hand, holds labs, art galleries and other work environments. Additionally, it has its own support facilities. Its bubbles provide some food and fresh air, but also serve as recreational facilities. Its decks have few permanent walls except around elevator shafts and airlocks; the walls unhook and reattach to ceilings and floors as inhabitants desire. The Huang-Marr conspirators' central headquarters and Argente Essem's secret transmitter are both in this section.

Station in Crisis

The initial Chromatic attack throws *Eyrie's* residents, the Eagles, into general panic. By the time Orgotek and the characters arrive, the most common activity inside the station involves running around frantically.

The Chromatic fighters' initial attack has severed the four main power conduits. That leaves *Eyrie* with a 12-hour backup power supply. But the ongoing assault damages even backup systems. Throughout *Eyrie*, illumination ranges randomly from perfectly normal to dim to flickering to out completely (and back again). Since *Eyrie's* infrastructure makes extensive use of biotechnology, weapon damage sometimes has unpredictable results. Light strips may cycle through the visible spectrum (and beyond), or pulse slowly on and off, or sparkle in small flashes.

You may allow a character an opportunity to improve her odds in a particular situation. At your option, have a player spend a **Willpower** point to ensure reliable lighting in a passage or room. This "lucky break" lasts for about five to 10 minutes; long enough to get a specific task done, but little else. The character doesn't ac-

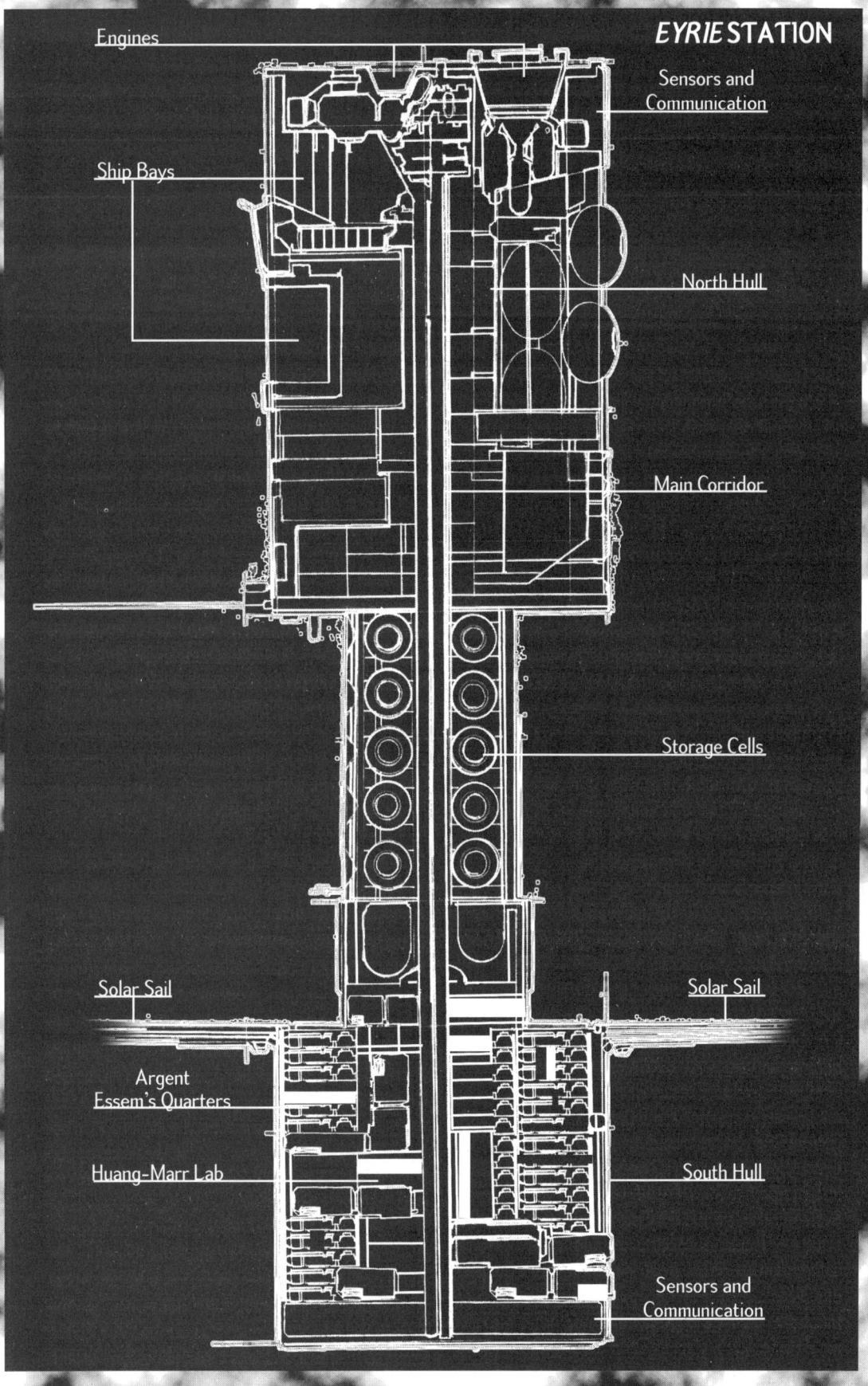

tivate the lights psionically; the option is simply cinematic license.

The station's air-circulation system is better protected than its lighting system is — after all, it's better to be in the dark than sucking vacuum — but it too wears down over the course of the Chromatic attack. Passages and deck sections cut off from power or air circulation go stale rapidly; their air is noticeably foul by the end of the battle. All **Stamina**-related rolls in such environments are at +1 difficulty. Rooms and passages nearest hulls are in most danger of stray hits from the battle

Combat Timing and Drama

The typical **Trinity** combat turn takes about three seconds, but not every turn is typical. During periods of pursuit or investigation between bouts of action, let turns take longer — up to a minute or more, in some cases. Doing so reflects the sustained tension and attention to detail that prevail, while keeping things moving when not every second is completely action-packed. You can also "fast-forward" through less intense events, abstracting and compressing as desired. The turn sequence is a framework around which to arrange your story. It's not a rigid structure that must be followed to the second.

outside, and may suffer anything from system failure to full decompression. Areas removed from both the hull and the central shaft may maintain local refresher systems throughout the battle.

All other support systems — water, sewage and so on — are also vulnerable. Inflict whatever degree of damage to them you feel is appropriate to enhance the scene's excitement and danger. A column of jetting water or steam, a growing pool of sewage, a sudden fire suppression spray, a strange smell — all can add significantly to the drama (for both the characters and their Chromatic foes).

Still, use discretion in deciding how much of this damage already exists by the time the characters arrive. Put in enough to be interesting, but not so much that it distracts from the primary mission of beating the aliens.

The Counterattack

Once Cassel realizes it's a Chromatic attack, his response is simple. He wants the aliens stopped

— and captured, if at all possible, so they can be examined. The Prexy also wants to make sure *Eyrie's* residents are safe. Cassel divides his forces into squads of six to eight people each. These squads enter *Eyrie* through maintenance airlocks on the South Hull and sweep toward boarding Chromatic forces from there.

The characters can choose their own course of action. Cassel gladly accepts their assistance if they offer it. If they decide to proceed independently, Cassel asks only that they stay out of Orgotek's way. He makes no effort to hide his disappointment and offers no assistance, but he doesn't try to stop them. Alert characters know that their vac suits have short-range transceivers that allow for communication throughout most of the station, so they can at least keep tabs of a sort on Orgotek's movements (and can call for help themselves if they're in a bind).

The Chromatic Advance

The Chromatic fighters with boarding squads dock — with a notable lack of skill — to different hatches off the North Hull hangar bay. Once inside, the squads spread out, some heading toward Essem's quarters in the lower South Hull, some venturing up into North Hull, others going through the middle to the service deck. Each squad spreads out as it goes, making forays into surrounding decks as members pursue human opponents, or to simply wreck important-looking things as they go. There are as many Chromatic squads as you want to make for an exciting time. If the characters somehow plow through the Chromatics too easily, have a few more squads appear suddenly.

Each enemy squad patrols separately. Those at full strength — six members — usually send a half-squad ahead to check out new territory, bringing up the rear half-squad, which makes sure that there is an open path of retreat. Chromatic culture is based on threes; the alien troops feel better able to defend themselves by staying in groups of three. The aliens are brave, but not stupid; a Chromatic goes solo only if everyone else in his squad dies.

The alien squad that secures the Doyen transmitter (an easy task of slaying a very surprised Argente Essem and packing the device and any of its bugs in a convenient case) heads back for the docked ships. Any other Chromatic squads encountered on the way withdraw similarly, blasting indiscriminately at the interior as they retreat. The entire alien force is comprised of volunteers who assume they have a slim chance of surviving (the only things that *must* return are the mother ship and the Doyen devices). Any squads left behind in the retreat continue working through the station, breaking things, hunting the enemy and hoping to die in a blaze of glory.

Victory Conditions

Despite Orgotek's assistance, the ultimate end of this battle depends primarily on the characters' actions. Those who stay outside take part in a dynamic battle over Earth, fighting off vengeful aliens. The debris from loose pressure bubbles presents a major complication. Fragments of synthetic tissue float about, buffeted by close calls with fighters. Tubes burst, spewing nutrients and neuromuscular fluid, obscuring visibility and creating ice pellets that inflict significant damage to anyone who has the incredibly bad luck to tumble through them with only a vac suit for protection.

The Chromatic mother ship makes up for its slow speed with an impressive weapons array. However, it stays out of the fight unless a human craft attacks it. (The Chromatic mission leader knows it's vital that the mother ship return to the homeworld; the alien isn't willing to risk the ship in direct combat.) The Chromatic fighters do their best to divert the Yellowjackets' attention (and while not as skilled, the aliens' superior number of craft make a difference at first). Yet the Yellowjackets' superior propulsion and weaponry eventually gain the upper hand. Surviving Chromatic fighters aren't above committing suicide by crashing into human ships or *Eyrie* itself. It's up to human pilots to knock the alien craft off course or to blow them up before the Chromatics destroy the station.

Chromatics within *Eyrie* pit their innate abilities and conviction against humans' technological advancement. Like Cassel and his forces, the characters can try to advance and can lay ambushes for the aliens. They can also attempt to rouse support among the Eagles (most are far too scared and confused to respond effectively). Still, each success on a standard **Command**, **Intimidation** or **Performance** roll gained against a group of residents earns the active assistance of a random Eagle. Few *Eyrie* residents have combat skills, but they're quite handy at support tasks (giving directions, operating machinery, interpreting data, providing supplies, tending to wounded). See *Eyrie* Defense, page 101, for details on groups that the characters may encounter.

Fighting Chromatics is difficult. They have advantages in both ranged and close combat. The aliens can disperse or reflect incoming energy attacks (lasers and heat, not electricity), have biotech weapons of their own, and can even generate laser beams psionically, without a weapon. Chromatics are small, fast, and have a field of view twice as wide as a human being's ("eye spots" all over their bodies act as rudimentary sensory organs and detect thermal energy — like body heat). They also have sharp natural claws. Furthermore, the aliens can use their mastery of Photokinesis to blend in with the environment, making them difficult to spot. Finally, they possess a resolute conviction in the righteousness of their cause.

Most energy weapons have no effect on the Chromatics (although tasers are electrical and outside the Chromatics' experience to defend against). Some psionic energy attacks — Biokinesis Modes, Electromanipulation, Cryokinesis, Telekinesis and Algesis — can inflict damage, bypassing Chromatics' defenses. Only those skilled in close combat would want to go hand to claw with a Chromatic (a Legionnaire or Norça might well find it a "worthy challenge"). The characters may also opt for something other than straight-up conflict, such as guerrilla raids or ambushes — although they're still difficult to pull off due to the aliens' impressive perceptive capacities.

The characters aren't likely to last very long if they insist on throwing themselves into the path of Chromatic lasers. The threat of death shouldn't escape the characters, especially if they insist on performing foolish or suicidal actions. Fools aren't the only ones to face death, though; sometimes the best-laid plans have tragic consequences. You must balance the concerns of heroic drama with faithful simulation of a combat environment.

Speaking of which, the station itself presents a challenge. Characters with experience in space combat know that using weapons such as lasers or autopistols isn't a good idea. Weapons such as screamers, tasers, flechettes and webbers are preferred to avoid hull breaches. For characters unwilling or unable to use these weapons, other choices include an Orgotek laser, close combat or fleeing.

The characters are most likely to first encounter Chromatics on the service deck. The biggest open spaces on the station, apart from the now-airless agricultural chamber, are here, as are various pieces of towering machinery. This is also where stray laser fire and similar random misses can cause the most damage to *Eyrie*'s integrity. A severely botched ranged attack damages a vital piece of machinery. The unintentional target explodes with half the force of a grenade and cuts off some essential service to part of the station. Up to half a deck could lose all light, air circulation, communications or power. The first botch effect should affect something on the service deck itself, to make the point clear. Use messages relayed from panicked people elsewhere on the station to keep characters apprised of further deterioration.

Eyrie Defense

Eyrie has no defense in the sense of planned resistance. Its designers never imagined that frontal assault would be a problem (in the post-Aberrant era, it was assumed that orbital security forces could handle any attack before it became a threat). Even so, *Eyrie* does have some defenders, individuals and small groups willing to do their part to protect their home.

- **Computer-Support Offices:** *Eyrie*'s resident computing experts include eight electrokinetics who don't care for the more political aspects of Orgotek's activities. They came to *Eyrie* to pursue their own biotechnological research, sharing a dream of organic computing. This group comprises the CSO, and works two shifts (members are split into two groups of four). Each group works at offices in one hull section for a week, then switches over to the other for a week.

The North Hull CSO facility is one deck down from the service deck. C.P. Carter, Cal Grinrye, Alana Nelson and Kevin Hughes use **Interface** to monitor the Chromatics' progress, and they lay ambushes. The teks can slam electronic doors shut, send an elevator plunging up or down, or trigger sprinkler and fire-suppression systems. None of this stops the Chromatics, but it does disorient, irritate and even cause minor injuries to some. Determine the damage some aliens suffer depending on how well the characters are doing (if the characters are somehow cleaving their way through Chromatics, provide full-strength opponents; otherwise, the characters come upon a few wet and battered aliens).

Alien Hostages

Capturing a Chromatic is more difficult than *killing* one; the aliens are waging a holy war. If injured and immobilized, a Chromatic begs its fellow soldiers to kill it rather than let it fall into the hands of its corrupt enemies. If grievously wounded, unable to move and with no fellow Chromatics nearby, the alien commits suicide by a shot through the head with a biotech weapon, or through a ritual technique. The latter involves building up a photokinetic charge over several turns and releasing it inward. This destroys the alien's insides completely, leaving a charred hide and vaporized organs. This technique drains the Chromatic considerably. If it somehow survives (unlikely since it can't soak the Lethal damage), the alien cannot attempt the ritual or any other Photokinesis effect for an hour.

If the characters want a captive, they must subdue the target quickly and disarm it. This includes not allowing the Chromatic to bring its own psionic ability to bear (successful only by keeping the alien unconscious at all times). **Telepathy** (use of The Muse, Mind Bomb, Brainjack or Will Control) might help command a Chromatic into quiescence. **Vitakinesis** (use of Contusion or Inflame) might render it unconscious. Attempts of this sort are at +1 difficulty due to adjusting to alien thought and physiology. Also, teks with **Electromagnetic Shield** can use it to disperse a Chromatic's suicide charge as it erupts. Each success that the electrokinetic's player achieves reduces the damage the alien takes by one Health Level.

Considering the aliens' determination and the characters' probable attitude toward them, it's unlikely that the psions will capture any Chromatics. Doing so would be quite an accomplishment, though — the first Chromatic ever captured alive! You are encouraged to present challenges that the characters can overcome through intelligence, courage, and above all teamwork.

The CSO staff can use **Transmit** to make contact with the characters through the intercoms in the Orgotek vac suits. (CSO staffers prefer to work with the characters rather than Cassel's forces due to professional differences.) After some discussion, the team and CSO may work out coordinated maneuvers, particularly ambushes in which the characters lead Chromatics into areas that electrokinetics can control.

• **The South Hull Volunteer Fire Department:** Although the name was chosen humorously, these people perform a very serious function. Fire is one of the most dangerous internal catastrophes that can strike a space station. It's second only to asteroid/debris impacts as the leading cause of orbital death and damage.

None of the tools at the VFD's disposal prove very damaging, but they help nonetheless. As the Chromatics march through the ship, an unsung hero in the VFD thinks to see what effect fire-suppressing chemicals might have on the aliens. *Eyrie's* fire-suppression systems release clouds of nontoxic vapors treated with bright colorizing agents to indicate the hazard at hand. The vapors are dense enough to seriously impair vision and the effects of lasers. All vision-related rolls require an extra success for each meter of vapor between observer and target. A laser loses one die from its damage effect for each meter of vapor through which it passes. The volunteers (and characters who know safety systems) can trigger extinguishers over a two-meter stretch of corridor or in a mid-sized room with a standard **Engineering** roll.

A Chromatic completely covered in spray cannot use its "eye spots" to sense for heat signatures (negating its special ability); it must rely solely on its two sets of eyes. Nor can the alien communicate clearly with other Chromatics — although it can still bark in surprise and panic.

Use the police-officer template in **Trinity** (page 306) for VFD personnel stats.

• **Heroic Individuals:** *Eyrie's* population includes many brave souls. They provide what defense they can. Most of their efforts fail, as the characters discover when they make their way through the station and encounter numerous scorched corpses. Finding human victims brings home the tragedy and horror of the situation. Yet encountering human defenders wears the Chromatics down, making them more vulnerable to the characters' and Orgotek's efforts. You can also heighten the drama by staging scenes in which the characters meet scared but determined Eagles gathering to mount an attack. By getting involved with the residents, the characters become involved in more than just a "bug hunt."

The End of Huang-Marr

The central installation of the entire Huang-Marr research network is on *Eyrie*, in the upper part of South Hull. A Chromatic squad passes through the area in its search for the Doyen transmitter. Huang, Beitz, Meeks and a couple of their subordinates mount a vigorous defense. In the grand cinematic tradition, the characters should be nearby, having followed a trail of destruction and bodies left by the very aliens the conspirators now face (not unreasonable, since the characters board the station on the South Hull side). The characters hear the sounds of conflict echoing down the corridor from some distance ahead, and arrive on the scene in moments.

The characters should recognize the ranking conspirators, having viewed their holograms a few times by now. Still, the characters presumably decide to deal with the Chromatic threat first. Considering the characters followed the Chromatics in, the two human groups should overwhelm the six aliens in a crossfire. (Characters who ignore Chromatics and deal with conspirators first may reconsider after a few well-placed alien laser beams.)

Addressing the alien threat doesn't end the danger, though. The Huang-Marr conspirators know they're being hunted by Æon operatives, and Beitz actually met the characters only days earlier in Montressor. A suite of offices off the contested hallway contains computers that hold all of the project's data, and adjoining lab facilities test particularly interesting innovations. In other words, the rooms contain irrefutable proof of these people's pursuits. The conspirators would normally be doomed — except the Chromatic attack provides them with the perfect opportunity to destroy their own facility, kill the meddling investigators and possibly even escape in the confusion. The conspirators therefore fight to the death.

The characters may intend to take the fugitives in, but may also be sick of chasing elusive traitors and have a little payback in mind. Whatever the characters' decision, Meeks opens fire before they act on it, and a second battle is joined. It's highly probable that the characters kill Meeks and Beitz in the conflict. Ella Huang, if she survived the previous firefight, is not suicidal and

ducks for cover; she gives up if given a chance. Any other conspirators may act as combat fodder at your discretion.

The characters may want to peruse the site, but have little opportunity as they hear chatter over the transceivers, and scattered bursts of violence; Orgotek forces continue to encounter Chromatic invaders. The best the characters can hope to do is download the archives into someone's minicomp (the files take up a *lot* of room, making it necessary to delete everything but basic functions from the computer), and bring Huang along. The fight for *Eyrie* continues elsewhere.

Characters who insist on remaining in the conspirators' suites to study evidence may do so. See Conclusions, page 107, for the information that's found. Sounds of battle rage on in the meantime, and Chromatic squads may even happen upon studious investigators.

The Final Engagement

The characters' face-off with the Huang-Marr cohorts takes place at roughly the same time that another Chromatic squad finds Argente Essem and the Doyen transmitter and bugs. Essem dies not knowing why the aliens are there. The Chromatics gather up the devices and head back to their ships, accumulating other surviving squads on the way. Although neither group knows it, the characters shouldn't be far behind the retreating aliens. (The characters may still encounter a few Chromatic squads that don't know of their compatriots' success.)

The final engagement between Chromatics and humans (with the characters playing a key role) takes place in the North Hull hangar as the remaining Chromatics — Doyen technology in hand — retreat back to the vessel waiting to return them to the mother ship. Some Orgotek personnel and *Eyrie* residents battle a couple alien squads, but allow the characters to spearhead the assault. The characters have enough support to carry the day, no matter how badly teammates are hurt. The fight should lead on board the Chromatic ship; the characters pursue the alien squad carrying a seemingly important, obviously human-made case.

As the characters battle the last few aliens inside the vessel (which is still hooked to *Eyrie*), a Chromatic makes a dying lunge for a strange control panel, hitting a glyph-like control. The characters see a blaze of light erupt outside the craft's canopy. It's immediately obvious that it isn't an explosion; rather, it seems to be some kind of plasma outgassing. Any character in a Yellowjacket outside *Eyrie* sees a surprisingly bright light flare briefly from the docked alien ship. An **Investigation** roll at +1 difficulty suggests that it is a signal of some sort, considering the Chromatics use light and pattern as their primary means of communication.

The flare is indeed a signal, indicating to the mother ship that the mission has failed. Although the Doyen device was of key importance to the Chromatics, saving their rare teleportation system is even more important to the aliens' plans. The Chromatic mission leader knows it's time to retreat, and the mother ship shudders as the teleporter is engaged. Rather than translating through subquantum space, however, the teleportation device triggers a succession of systems failures. The series of biotech engines throb dangerously out of tune, power conduits short out and spew bioelectricity, and weapons arrays explode in a spectacular display. The subquantum energy drawn by the failed teleport floods through the ship, amplified by the teleportation mechanism itself, and shreds the ship apart in a massive explosion. In the aftermath, only twisted pieces remain, tumbling into decaying Earth orbit. All psions within **Attunement** range suffer a backlash effect when the mother ship blows.

The destruction of the ship is a mystery for the moment. Most characters may even assume the Chromatic on *Eyrie* triggered a self-destruct device on the mother ship when it hit the control. The characters learn what caused this accident, but not until they pursue further investigations themselves. Thus ends the Chromatics' first effort at revenge against the enemy's homeworld. The shocking truth behind the mother ship's explosion is revealed in **Ascent into Light**, the next in the **Darkness Revealed** series.

The Cleanup

The excitement of combat is over, but there are still a few things the characters must address. Most immediately, survivors must escape *Eyrie* before the place literally falls apart. Additionally, the characters have a couple of important discoveries to make.

The Doyen Equipment

Unless the characters were victims of unfortunate dice rolling, they have probably defeated the Chromatics and have at least one damaged but functional alien ship in their possession. They also have the case that the aliens were so intent on stealing. Considering the Chromatics didn't seem interested in anything else (going out of their way to destroy other things, in fact), the characters are sure to want to find out what the aliens tried to steal.

Make sure that Cassel is on hand when the characters open the container. While the strange devices (described in detail on page 114) look totally unfamiliar to the characters, the Prexy recognizes them immediately. The characters may simply be puzzled by the strange pieces of bioware, but they should be utterly surprised by Cassel's reaction to them. The proxy is caught completely off-guard by the sight, succumbing to a mixture of wonder, fear and bewilderment. In a very, very rare moment of lost control, Alex Cassel curses: "Son of a bitch! *Doyen*." The characters have seen the Prexy angry, concerned, sad and driven. This naked shock is something brand new. They should wonder just what sort of thing might inspire such a reaction in a man of Cassel's obvious power and capability.

The characters can take advantage of Cassel's momentary loss of composure and urge the Prexy to provide an explanation. The Doyen section, page 81, describes what Cassel knows (and more — note that none of the proxies are aware of the aliens' recent contact with the Chromatics). Cassel tells what he knows slowly and reluctantly. This is, quite literally, the first time he has ever spoken of the Doyen to anyone other than a fellow proxy, and he does so now only because the current surprise imbalances him.

Based on Cassel's explanation and the Chromatics' efforts, the characters may deduce that the Chromatics receive technical support from the Doyen (if this slips by them, have Cassel suggest it). Once conversation achieves that point, the Prexy regains his composure. Anything else the characters ask about the Doyen goes unanswered. Questions about how the Aberrants first came to the Doyens' attention, the circumstances of the proxies' encounters with the Doyen, how the proxies know what the Doyen are up to, and most importantly about what else Cassel knows but isn't saying all lead to immediate silence on his part.

If pushed, the Prexy becomes angry (complete with subconscious power manifestations as when he confronted Disbray at the Blight Project). Characters with a sense of self-preservation know to back down — they should never forget that Alex Cassel is a powerful individual in more than just a psionic sense.

To redirect attention, Cassel points out that survivors must find and treat any injured, and must collect Chromatic captives and equipment for study before the station breaks up. As part of these cleanup efforts, Cassel calls in Yellowjackets to take Chromatic captives or bodies and alien technology lying around — including the Doyen transmitter. The Prexy claims to be within his rights to make this decision over any protests. If the characters try to throw their weight around, Cassel reminds them that the Æon Trinity is not a governing body. If any of the characters are government representatives, the Prexy reminds them that they're on a private installation outside of governmental jurisdiction. He ends any arguments by pointing out that using his ships is simply the most expedient way to get recovered items down to the planet for study.

Cassel isn't concerned if characters insist on riding back with the evidence, but whatever they do, the Prexy keeps the Doyen devices. He plans to turn over all recovered Chromatic evidence for study, but doesn't release the Doyen gear until he's determined its function. Cassel is not above growing a bioware component that resembles the transmitter and turning it over instead if the characters convince the Æon Trinity to push the issue. He even uses hologram technology to create scenes around the device so that any telesthetic scans don't discover the switch.

The Fate of *Eyrie* Station

The subquantum wave that first alerts the characters to the Chromatics' attack is felt throughout near space. Human forces scramble to respond when the aliens attack the Moon and Asia. The fighting there goes more quickly than it does around *Eyrie* due to the superior human forces in the regions. Ships converge on the station from elsewhere in orbit, but the battle for *Eyrie* is over by the time they arrive. The newcomers evacuate the station before its orbit decays.

The challenge here is to make sure that nobody is left behind. The battle likely drained most psions of their energy reserves, and *Eyrie* has suffered sufficient damage that scanning it psionically for survivors is not enough. Rescuers explore *Eyrie* physically as well. The characters need not take part in the search, but if you wish to promote the constructive side of psion activity, you should encourage them to do so. Furthermore, taking part in the search is possibly the only way the characters can learn where the Doyen transmitter came from.

Several dozen people await rescue, spread throughout isolated sections of the station. Characters who help out earn favorable media attention and the thanks of whatever groups with which survivors are associated. The characters' efforts also raise their standing in the eyes of the Æon Trinity, which strives to promote precisely this sort of unity in the face of adversity.

Eyrie's orbit decays slowly during the entire process. There's a sense of urgency to the evacuation, but not panic. Rescuers are confident that everyone will make it off safely before the station's orbit fails completely. At that point, some judicious shoves adjust the orbit so that *Eyrie* fragments rain harmlessly over Antarctica and part of the southern Pacific Ocean.

The Fate of the Chromatics

Everyone has noticed that the Chromatic ships and weapons bear a striking resemblance to human biotechnology — much more so than can be explained by coincidence or parallel invention. The remains of the mother ship, the fighter craft, the weapons and the Chromatics themselves all undergo very, very careful examination.

A potentially long, heated debate over who gets the Chromatics is short-circuited as the Æon Trinity (backed by the UN) declares that, despite recent allegations, the Æsculapians' Montressor Clinic is the logical place to take the aliens and their equipment. The docs have performed Chromatic autopsies before and have cutting-edge medical and research technology with which to gather information about the enemy. Cassel admits that many small items are already on their way to Orgotek's San Francisco facility, but he orders it all forwarded to Basel. All this waits until after *Eyrie's* immediate status is resolved, though.

The Fate of Argente Essem

While the characters search *Eyrie's* lower South Hull (other rescuers already cover other areas), they discover a battered and laser-burned door. It's obvious that Chromatics were determined to smash it down, which seems contradictory to their random attacks elsewhere on the station.

The characters step through into a living room. To the left is a small food-preparation area. To the right are two doorways: one to a bedroom (with a tiny bathroom), and another to a small office. There are more scorch marks around the latter door. Beyond it, the characters find a man in his mid-30s, dead from multiple laser wounds. A cabinet in the corner was obviously rent open. A standard **Investigation** roll confirms that a vacant spot within is perfect for a container the size of the one that held the Doyen transmitter.

A clairsentient who uses **Psychometry** confirms that Chromatics burst into Essem's apartment (the characters can learn his identity easily by looking through his numerous personal effects and by perusing his minicomp — allow players to read Essem's diary now) and went straight to the cabinet. Killing Essem seemed almost incidental. They found the Doyen transmitter and bugs inside, packed them into the container, and left.

The only mystery remaining is how Essem got the items in the first place. Once the characters find his private journal, however, it seems apparent that the Doyen used him as a tool for quite some time. Alex Cassel would dearly like to know this little tidbit of information; of course the characters aren't obligated to tell him — or anyone else, for that matter.

choice of branches, since field groups are often comprised of a mix of Neptune (team leaders), Triton (investigators) and Proteus (support and security) agents. If the characters turn the offer down, Æon remains willing to work with them. Even as associated members, the characters may still assist with the new Chromatic situation.

Orgotek

The characters have developed a complex relationship with Alex Cassel in a very short period of time. The Prexy's demonstrated courage and goodwill during the battle for *Eyrie* Station should carry some weight with the characters. But the problems of the Huang-Marr conspiracy remain, and though the record seems fairly clean on his end, there is *always* room for doubt about such matters. Additionally, Cassel's quick control of the alien equipment shows the characters that they should never underestimate a proxy's power. The Prexy values associations with active people of good intent such as the characters, but wonders what further secrets they might uncover if they continue to poke around his order. Cassel prefers that they direct their attention away from Orgotek — to the captured Chromatics, for instance.

Conclusions

The battle for *Eyrie* Station brings an end to the Huang-Marr conspiracy. Despite the deaths of almost every conspirator, the characters have amassed a large amount of incriminating evidence. The data downloaded from the lab on *Eyrie* confirms almost everything the characters have uncovered to date (if the characters didn't access this information, Ella Huang admits to it). The characters must wait until after they're off *Eyrie* before they have a chance to thoroughly peruse information from the lab. In the final analysis, the characters should feel confident that they have seen the last of the Huang-Marr Project.

Æon Trinity

The characters have established very deep ties with Æon. Whatever the characters' initial doubts and concerns, they should now know that the Trinity is a necessary and desirable balancing factor for the psi orders. Meanwhile, Æon recognizes the characters' abilities and willingness to pursue its goals in the face of opposition. If the characters have not previously joined, the Trinity now offers them full membership. They have their

Character Development

A player may spend experience points on his character to signify permanent benefits from recent efforts. Any Abilities or Aptitude Modes that were used are obvious choices for development.

The Allies, Contacts and Status Backgrounds may also be purchased to indicate the results of intense involvement with the Æon Trinity or Orgotek. (Even if a player passes on this option, he should know that his character can get help from these groups when in trouble — though not as often as those who develop the relationships fully.) Influence is also appropriate, since the characters have been the focus of much media coverage, making them the celebrities of the moment.

A character may be so impressed with the Æon Trinity, or with Cassel and his operation, that she decides to change her Allegiance. This isn't always easy, but is appropriate in this instance. See **Trinity**, page 175, for information on changing Allegiance. **America Offline** also has detailed information on Orgotek and groups to join within the organization.

Even so, Cassel's appreciation for the characters' help is sincere. He makes it clear that the characters may call on Orgotek in times of need.

Aftermath

Unfortunately, the Huang-Marr conspiracy has been exposed to the public. Society has become increasingly concerned over the past few weeks that more psions may have been corrupted as the Chitra Bhanu were. It doesn't take much conjecture to propose that all of these events are simply evidence that the Gifted are headed down the very same path that the Aberrants took. The characters know that the Huang-Marr Project was limited to a relatively small group of people, but that knowledge doesn't change the fact that Joe Hologram's confidence in psions is shaken seriously. The best the characters can hope for is that the United Nations investigation confirms what the characters already know, and that humanity will once again agree that psions are committed to its aid.

At least the Chromatic attack could steer public attention away from the UN hearings. The aliens' appearance in our Solar System is an incredible surprise — from what anyone knows, only humans have any kind of teleportation technology. Now that the Chromatics have apparently developed it as well, Earth has yet another threat to face aside from Aberrants. This is a terrible concern and mystery. How could an apparently low-tech race like the Chromatics develop teleportation? And if it's a natural psionic ability, why haven't they used it before? The Doyen obviously play a vital role in this, since it was apparently they who provided the Chromatics' "gifts." The characters should be very interested in learning more about both alien races. Thanks to their recent successes in the Huang-Marr investigation, they have the clout with Æon to get involved in these new pursuits, which are explored in **Ascent into Light**.

Other Endings

This story does not have to end as described here. There are a number of alternate directions that it can take.

• **The conspirators escape (again):** You may wish to draw out the cat-and-mouse game. Although Beitz and Meeks exhausted most of their options by retreating to *Eyrie*, they are not without friends elsewhere in settled space. You could develop one or both into major long-running opponents for the characters (the duo certainly has reasons to exact vengeance on the characters).

• **Round up the others:** Among the information the characters find in the main Huang-Marr database, they learn the locations of other research facilities. This could range from a couple sites with only a few researchers each to a Byzantine network of locations in North America, Europe, Asia, Oceania, the Asteroid Belt and beyond. The extent of conspirators depends on how far you choose to spread the corruption — the more widespread, the greater the outcry and the worse psions end up looking to the public.

• **More Chromatics:** One (or more) of the alien fighters may escape destruction, either during the battle for *Eyrie* Station or in the Lunar or Asian attack. Trapped in the enemy's Solar System, the Chromatics cause as much trouble as possible. Again, they're not dumb; they go to ground and plan quick strikes on various human urban centers. The fighter could have up to nine aliens on board, who hop off and sneak through the countryside, terrorizing the populace.

Dramatis Personae

The following are profiles and statistics for key individuals involved in the events of *Signals and Flares*. There are a number of people with whom the characters can interact, not only in their official investigation but in any other stories you wish to run at the Blight Project or on *Eyrie* Station.

Ella Huang

Intense and driven, Ella Huang always had an unquenchable desire to *know*. She finally came to the attention of an Orgotek recruitment team. They tested Huang, who possessed a tendency for Vitakinesis. Orgotek usually informed its fellow orders of an appropriate latent; this time was no different. After seeing Huang's test results, the Æsculapians (Beitz, in fact, who was in charge of new recruits at the time), extended her the offer to join.

Huang's curiosity only increased after experiencing the Prometheus Effect; psi gave her a whole new perspective from which to view the universe. The more she studied, the more she wanted to know, and this thirst for knowledge soon overshadowed her life.

Huang sees greater awareness of the universe as the ultimate goal to which humanity should aspire. Her efforts in the Huang-Marr Project are devoted to the pursuit of knowledge; she sees nothing unethical or immoral in that.

Cassel's Motives

The Prexy's personality should be a constantly unfolding enigma to players and characters. **America Offline** contains a detailed look at Alex Cassel. The following is a brief overview, sufficient for you to roleplay him well during the events of this book.

Cassel dreams of a human race prospering in every sense of the word — free of the Aberrant menace; expanding throughout the universe; living long, full, satisfying lives. He wants to abolish tyranny and poverty and everything else that keeps people from fulfilling their dreams. The Prexy is willing to do almost anything to accomplish these goals.

Yet even his virtue has limitations. He balances his moral books carefully. The potential good gained in a given course of action must assuredly outweigh the known harm it could cause. Nor is Cassel willing to engage in general evils: He risks specific bad acts in pursuit of good rewards, but doesn't enact general policies of ongoing brutality or suffering in the hopes that it might pay off "someday."

In short, Cassel is not a villain. He has a moral code that stops him from taking the convenient or expedient course of action if it may harm others. Cassel is not a hero in any conventional sense, though. He's willing to make very hard choices for what he considers the greater good (which sometimes involves actions appalling to those who don't share his morality).

You can also have him do almost anything imaginable associated with Electrokinesis (within relatively broad limits), if you feel it's necessary or desirable for the story. Cassel is a proxy, after all. He's a master of Electrokinesis' three Modes, and is very skilled at manipulating subquantum energy in manners that other electrokinetics can scarcely imagine.

Rita Disbray

Disbray is a young woman who gets things done. She always had a knack for seeing the simplest, most expedient solution to any problem. Due to somewhat weak morals, Disbray's choices were often outside the bounds of conventional law. There was a demand for her kind of initiative and problem-solving, and Horace Meeks had a keen eye for talent.

Meeks brought Disbray on board as an "administrative assistant" in 2115. In reality, he used her to carry out all manner of covert tasks. As far as any records were concerned, Disbray was just another flunky. In reality, she helped Meeks accomplish many of his project "saves" by applying pressure in the right places, by gathering (or losing) data and resources, and by generally taking whatever steps were necessary to solve the problem at hand.

However, she has been bored with her role until recently. She cares little about the Huang-Marr Project, learning only what she must to be useful if cleanup or coverup is required. Disbray spends much of her time studying noetic theory. Although a neutral, she finds psionic phenomena fascinating. She has thus discovered new interest in her work; she now considers her tasks a challenge of her unaugmented mind against the psionically enhanced.

Image: Rita Disbray is an slender woman of medium height. She has piercing eyes, a sharp chin, short-cropped dark hair and an athletic build. These qualities combine attractively, although not in a conventional sense. Disbray wears classic styles that look good no matter what the current fashion is. She doesn't like being flashy, as suggested by the subdued tones of her clothing.

Roleplaying Hints: You take great pride in the fact that you can get out of almost any situation on your own. That doesn't mean you ignore offers of help, just that you seldom need them. You're not so full of yourself that you ignore the danger of being involved in Huang-Marr. If you get caught, you know the best thing to do is downplay your role (but don't lie; you've read enough on Telepathy to know how it works), and do your best to work with the authorities. You have a long life ahead of you, and if you play your cards right, you won't spend it in a cell.

Nature: Analyst
Allegiance: Self

Physical Attributes
Strength 2
Dexterity 4
Stamina 3

Abilities
Might 2
Athletics 3, Drive 3, Firearms 4, Legerdemain 3, Martial Arts 4, Melee 2, Pilot 2, Stealth 3
Endurance 2

Mental Attributes
Perception 3
Intelligence 3
Wits 3

Abilities
Awareness 3, Investigation 5
Academics 2, Bureaucracy 2, Engineering 2, Intrusion 4, Linguistics (Spanish) 1, Survival 3
Arts 2, Rapport 2

Social Attributes
Appearance 3
Manipulation 3
Charisma 2

Abilities
Intimidation 2, Style 1
Subterfuge 4
Etiquette 1, Savvy 2

Willpower: 9
Psi: 1
Backgrounds: Allies (Meeks) 4, Cipher 4, Contacts 4, Resources 4, Status (Orgotek) 2
Gear: Casual work suit (reinforced), fighting gloves, Orgotek Wasp 11 pulse laser, Wazukana DX70 minicomp (with 007 agent and cell link), radio detonator

Horace K. Meeks III

Meeks has been with Orgotek since the early days; he was hired by Tekne Group in 2109. Since then he's moved from one division to another, bringing formidable organizational skills and an utter lack of social grace with him. He straightens out disorderly situations, contributing substantially to the success of marginal operations. Wise supervisors then move Meeks along; his habitual rudeness and aggressive favoritism create enemies.

Despite a highly successful career in Orgotek, Meeks considered his college days the high point of his life — at least until he joined Huang and Marr as one of humanity's secret saviors (as he views his role on the project). Meeks was especially well-suited to the project. He considered humans too stupid and sluggish to save themselves; his skills were vital to this effort to save mankind's worthless hide. Due to Meeks' fundamentally duplicitous nature, the conspirators had readily available resources as well. Meeks always left backdoor codes in the computers of departments that he reorganized. Every place he's ever worked for Orgotek is therefore a source of goods, personnel and resources. Meeks' psionic talent is middling at best; his significant planning and strategic skills make him beneficial to Huang-Marr.

Image: Meeks is in early middle age. Contrary to his Anglo name, his appearance reflects his predominantly Armenian heritage. He has two prominent scars on the left side of his face (the result of his experiences in an unauthorized unlimited dueling league at Yale).

Roleplaying Hints: While a tremendous boon to Orgotek's bottom line — no project you were brought in on failed after you became involved — you invariably infuriate your colleagues. You care little if your methods don't sit well with others; you're here to do a job and everyone should get out of your way. If someone gets caught in the middle, it's his fault. You're a visionary; all these dullards just slow you down.

Nature: Architect
Allegiance: Huang-Marr

Physical Attributes   **Abilities**
Strength 2   Brawl 2
Dexterity 2   Athletics 1, Drive 2, Firearms 3, Pilot 3, Stealth 2
Stamina 3   Resistance 2

Mental Attributes   **Abilities**
Perception (Astute) 4   Awareness 4, Investigation 4
Intelligence (Discerning) 4 Academics 4, Bureaucracy 5, Engineering 5, Intrusion 4, Linguistics (Arabic, Chinese, French, Turkish, Portuguese) 5, Medicine 1, Science 4
Wits 3   Arts 2, Rapport 2

Social Attributes   **Abilities**
Appearance 3   Intimidation 4, Style 1
Manipulation (Devious) 4   Command 3, Subterfuge 4
Charisma 3   Etiquette 3, Savvy 3

Aptitude: [Electrokinesis] Photokinesis 1, Technokinesis 3
Willpower: 7
Psi: 5
Backgrounds: Allies (Disbray) 4, Cipher 2, Contacts 4, Influence 3, Resources 4, Status (Orgotek) 5
Gear: Tailored suit, Orgotek Wasp II pulse laser, Wazukana DX70 minicomp (with Friday agent and cell link)

Dr. Gustaf Beitz

Beitz is the Huang-Marr Project's guardian angel and was one of Zweidler's closest advisors. Indeed, he provided the business expertise necessary to keep the Montressor Clinic running in its lean, early years (it was Beitz's idea to base the clinic's initial operations on plastic surgery). Pierce Monahan handled the clinic's legal angles, Beitz took care of long-range planning, and Zweidler covered medical requirements. Beitz is also a doctor and a psion, though he talks about himself and his capabilities as little as possible. Beitz usually remains in the background and makes his points quickly and quietly — histrionics are for Meeks. Beitz comes off as a moderate; controversy doesn't get things done.

Beitz introduced doctors Huang and Marr, took experiments ever further afield, incorporated Meeks and Orgotek personnel into the biorg research, took advantage of Schilltronix's resources — in short, Beitz has been behind all aspects of Huang-Marr. He's aware of everything from the initial research proposal (he designed it) down to every experiment's results (he double-checks the findings).

Image: Beitz is of medium build and slightly above-average height. His Germanic heritage is apparent, but is displayed in a calm, unassuming fashion. He has brown hair, silvering slightly in a distinguished manner, a gentle, almost effeminate smile, and pale eyes that disguise the staggering intellect and amorality beyond them.

Roleplaying Hints: You pride yourself on your brilliance. You are, by design, a man whom history has largely overlooked. You are interested in true power, not its trappings — Zweidler can be the head of the Æsculapians; it's you who will guide them into the future. At least, that was the plan until some meddling upstarts exposed it all. You don't panic, though; you planned for the project's exposure. While Huang-Marr may be shut down, you intend to pursue your personal agenda after this current inconvenience is past.

Nature: Visionary
Allegiance: Huang-Marr

Physical Attributes
Strength 2
Dexterity 3
Stamina (Hardy) 4

Abilities
Athletics 3, Drive 1, Firearms 3, Pilot 2, Stealth 2
Endurance 2

Mental Attributes
Perception (Observant) 4
Intelligence (Brilliant) 5
Wits (Shrewd) 4

Abilities
Awareness 4, Investigation 3
Academics 5, Bureaucracy 4, Engineering 2, Intrusion 3, Linguistics (Chinese, English, Turkish, Portuguese) 4, Medicine 4, Science 4
Meditation 3, Rapport 4

Social Attributes
Appearance 3
Manipulation (Authoritative) 5
Charisma (Genial) 4

Abilities
Intimidation 2, Style 3
Command 4, Subterfuge 5
Etiquette 4, Savvy 1

Willpower: 9
Psi: 6
Backgrounds: Allies (Huang-Marr Conspirators) 5, Cipher 3, Contacts 5, Influence 4, Resources 5, Status (Æsculapians) 5, Status (Huang-Marr) 5
Gear: Tailored suit, Orgotek Stinger flechette pistol, Wazukana DX70 minicomp (with Pasteur agent and cell link), vocoder (French, Korean, Qin, Nihonjin), t-blocker

Chromatic Warriors

The Chromatics are alien beings. Their culture, their very way of thinking, is foreign to humanity. A detailed discussion of the Chromatic race would take more space than is available here. The section entitled Chromatics, page 81, explains how the beings started their war against humanity, and what brings the aliens to *Eyrie* Station. The Chromatics who volunteer for this mission are among the most courageous and dedicated warriors of the race.

The attackers are split between troopers and squad commanders. Use the Chromatic template in **Trinity**, page 306, for the troopers. Squad commanders' statistics are listed below. The main distinction between troopers and commanders is that the latter demonstrate the proper combination of innovative thinking, solid tactical planning and unswerving loyalty to superiors.

Image: Soldiers include both genders, but since their genitalia are internal, the difference is not apparent to human observers. They average 1.75 meters in height, and have mottled hides of gray and brown highlighted with often startlingly bright splotches. These "eye spots" don't actually look like eyes, but form natural yet distinctive patterns over the Chromatics' bodies. The spots often glow in bright luminescent patterns, and provide Chromatics with sensory input from all directions by picking up heat traces. The aliens have two sets of actual eyes; one pair on the front for binocular vision, the other on the sides for wide-angle sight.

Most, though not all, squad commanders are larger than troopers. They also tend to be visibly scarred; Chromatic culture values courage, and direct engagement with the enemy offers many opportunities to demonstrate it.

Roleplaying Hints: You are a chosen guardian of your race. You take this mission *extremely* seriously. You will give it your very best, and will not conserve your forces or yourself. You don't expect to survive the conflict, but you're willing to give your life for your race. That doesn't mean you take ridiculous chances, though. Courage and cunning are your greatest weapons against the corrupters.

Nature: Leader
Allegiance: Chromatics

Physical Attributes	Abilities
Strength 4	Might 2
Dexterity 4	Athletics 4, Firearms 3, Martial Arts 4, Stealth 3
Stamina 4	Endurance 4
Mental Attributes	**Abilities**
Perception 3	Awareness 4
Intelligence 3	Bureaucracy 1, Engineering 1, Medicine 1, Survival 3
Wits 4	Meditation 2, Rapport 2
Social Attributes	**Abilities**
Appearance 1	Intimidation 4
Manipulation 3	Command 3, Subterfuge 4
Charisma 3	

Aptitudes: [Electrokinesis] Electromanipulation 1, Photokinesis 5; [auxiliary Mode] Pyrokinesis 1

Special Abilities: Every Chromatic has the ability to generate lasers and disperse energy attacks. Used properly, the Photokinesis and Pyrokinesis powers described in **Trinity** are sufficient to create those effects. Below are two additional powers that every Chromatic has.

Thermal Sensing: A Chromatic uses the "eye spots" on its body to sense light and heat emissions, even those from another living creature. It's virtually impossible to sneak up on one of the aliens (think of the being in the movie *Predator*, except with 360° perception). A Chromatic gets an **Awareness** roll no matter from what direction a target approaches. If successful, the alien perceives the thermal signature and may react appropriately. Heat suppressants (such as flame-retardant foam) apply a +3 difficulty to **Awareness** rolls.

Blending: As part of its photokinetic mastery, a Chromatic can manipulate light to become virtually invisible. Spend a **Psi** point and roll **Psi**; each success equals a difficulty added to all **Awareness** rolls made to perceive the Chromatic. Blending lasts for a number of minutes equal to the successes rolled.

Willpower: 9
Psi: 8
Backgrounds: Mentor (Doyen) 5
Gear: Primary gun (equivalent to L-K Vindicator 11 laser carbine), secondary gun (equivalent to L-K Personal Protector laser pistol), weapon harness

Technology

Weapons

• **Orgotek Shrike Sonic Pistol:** Orgotek created the Shrike to compete in the growing sonic weapons market. Although made of biotech components, the Shrike functions just like a hardtech screamer. It benefits from formatting like any biotech weapon (see **Trinity**, page 264).

Tech: Ψ, Accuracy: 0, Damage: 5d10 B**, Range: 50, Maneuvers: Ms Tw, ROF: 1, Clip: 25, Concealability: J, Mass: 1.5, Cost: • • •

• **Orgotek Electric Eel Taser Baton:** Orgotek saw the success of Banji's stunner baton (combining a ranged taser with a billy club) and created a variation on its own Eel pistol. This version is exactly the same as the Eel pistol, except in a durable baton shape.

Computer Agents

• **Orgotek Universal Agent:** The Orgotek Universal Agent is the tool of choice of Orgotek management, and has gained market share ever since its release to the general public in 2118. The Orgotek Agent projects a neutral-race and gender human bust, with just a hint of Cassel's facial structure. Its voice pitch and (upper) body language adapt to match its user, so that the user sees an agent that resembles himself within a few hours. The Orgotek Agent's personality is friendly and accommodating, though it has an option to monitor patterns of request and offer recommendations when user reaction time seems unusually slow (Orgotek management calls this the "hangover watch"). Tech: Ψ, Cost: • • • •

Performance: 5

Applications: Administration 4, Business 4, Culture 2, Discern Truth 2, Law 2, Negotiation 3, Organization 3, Procedures 4, Quick Search 3, Romance Languages 3, Writing 2

Doyen Biotechnology

• **Transmitter:** The Doyen transmitter hums and vibrates noticeably when first discovered; this slows to a stop over the course of a day or so after the raid. It's biotech in design, but based on a very alien biology. The exterior is a spherical carbon lattice that is 30 cm in diameter. It contains a green sludge. Analysis identifies this material as a methane clathrate, an ice holding a methane compound in very dense solution. It's also laced with traces of molecules that are orders of magnitude more complex than DNA.

• **Listening Devices:** The Doyen-supplied "bugs" are even stranger than the transmitter. Each is a dull-blue spike about five centimeters long and a few millimeters wide. One end lights up with a soft red glow when activated. Placed against a wall or other surface and twisted for activation, a listening device melts into the surface, dissolving into microscopic nodes linked by monomolecular fibers. The probe spreads out just beneath the surface of whatever it's attached to, covering a roughly circular area a meter across. While active, the probe is all but undetectable; there's less of it per unit of surface area than of typical airborne pollutants.

Each node records input in molecular memory — a heavily engineered form of RNA. When the person who activated the bug taps the affected surface area, the device pulls loose and reassembles into its spike form. The data gathered allows for the creation of a three-dimensional projection of the surrounding space, displaying the movement of living beings with 15 meters and transmitting all sounds emitted in the vicinity.

Vehicles

• **Orgotek Yellowjacket Interceptor:** The Yellowjacket is a mid-size hybrid transport. It has a two-person cockpit with additional seating for eight or a 600-cubic-meter cargo area. The Yellowjacket can be used as a commercial transport or as a support craft.

VT: Hybrid
Tech: Ψ
CS: Mach 1.5
TS: Mach 1.7
VS: 4
Handling: +2
Mass: 40
Tolerance: ••••
Cost: •••••••
Armor: 3 [5]
Weapons: Dual front and rear medium laser cannons (Accuracy: +2, Damage: 6d10 [5] L)

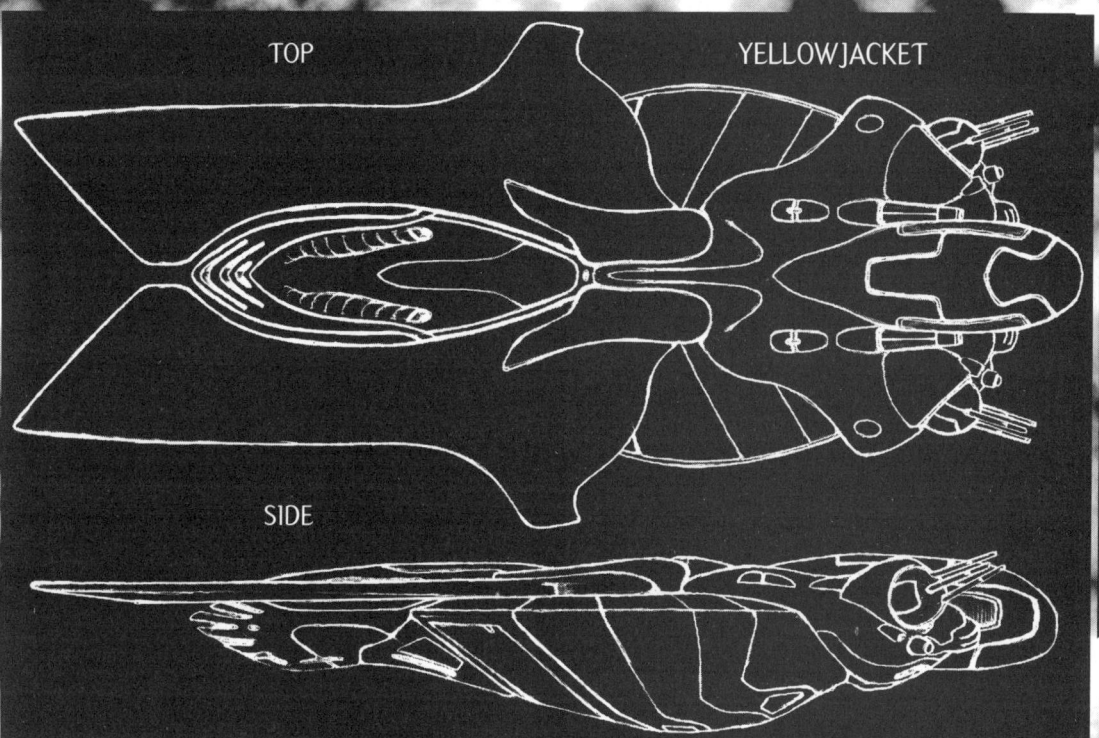

• **Orgotek Cruiser 17:** This is the most successful passenger version of Orgotek's research into vertical-takeoff-and-landing (VTOL) aircraft designs. The craft's hull texture bears some resemblance to a conch shell; in fact, Orgotek labs grow the hulls as single units in a mineral-deposition process involving tailored bacteria. Unlike the more rugged style common to the Cicada ATV and other commercial vehicles, the Cruiser 17 shines brightly iridescent in sunlight. The Cruiser 17's leg gear are similar to those of the Cicada, but are covered with soft plates of hull material to present a more aesthetically pleasing image.

The Cruiser 17 has a two-man cockpit. Although the craft requires only one pilot, Orgotek has introduced a copilot as well. The aircraft's public cabin has luxurious seating for 16, with the rear section divided into four small but comfortable private cabins, plus two fully appointed bathrooms. The bottom storage bay holds up to 400 cubic meters of cargo.

VT: Jet (VTOL)
Tech: Ψ
CS: Mach 1.5 (50 km altitude)
TS: Mach 2
Handling: +1
Mass: 40
Tolerance: ••••
Cost: •••••••• (vehicle)

Chromatic Ships

The Chromatic fighters are entirely biotech. It seems that the Chromatics have little technology of their own; whatever they were given by their "gods of light" appears to be based on human biotech designs. As a result, Chromatic vessels suffer from reduced thrust and offensive capabilities compared to human hardtech engines and weaponry.

The details of any ship's engines or the mother ship's teleportation capabilities are a mystery to any captured Chromatics. They are warriors, not servants to machines. Chromatic mechanics wouldn't presume to tell troopers how to fight, and the warriors return the courtesy concerning flying.

Chromatic spacecraft are eerily similar in design to human biotech ships. The controls, while designed for the smaller aliens, are actually relatively simple and not much different from controls in a human craft.

These vessels are unique in one respect. Chromatic ships can "heal" minor damage; a result of the biotech craft performing self-repair procedures. A craft can repair one Structural Level every turn. However, doing so reduces Vacuum Speed by one and restricts the ship to Cruising Speed ("healing" puts significant demands on the ship's engines).

- **Chromatic Fighter:** This craft is designed to do significant damage as quickly as possible. It has a primary pilot and two copilots, with cargo space for up to six battle-ready Chromatics.

   VT: Hybrid
   Tech: Ψ
   CS: Mach 1
   TS: Mach 1.1
   VS: 3
   Handling: 0
   Mass: 29
   Cost: Not available to humans
   Armor: 4 [5]
   Weapons: Three laser cannons (Accuracy: +1, Damage: 7d10 [3] L), two in front and one in the rear

- **Chromatic Transport:** Larger and not as sleek as the fighter, the transport was designed as a ferry. It can carry up to 1,800 cubic meters of cargo or 60 Chromatic passengers.

   VT: Hybrid
   Tech: Ψ
   CS: 560 km/h
   TS: 690 km/h
   VS: 3
   Handling: -1
   Mass: 50
   Cost: Not available to humans
   Armor: 4 [5]
   Weapons: Two laser cannons (Accuracy: +1, Damage: 7d10 [3] L), both mounted in front.

DARKNESS REVEALED 2
PASSAGE THROUGH SHADOW

Episode One: *Friends in High Places*

Setting material	1
Rules information	17
Dramatis Personae	51

Episode Two: *Signals and Flares*

Setting material	57
Rules information	73
Dramatis Personae	109
Technology	114

Credits

Writers: Bruce Baugh (*Signals and Flares*) and Richard E. Dansky (*Friends in High Places*)
Developer: Andrew Bates
Editor: Ken Cliffe
Vice President in charge of Production: Richard Thomas
Art Director: Aileen Miles
Cover Art: William O'Connor
Front & Back Cover Design: Pauline Benney
Layout and typesetting: Pauline Benney
Artists: James Crabtree, Langdon Foss, Jeff Holt, Leif Jones, Jon Carroll

Author Dedications

Richard Dansky: To the folks on DragonMUD, for putting up with the psychotic who logged on occasionally while writing this.

Bruce Baugh: To Mom and Dad, with thanks for support and encouragement on what must have sometimes seemed awfully peculiar work, and to the Eyrie Mafia for ideas, feedback and distractions at just the right times.

735 PARK NORTH BLVD.
SUITE 128
CLARKSTON, GA 30021
USA

© 1998 White Wolf Publishing, Inc. All rights reserved. Reproduction without the written permission of the publisher is expressly forbidden, except for the purposes of reviews. White Wolf, Vampire the Masquerade, Vampire the Dark Ages and Mage the Ascension are registered trademarks of White Wolf Publishing, Inc. All rights reserved. Werewolf the Apocalypse, Wraith the Oblivion, Changeling the Dreaming, Werewolf the Wild West, Trinity, Hidden Agendas, Trinity Technology Manual, Trinity America Offline, Darkness Revealed, Descent into Darkness, Passage Through Shadow, Ascent into Light and Trinity Universe are trademarks of White Wolf Publishing, Inc. All rights reserved. All characters, names, places and text herein are copyrighted by White Wolf Publishing, Inc.

The mention of or reference to any company or product in these pages is not a challenge to the trademark or copyright concerned.

This book uses science fiction for settings, characters and themes. All science fiction, geopolitical scenarios and psi-related elements are fiction and intended for entertainment purposes only. Reader discretion is advised.

Check out White Wolf online at http://www.white-wolf.com; alt.games.whitewolf and rec.games.frp.storyteller

PRINTED IN CANADA.

TRINITY BATTLEGROUND

YOU ARE THE WEAPON
LET THE BATTLE BEGIN

These are the opening volleys in a war that will determine the future of mankind — and the outcome is up to you. Trinity: Battleground is an in-your-face battle of psionics and biotech weapons against the twisted powers of the Aberrants. Battleground is a stand-alone miniatures game that's fully compatible with the Trinity RPG. Your roleplaying character can be converted easily into a heroic Battleground warrior — not a faceless minion — who takes the fight to the Aberrants, once and for all.

The Battleground boxed set contains 20 hand-cast high-definition plastic miniatures, terrain, rules, dice — everything you need to play. Also look for forthcoming Trinity: Battleground Terrain Sets and blister-packed pewter miniatures.

AUGUST

White Wolf is a registered trademark of White Wolf Publishing, Inc. Trinity, Trinity Battleground and Trinity Universe are trademarks of White Wolf Publishing, Inc. All rights reserved.

ABERRANT